HAINT BLUE

HAINT BLUE

A NOVEL BY

CARL E. LINKE

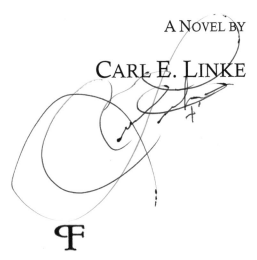

ℙF

Philip-Forrest Publishing
Chapel Hill

℉ Philip-Forrest Publishing

Published in the United States by Philip-Forrest Publishing
P.O. Box 2053
Chapel Hill, NC 27515-2053
Visit our website at: www.carllinke.com

De Nyew Testament, (The New Testament in Gullah) translation © American Bible Society 2005.

Book Design by Carl E. Linke
Photography by Jack Howison

ISBN-13: 978-0-982-74216-7

PRINTED IN THE UNITED STATES OF AMERICA
First Edition: (June 2010)
10 9 8 7 6 5 4 3 2 1

This book is dedicated to my amazing wife,
Penny, and our two children – Jay and Carrie –
personal inspirations for writing, who allowed me
time to put more than just my nose in a book.

Oona mus do ta ebrybody
jes like oona wahn dem fa
do to oona.

*Do to others as you would
have them do to you.*
LUKE 6:31
De Nyew Testament

Black blood 'pontop'ui dis' tredjuh
gwine bu'n dem'own veins, bone en'
body 'tell de't uh nobody wuh nebuh
fails nyuse de tredjuh fa sabe dem en
slabery 'pon dis' Lan'.

*Black blood on this treasure will burn the
veins, bones and flesh to the death of
anyone who fails to use the treasure to
ransom those enslaved on this Land.*
—loosely translated from *The
Legend of the Gullah Treasure*

—

CHAPTER 1

In autumn, life starts the same way every day in the Lowcountry of South Carolina. When the blackness of night bleeds into the marsh, the dawn unveils the blue-gray contour of the wood line across the islands and sheds its watery skin of dew — a reminder of how hot the day before had been and an omen of what the day's afternoon would become. Beneath the colors and clouds of a kaleidoscopic sky, a muted dissonance unfolds — the bark of a lonely dog, the crow of a dominant rooster, the crescendo buzz of cicadas left over from the dog-days. Chirps and tweets echo across treetops as a white ibis, like a circus clown on stilts, pecks at oysters spitting in the marsh mud. A great blue heron, slowly flapping its outstretched wings in the soft morning air, soars higher and higher in lazy flight above the marsh. All in all, it was a splendorous ballet of nature, lost on an audience too preoccupied to notice.

"It may be 1992 and all," Micah Pruett said, "but ain't no way in hell no skinny-ass black man is goin' to own no bidness like that in this town, Gunny. It don' make no difference what you done."

"So it don' sound like you cooled off any from last night?" Gunny Brewer said to his childhood friend.

"Hell no. I still be pissed. You just be talkin' all crazy and shit, talkin' 'bout buying that old, run-down factory, anyhow." Micah tossed his brown-bag lunch under the truck seat, as the two exchanged their morning hand slap, grab, and dap, the same routine they shared since middle school. The hinges on Gunny's truck doors never quite worked, so Micah had to lift the passenger door by the armrest and then pull it closed with a metal-on-metal clunk. Then he slouched deep in the seat.

"You managed to roll your bony body out of de sack before I could bang on de door dis time," said Milan Garrett Brewer, the wiry black man from St. Helena Island who was known by most as "Gunny," a nickname he earned as a Marine in Vietnam—along with a checkerboard of deep herringbone scars across his chest.

"Ain't talkin'," Micah said. He closed his eyes.

Gunny slipped the truck into reverse. He wrapped his arm over the back of the seat and twisted his torso to look through the back window, a move that always irritated his "Arthur Itus," which had taken up permanent residence in all of his joints, neck to toe.

Out of the drive, the truck's headlights, though not properly aligned, searched the scorched pavement for the bend on Highway 802, just before Sam's Point Landing, the roundabout with a concrete ramp leading down into the Coosaw River.

Like a pit crew on NASCAR Sunday, when they hit the ramp, it was all business. Micah was out of the truck, arms flapping and hands spinning in a pantomime of signals. Gunny turned the wheel to the left and then abruptly to the right, to align the trailer with the ramp.

Soon, with the tailpipe spitting salt water into Micah's face, Gunny's rehabbed Boston Whaler—the Tentacle Tattoo—began to drift. Gunny parked his truck between a stack of rotted pilings and a volunteer palmetto, pulled on his rubber knee-high boots, waded through the thin oil slick left by his boat, and rolled over the side of it to take the controls. Respectful of the dock house at the ramp, even though it had been boarded up for over twelve years, Gunny just nudged the throttle. The launch was a two-minute drill performed in near silence—an exercise which, in the presence of fog, rain, or sand gnats, sometimes looked like a comical silent movie.

With the Sam's Point bridge well behind them, they passed Coosaw Island and Goat Island and worked their way down Lucy Creek, headed south. Gunny stood spread-legged behind the controls. A soiled Philadelphia Flyers baseball cap covered his horseshoe ring of short, nappy hair. Still slim, but no longer well-toned at forty-seven, he showed the signs of his rugged past written all over his body. He stood strong still, but slightly slump-shouldered, as if weary from some enormous weight. His face was prematurely wrinkled from days spent in the sun.

When they reached Mugg's Hole, a deep pool from the phosphate mines that flourished in the 1800s, Gunny jerked the wheel to the right, slued the boat around a sandbar, and shook Micah back into their conversation— from right where they had stopped.

"So tell me again, why you even thinkin' about buyin' dat factory, Bro?" Micah asked with a yawn.

"Been something I wanted to do since we was kids," Gunny said, as he took aim at a barnacle-covered, white buoy that marked the spot for his first crab pot up ahead.

"You ain't never run nothin' 'cept a bunch of grunts in Nam. I mean dat bidness gots books to be kept and bills and things," Micah said, as Gunny slid the boat next to the buoy and slapped the throttle back to neutral. Micah grabbed the broomstick handle retrofitted with a metal hook on the end, snagged the rope below the Styrofoam buoy, and hoisted the crab pot from the creek bottom.

"There's been rumor dem be closin' de factory, ya know. Been hearin' dat for years now," Micah said as a cloud of oily, blue-and-white smoke from the Evinrude 75 drifted over the boat.

"Yeah, I asked 'bout de rumors, and all Mr. Drummond ever say is dat dey is no plans to sell de place," Gunny said.

"So why you t'ink you can buy it? I mean what you goin' to do with dat piece of shit place, Bro?" Micah asked as he strained to hoist the heavy pot made of chicken wire, hand over hand, from the creek mud seventeen feet below. He manhandled the pot into the boat, flipped open the trap door, and shook several crabs into an extra large cooler half-filled with marsh water. Two crabs fell onto the deck, which spurred Micah into a herky-jerky tap dance to avoid their swashbuckler claws before he could scoop them up with a nearby net.

"OK, Bro, forget it," Gunny said. "We're right back to where we was last night. I ain't goin' to convince you of nothin', and you ain't goin' to convince me. So save your breath. Let's get dese pots picked up."

Micah threw the pot back over the side. Before the splash settled, Gunny slammed the throttle forward, hard. Micah lost his footing on the slippery deck and landed hard on top of the cooler of crabs, his head between his knees. "Dishyuh shit be gettin' old, Bro. We been doin' dis for twenty years, every day, out here haulin' dese traps. Why we keep doin' dis?

"Hey, just be t'ankful to de good Lord for eb'ry'ting we have," Gunny replied. "He giveth and He taketh away. He give us a home, a family, and a job, even though it don' pay much. Be thankful, Bro," he said with a chuckle. "Ain't no pot of gold under no rainbows 'round here. You just be t'ankful for them crabs."

Micah shook his head and laughed, flicking his hand to make his fingers snap; then he smacked the cooler a few hard raps and said, "Shit. T'anks, you fuckin' crabs. You some kinda good deal for me."

After a good, long laugh, Micah added, "Hey, may not be no pot of gold under no trees 'round here, but you always got dat lottery ticket from dat fat Nam brother of yours from Philly."

Micah laughed again, and as Gunny steered wide of the marker around the Little Elba sandbar, he asked, "Don't he brings you one eb'ry week? Why he do dat?"

"I told you before," Gunny said. "I saved his white ass over there, and this is his payback. Says he sure as hell will never make any money drivin' dat rig of his or bettin' de horses." He jammed the throttle to the wall after they passed the "No Wake" zone by all the docks of the big houses on the bend in Lucy Creek.

Over the whine of the Evinrude, he yelled, "At a dollar a week, dat makes his ass worth a little over a thousand bucks by now! Overpriced!" They both laughed.

The boat sped off toward the next buoy, and then the next, and the next—twenty-seven of them altogether. With the last pot back in the water, they reversed course and headed back to the boat ramp. There, they waited in a long line of latecomer leisure boats at the ramp before they could get the Tentacle Tattoo back on the trailer and head off to work.

Out on the highway, they stopped at Van Hatten's Seafood Shop to sell the crabs. Micah earned enough from their sale to buy a few forty-ounce malt liquors. Gunny would stash his share away toward his down payment on a business.

The Lady's Island Oyster Factory had long outlived the adjective "pretty."   Weather-beaten, rust-brown flaps of twisted corrugated metal overlapped a skeleton of scaly iron beams and rotting wooden timbers—all surrounded by mounds of shells that looked like dunes from a distance. The building itself was a mix of tabby walls, steel trestles, and corrugated metal plates slapped together in a patchwork fashion, representing nearly seventy years of growth, additions, and changes. The original building was built in 1924, three years before the bridge from Beaufort to Lady's Island was constructed. The parking area consisted of crushed oyster shells and clusters of dilapidated car bodies with windowless doors, which, in the mist of the morning, were all shades of a salmon- and rust-colored primer with patches of Bondo putty and duct tape.

In spite of the building and the man-made relics surrounding it, the natural beauty of the site was the pride of the Lowcountry. There were gargantuan live oaks with trunks wider than the height of most men and gnarly, century-scarred branches that blocked the sun and offered cool shade. Water oaks sixty feet high lined the banks of the river. Magnolia trees showed their waxy green foliage and their nestlike fragrant flowers. Directly across the Beaufort River, cushioned by the marsh grass, the antebellum houses of Beaufort still stood in white splendor.

Gunny and Micah rolled into the parking lot of the Lady's Island Oyster Factory before all the other workers. As they pulled in, Micah noticed a white service truck on the far side of the lot—where the owner, Kip Drummond, normally parked.

"Who truck is dat?" Micah asked as Gunny drove his truck and trailer over the lot and stopped near a pile of dead palm fronds.

"Beats me. Never seen it before," Gunny responded.

They grabbed their lunch bags and walked over to the white truck with boxy storage bins in the bed. On the side of the truck, in green letters, a sign read, "ACE Basin Surveyors," and gave a phone number. Cigarette smoke drifted out of the four open windows on the crew cab. As Gunny and Micah approached, a short white man in camouflage pants and a dark green T-shirt that looked as if it were painted on his ponderous gut opened the driver's door and hopped out. He tossed his cigarette to the ground, away from the truck.

"What can I do for you, Brother?" Gunny asked, his eyes first on the cigarette that smoldered in the pine straw; then he looked up.

"Yeah, man. Name's Buzz Sampson. We're here to survey this piece of property. Sheet says to meet this guy Drummond here." He held out his clipboard and pointed to a sheet of paper with notes typed on it. Gunny scanned the sheet and noticed the contact info listed a company in Philadelphia; its name—Taggett & Vystroon, LLP—did not ring a bell.

"Mr. Drummond is not here yet. Is he expectin' you?" Gunny asked, his curiosity rooted deep.

"Not sure. I reckon he is. Guess we might be a little early. OK to wait for him here? We need to get this done today, man."

Gunny nodded in approval, "Whatever, Brother."

He and Micah walked around the heaps of oyster shells that were taller than the roofline of the factory. As they walked, Micah said, "What's dis all about, Bro? Sure sounds like somebody be fixin' to buy dishyuh place. Thought you said Drummond told you he wasn't sellin'."

As they continued to walk, they noticed a few bateaux tied to the dock in back, gave their crews a friendly high sign, and came back around front. Gunny unlocked the door to the retail store at the front of the factory building and told Micah to open the dock doors to get those loads processed. Gunny went back out to the surveyors' truck. If there is going to be any selling, it will be to me.

Before long Kip Drummond, the contact the survey team needed, drove up. He noticed the strange truck parked in his usual spot. As he got out of his truck, he noticed the ACE Basin Surveyors sign on the side of the truck and saw Gunny standing there. He wasted no time.

"Mornin' Mr. Drummond," Gunny said, prepared to introduce Buzz Sampson and his crew.

"Who sent you here?" Drummond demanded. But before the crew chief had a breath to respond, he continued: "Never mind; I can guess who sent you here. I told them, and I'll tell you, there is no need to send anyone out here until I am damn good and ready, and I am not ready. So take your crew on out of here. You tell those guys that sent you that I kicked your ass off the property and told you not to come back until I call you.

You got that? Until I call you!" Kip tapped the team leader's clipboard like a woodpecker. Gunny stepped back to let the confrontation run its course.

Buzz Sampson did not say a word. He climbed back into his truck, cranked up the diesel engine, and steered back out of the lot, mindful of the workers as they arrived on foot and the other beat-up clunkers.

Kip watched the dust trail of the ACE Basin truck as it made its way down the sandy Oyster Factory Road until it turned left onto Highway 21, headed toward Sam's Point.

As the two men walked back toward the sales room, Kip turned to his foreman and said, "Gunny, why don't you come up to the office in about an hour or so."

"Sure thing, Mr. Drummond. Let me get things movin' down on de floor, and I be up."

As he climbed the stairs to his mezzanine office, Kip wrestled with doubts about his unwanted visitors. How much did Gunny learn from the survey team? I don't need him to know anything. If they told him anything, I need to do some quick damage control.

■　■　■

"That you, Khouri?" Alex Stringham asked, having put Manny Ventresca on hold for a moment.

"No, it's the ghost of Christmas Past, you asshole. Do you not know what time it is out here?" Mazan Khouri spared no time in expressing his disgust.

"Listen, Sleeping Beauty, just had a call from the survey crew chief in Beaufort. Drummond threw him off the oyster factory property. Manny, you still on the line?" Stringham asked.

"Yeah," Manny Ventresca said. "So much for Southern hospitality. This guy is an idiot. He has all his money tied up in that run-down factory."

"OK, the guy's a moron," Stringham said. "No chutzpah. No balls. He is too chicken shit to close the place. He thinks the place is a landmark. Most of those people have been working there for decades. It's a sanctuary. Hell, they probably see more tourists than they see oysters."

"He's a one-trick pony in real estate," Manny said. "Made some quick coin and bought himself a goddamn run-down oyster canning business in Podunk, South goddamn Carolina—built back when Coolidge was president. It just happens to be on prime real estate for waterfront lots with deep-water access."

"Okay, okay. Enough about him. Mr. Tanaka said he would have our balls if we didn't close on that property by the end of the month. He is not playing games. We have his weekly call tomorrow. That gives us twenty-nine days to close it."

Despite their junior status within the pantheon of corporate scoundrels, Alex Stringham, Mazan Khouri, and Armando "Manny" Ventresca dominated the "Art of the Close" at Taggett & Vystroon, a subsidiary of the global conglomerate Yatsuki LTD. The only pride Taggett & Vystroon spoke of was their ability to close a deal and make money. It wasn't about big or small, although size drove the teams; it was about making money. Whatever it took.

"We need to accelerate our plan like we did at Newport in California and that chunk down by Naples, Florida," Stringham said into the phone as he fumbled through folders on his desk.

"We need to start squeezing this guy. Up the ante and make him pucker," Khouri said, the hum of an electric razor in the background.

"We have deals with every one of his suppliers to back off," Manny Ventresca said. "No oysters starting day after tomorrow. That pressure settles in about the time we meet with him in Charleston."

"He will be dead in the water by then. It will take him weeks to find new suppliers," Khouri added.

"I think we have all those local bateaux drivers scared shitless to do business with Drummond," Ventresca said. "Besides, we gave them more than he would pay and hooked up that deal for them to sell everything direct to the guy at that Dockside Restaurant down there. I took care of the Dockside incentive. They'll buy everything those boys bring in, guaranteed."

"When we talk to Tanaka tomorrow, I'll make sure he knows," Stringham said. "I have a lead on someone to keep an eye on the idiot's wife and kid. Plus, I think we can get a little more out of this guy. I will finalize the plans for the meeting in Charleston. Manny, make sure you and your guy get in the country ready for action,

ASAP. Get your thoughts together and make sure you are on time for that call tomorrow. We'll talk then."

Chapter 2

Sparta, the telepathic, wire-haired pointer, trotted down the stairs from the second-floor hallway and splayed with a groan inside the carport door eleven minutes before it opened.

"Attack, Sparta. Attack!" Sandi Drummond said, with a German accent like that of Der Führer himself.

The whiskered, floppy-eared pooch stood on his hind legs and slapped his paws against Kip's chest to pin him against the wall before his second foot crossed the threshold.

"It's about time. It's Friday night. The weekend's already started," Sandi said, turning to look at the clock on the wall behind her.

"Hey, if I don't do the work, nobody will," Kip replied.

"And so—" she paused. "If nobody does, what difference would that make?"

"It's a business. And businesses need to make money, or they don't remain a business in business." He tossed his briefcase in the corner, pealed the dog off his chest, rubbed him vigorously on the head and shoulders, then slapped him hard on the rump—the signal for Sparta to bring him one of the many fuzz-free tennis balls lying around the house.

"Besides, the longer I stay at the office, the less you have to put up with me around here."

He started down the main hall, and as he turned into the kitchen, Sandi met him with one of her Deep Throat kisses that would stiffen most men. But Kip responded with his usual unimpassioned hug. He turned away. He could smell the alcohol over her heavy spritz of perfume. Sandi rounded the corners of her ruby-red lips in a childish pout, fluffed her sun-bleached blond hair, and returned to the butcher-block cutting board. There, she finished off a tall gin and tonic with a few hefty slugs.

"Evelyn brought some gorgeous shrimp today when she came to clean," Sandi said. "I made some Shrimp Rosemary and a great pasta salad. I thought we could eat out on the porch if it's not too humid."

Kip had his nose in the mail and missed most of what she said.

"Yeah, sure, that's fine," Kip said. "Hey, what's this invitation from Marga Snelling for a LIARS party?"

"We can't go. I already told you we received an invitation from Armando Ventresca from Taggett & Vystroon for a weekend getaway in Charleston. A suite at the Mills House—on their nickel." Sandi tossed the shrimp in the copper skillet.

"The LIARS party is a different weekend," Kip said. "Besides, I already told you I could not take time off to go up there. I said you could go if you wanted to get away, but I have too much work to do. I can't go." He glanced up from the mail.

Sandi grimaced. "Kip, we never get out of here, just the two of us. I told you when we were married that I would move here, but I did not agree to be a prisoner in this house."

Being a homebody did not settle well with Sandi. She was, with emphasis on the past tense, a social butterfly. As a child, she lived in the shadow of the Charleston Country Club. While her parents played golf, she enjoyed the amenities for the young clubbers—Easter egg hunts, Halloween pumpkin carvings, pool parties, and teen tennis lessons. Her "coming out" debutante ball took place in the main ballroom, less than a hundred yards from where she offered her virginity that same night to her tall, dark, and handsome escort from the Citadel. Charleston was her home—her real home. The social life that came from "old-money" Charleston was her style, with many thanks to Daddy. She enjoyed the company of authors and composers, tennis stars and playwrights. She enjoyed the nightlife, the lounges, the music, and the people. She enjoyed none of that in Beaufort. The two cities existed an hour apart by car—and centuries away by the clock. There was no nightlife in the Lowcountry city, and the people were transplanted, retired northerners or the poor black people whose roots on these islands traced back to the African slave trade of Sir John Hawkins and Sierra Leone.

"Ah, but you did agree to come here if you could live in a historic house," Kip said. "And is this not a historic house?" He broke eye contact and looked nose-down at the mail.

"Come on, Kip," she said, shaking her head. "You know I can't stand those people. Even the name disgusts me. Really. The "Lady's Island Anglers and Recreation Society"? It's not a society! It's eight couples for Christ's sake! Sixteen people—most of whom are social retards that have two things in common. They drink, and they have all lived on Lady's Island. I mean, come on." She wiped shrimp guts and veins on her apron. "Can't we for once just go somewhere and do something that has a little more class than chips, dips, and newspaper shrimp?"

"Hey, I have spent the better part of my day on the phone haggling with those three bastards from Taggett & Vystroon," Kip said. "They think they have this deal sewed up. Hell, when I pulled into the parking lot this morning they had a survey team there at the door waiting for me so I could sign some waiver for them to survey the property. Of course, that was after Gunny had a chance to talk to them first. I have no idea what bullshit they told him, but I called him up to the office, and he had all sorts of questions about selling the place."

"So why not just sell the damn place!" Sandi said anxiously. "Take the money, and then we can get out of this place!"

He paused long enough to roll his eyes behind closed lids. "Easy for you to say. As soon as I finish with those shysters from Philly, I walk out of the office, and one of those black ladies corners me about how much she needs her job and how much the place means to her. Happens all the time. Then I come home, and you're riding my ass about this deal."

"I'm not riding your ass; I was talking about your damn LIARS. I just said . . ."

Kip slapped the fist full of mail on the counter and turned toward Sandi. "For the life of me, Sandi, I don't know why you resist this place so much. Give Beaufort half a chance; it's a great little place. And the LIARS? If you don't like the name, then just forget the name. They're our friends. Lighten up. They're just good, fun-loving people. They don't put on airs, most of them." He puffed his cheeks and exhaled slowly and deliberately, like letting the air out of a balloon.

"Finish fixing dinner," Kip said. "It sounds great. Smells wonderful. We can eat on the porch if you'd like. There is a bit of a breeze off the river; the bugs shouldn't be too bad. We can sit there and just enjoy the view."

Kip clapped and whistled for Sparta as he walked toward the hall. "Where's Chris?"

"My son," Sandi said, her nose wrinkling, "is over at Trevor Elliott's house for dinner. When you never showed to take Chris out in the kayaks, he and Trevor decided to go see Wayne's World at the Pelican Theatre."

"Oh shit! I got wrapped up with the deal," Kip said. "The kayak thing completely slipped my mind. Sorry. Let's go, Sparta."

He looked down toward the dog and motioned with his chin. The dog hopped up from a crouch and trotted down the hall, tennis ball in its mouth.

"Call me when dinner is ready, will ya? I have some things to do in my office."

Though the recipe called for chopped onions, by the time Kip turned from Sandi's stare, she had minced them to a mush of pulp. The knife in her hand gave her cause to hesitate. Instead, she threw it into the sink and headed to Kip's office. Sell the damn business. I don't need this place, or you. All I need is the money.

"You are not listening to me. I'm not going to that LIARS party," Sandi said, standing akimbo in the doorway.

"What are you talking about?" he said with a puzzled look. "It's a party."

"I said I am not going to the damn party. I told you I can't stand those morons. If you can't take a little time out of your precious busy schedule to leave that precious little factory of yours to take your son out kayaking or to enjoy a getaway with me in Charleston, then I am not going to bore myself with the usual gossip and drivel with your LIARS."

"OK, OK, OK, let's just start over. Forget about the parties. Forget about the trips," he said as he flashed ten fingers to ward off her assault. "Let's call a truce and just have a nice, quiet dinner, OK? I am beat."

He turned his attention back to his desk, which like the walls, was cluttered with the typical male "I love me" memorabilia.

"Beat from what? Shuckin' oysters all day?" Sandi asked. "You just said you spent all day on the phone with those guys from Philly. You are out of your league. Those guys are an international conglomerate, not a mom-and-pop operation. Sell them the damn business and be done with it."

She relaxed her stance, but the alcohol in her kept talking. "You've been going round and round with this offer for months."

"It is a big deal!" Kip hollered, his face tight and steamed.

"They have offered you more than you put into it. Take the money."

"It's more than the money; I already told you that."

"Yeah, and while you play your puny games with those three, I'm stranded here."

"You're not stranded."

"Come on, Kip. All I ask is for one weekend, alone."

"Well then, go, go alone," he replied, but he never bothered to look at her.

"That's not what I meant. I don't want to be alone. I want to enjoy a weekend in a suite at the Mills House, the poshest hotel in Charleston." She stiffened, frustrated with his unwillingness. "We have not taken a vacation since we moved here. This could be so good. We need some time away from this place, together, just the two of us."

Kip turned toward Sandi, his voice two decibels short of a rioter's yell. "That's just it. It won't be just the two of us, Sandi. Stringham, Ventresca, and Khouri will be there."

"Not the whole time."

"It's not that simple. You don't think they will leave us alone, do you? The point is to get us there so they can put the squeeze on me with this deal. These guys, they would find a way to drag you into the middle of this. Throw in a little alcohol. Have me drop my guard. Simple tactics. I can't afford to give them the chance. I have them in a corner. They need to up the ante, and they know it. I saw this when I was in real estate. It's an art. The key is for me to drive up the stakes. At some point, something's got to give. They are not about to let a small fish like me rule their big pond."

She smelled the shrimp and glanced back looked back toward the kitchen, distracted by the dinner half-prepared.

"Then why not let them treat us to a good time?" Sandi asked.

Kip squeezed his eyes closed tight, then opened them. "How about if we compromise? If you go to the LIARS party, then I will take off work and go to Charleston. Would that make you feel better?"

Without hesitation, Sandi agreed with a nod, then qualified her acceptance. "OK. I will think about it," she said, her voice still filled with anger and doubt.

"But so help me God, if another one of your nonsensical catastrophes comes up at work and you welsh on this one, Kip Drummond, I'll go to Charleston without you. I'll live high on the hog," she said with a scowl, her finger pointed toward him as if he were the accused.

Relieved, somewhat, she flashed a conciliatory smile before she returned to her unfinished business in the kitchen.

Kip went back to the stacks of papers on his desk. He knew he would never go to Charleston. His willingness to appease her was short-term and tactical. He just wanted her off his back. His strategy for working the deal remained unchanged.

With the tensions of their discussion behind them, they dined peacefully on the porch until the winds picked up ahead of a storm that proved to threaten all the outdoor activities in the Lowcountry that night— including Gunny's employee cookout, which Kip blew off, again.

CHAPTER 3

Yo, Gunny. Looks like we gots us an old party crasher," Walter Goodwine hollered from the back porch.

"If it ain't my main man, Obadiah Whyteson. What you doin' here Obadiah?" Sam Stone said, his voice filled with bravado and disapproval. Sam and a crowd of a dozen black men near the horseshoe pit along the far edge of the yard watched the old man as he approached.

"Ain't nobody invite you," Sam went on. "This is Gunny's party, old man. It be for working peoples from the factory and dem families."

"You know'd you need me here," Obadiah said. "Sho, Gunny just fuhgit to invites me, dat's all. Why, I be de life of dis yuh party, you knows dat."

The bony black man with hair like a peppered-gray Brillo pad gave a full arm wave as he hobbled past the porch and toward the pit. A stroke, years earlier, had left his right leg crippled and two fingers on his right hand bent and frozen. Behind him, black clouds smeared the sunset.

"We always appreciate you being 'round, Obadiah," Gunny said as he raked the sand in the pit. A stern look from his wife, Joetta, indicated he should be nice. Joetta had a soft spot in her heart for Obadiah because of a "condition" he had. He was a little "touched" in the head; "his bread wasn't quite done."

"Grab you a beer, Obadiah," Gunny said, then looked back toward his wife, who was speaking with a short, burly white man with a closely shaved flattop.

"Hey, Picorelli!" Gunny called to Al "Pico" Picorelli, his barrel-chested Vietnam buddy. "Leave my lady alone and get your greasy white butt over yuh. Time to toss some horseshoes for de Corps."

Gunny raised his arms, horseshoes in both hands. He looked toward the would-be challengers, and added, "Just so you scum-sucking chumps know, dat leetle meatball from Philadelphia was de 'Rocky' of de horseshoe pit in Vietnam—he was THE regimental champ. You two loud mouths will be whining for yo mamas before dis game is over."

"Aye, aye, Semper Fi! Let's do it," the squatty ex-Marine acknowledged.

He headed toward Gunny with his fist raised in mock defiance, then two fingers flipped up, spread outward in a "V"—the sign of victory, not peace. He grabbed a set of horseshoes and banged them together hard. When his arms traced circles like a windmill in a storm to loosen his shoulders, his USMC tattoo flashed from under the rolled up sleeve of his Philadelphia Flyers T-shirt. The more he stretched, and the more he grunted and groaned, the more he sounded like a pig in a wrestling match. This oversized version of an Italian leprechaun danced a jig and clanged the horseshoes together to energize the spectators. The onlookers, in an exchange of cheers and jeers, polarized into two camps, one more loyal to their homeboys than to Gunny and his spark plug Italian friend. The cookout became a bookie's paradise — bets and bills everywhere.

"I see you're still drivin' dat big rig of yours through here eb'ry week. Guess dat lottery bidness of yours ain't comin' along so good there, GI," said Wallace Pearsall, one of the challengers. "Think your luck be any better at horseshoes, old man?" The crowd roared with taunts and barbs.

"I'm goinna wale all over your loogie suckin' puss, ya hushpuppy-eatin' rookie," Al said. "I made a promise to Gunny. And I got twunny here that says you lose this game, Brother."

Along the horseshoe pit periphery, money flew between hands faster than buy-sell orders at the New York Stock Exchange. One camp of bystanders heckled, while the other encouraged the trucker from Philadelphia.

"OK, old man. Let's see if you got anything left in you den," Titus Dawlin said. He jogged a dozen steps to the far end of the pit, a tall can of Colt 45 in tow. "See if you can reach dishyuh end of de pit. I know you old guys can be forgetful. Remember, closest shoe to de stake gets to choose to pitch first. Doubles rules, alternate pitch. Gunny, man, you want a handicap?"

"I already have Pico; that's all de handicap I need," Gunny said as he slapped his old friend hard on the back, then grabbed him by the scruff of his neck. "I don't need no extra points or nothin' if dat's what you mean. Let's play. I have food be git cold and those clouds be gittin' darker."

"Hey, Lewis! You and Theo haul that tub of beer over here, Brother," Titus shouted, then wandered to the end of the pit, ready to throw.

The female guests had seen similar displays at previous cookouts. They stayed clear of the testosterone zone, quite comfortable just to organize their potluck creations on a weather-beaten, dried-out picnic table by the back door, a few yards from the periphery of the horseshoe pit.

"So, Joetta, what you heard 'bout de factory?" Jackie Goodwine asked, under her breath. "I keep hearing all sorts of bad t'ings. What do Gunny tell you?"

"Gunny don't talk much 'bout the factory. He leaves dat all behind when he comes home," Joetta said as she fanned a pesky fly from her face. "He ain't goin' to let nobody close it. He is goin' to take care of dem good peoples. He ain't leavin' dem."

Jackie slurped up the last drops of her lemonade. "Yeah, but we heard Mr. Drummond be thinkin' about sellin' out. Sadie, you 'member Sadie Mendage—she one of de two counter sales ladies—she said she overheard a conversation jus' today, when she came into de factory today. Somethin' 'bout somebody come to survey de lot and all."

"That's odd. Gunny didn't say nothin' 'bout dat to me," Joetta said, taken aback. "But we been busy gettin' ready for dis cookout and all; he probably just don't have time."

"Well, Gunny ought to go talk to Mr. Drummond and set dat man straight," Jackie charged.

"If you feel dat way, den tell Walter to go tell Gunny," Joetta said, her voice mellowing her temper.

Just as Jackie was about to drag her fake nails over Joetta's face, a shock wave of heehaw laughter from the horseshoe pit suspended their dispute. Jackie spun around and stormed off toward her husband, Walter. Joetta growled and shook her head, pleased that nobody else had witnessed their quarrel.

"Gunny, better change dat technique of yours," Titus said. "This ain't hand grenades. Gotta aim a little closer in horseshoes. Guess my team be goin' first."

"Go ahead, Pico," Gunny said. "Put de damn-damn on dese jive-ass turkeys. Dis is going to be like taking candy from a baby." He punched a fist at Pico's sternum for encouragement.

With his arm locked and cocked like a mechanical sling, Titus chucked his first horseshoe with such a high arc that it flipped end over end and landed thirty-seven feet away, perfectly positioned around the post.

"Oh, dat be a ringer!" Wallace shouted, and he danced a little "happy dance," pumping his fist in the air.

Just as "the Babe" called his shot in the '32 World Series, Pico anteed up, "I'll sees your ringer . . . and raise you . . . a ringer." Then, eyes focused, he heaved the shoe. Despite clumsy footwork and a stroke so awkward that his arm hit his leg, Pico delivered a low line drive that grabbed the stake around the top with a clank and then whirled around it until it came to rest on top of Titus's shoe.

"You're dead, mofo!" Pico said, and he raised his hand, first finger pointed like a pistol, and "fired" at Titus; then he blew the imaginary smoke away from his fingertip.

"Bro, you got lucky dat time," Wallace said as he placed his beer on the ground.

"Pico, no slack, Jack," Gunny said. "Just whip those punks de old school way, like there ain't no tomorrow. Toss it higher next time!" Then he choked on his first-round throws. Pico gestured some adjustments to his approach and grip.

"No points there, Blood," Wallace said. "Guess you done shot your wad in de warm-ups. Try dis."

In super-slow motion, Wallace mimicked fat Pico's coaching tips to Gunny. He bent his knee in an exaggerated, but dainty, curtsy, then rose up, swinging his arm in full range as if to lob a slow-pitch softball to some target over the moon.

"But don't let your skirt touch de ground, big dog," he said.

The crowd howled to single out the only white man at the party and the butt of their joke.

Unfazed, Pico played to the crowd. He strutted to the foul line, then stood "at attention" perfectly still, like a "maggot" on the first day of Marine boot camp. Eyeballs straight ahead, he saluted sharply with his right hand, and as he lowered his salute, he flipped the horseshoe upward with his left hand and shouted, "Sir, yes sir!"

With a trajectory that took it twenty feet into the air, the shoe flipped once and scraped the side of the stake. A leaner. Two points.

"OK, suckers, we'll give you dem points, Pico," Titus said. Time for my a-tomic bomb." He held out his beer can for his partner to tap in a toast.

"Sorry about dat, Mister Pico," he said. "You can kiss dem points goodbye. And for Bro Gunny, dis one's fuh you."

Not to be outdone by Pico, Wallace called his shot. He slammed a low-ball toss, and with one skip in the sand, the shoe bumped Pico's leaner out of the pit, then horse-collared the stake. "So you Bloods have any more 'citement up your sleeves?"

"Yo, Wallace! Ever heard of Minnesota Fats?" Pico asked.

"Sure, dat pool player dude?"

"Yuz ever see him play? I tell you what, how about we up the wager on this game? If yuz is so cocksure of yourselves, let's make this a bet."

"Beer or bucks, Brother?" Titus asked.

"In my world, they're just about the same, but for my friend Gunny, better go with bucks. What do yuz say? Twunny bucks?"

"Ooo, you make dis a big-time game, Brother. Dat's about half a day pay, ain't it?" Titus said, tight in the throat.

"Don't you worry about me, Blood," Pico said. "Just figure how much of a hole that'll burn in those bloomers of yours. Your momma find out you done 'screwed the pooch,' she whip your bootie."

He dropped his horseshoes, walked over to the scrub oak beyond the playing pit, then grabbed his bottle of Bud Light and chugged it. .

Micah shoved another bottle into the Italian dynamo's hand and then headed toward Gunny. But before he could reach him, Pico slapped him on the shoulder and said, "You're a good man, Micah. I don't care what these other jamokes say about ya!"

"Gunny, did ya talk to Drummond this afternoon?" Micah asked as he handed Gunny a Bud.

Gunny flinched with a double take, unsure of what Micah was talking about, but he knew it wasn't about horseshoes.

"I mean 'bout dem surveyors in de parking lot dis morning. Did you talk to him 'bout dem surveyors?"

"Later, Micah. I'm in de middle of somethin' here." He walked away to rejoin the game.

"Are yo in, Gunny, or is you just goinna talk 'bout how my momma raise her child?" Wallace said as he motioned for Gunny to return.

"We're in, but we ain't startin' over," Gunny hollered to Wallace. "We play to forty points." Then he turned back to Micah and said, "I'll fill ya in later."

Wallace pulled a small wad of bills from his pants pocket, took out a ten-dollar bill, and motioned to Titus to do the same.

Zeke Gilmore, quiet until now, strolled out from the tree on the back side of the horseshoe pit and nudged Obadiah Whyteson gently on his shoulder.

"Where's your buddy Rootie Kazootie?" Zeke said, eager to mess with the old man's head.

"Oh, he be 'round. Yes, sir. He be doin' fine," Obadiah said, unaware of what Zeke intended.

"I saw him this afternoon," Zeke said, then turned away. "He was out there directing traffic in the middle of Carteret Street in the heat with his baseball cap and whistle, just waving cars by and giving everybody a howdy do."

He looked back and cautioned the old man, "Now, you make sure Rootie don't go showing up here."

Zeke, like Joetta and all the others, was well aware Obadiah had a "condition" — some disease or habit or spirit inside him, a second personality the locals nicknamed "Rootie Kazootie." One minute, Obadiah would talk to one of them "just as normal as could be" — the usual jabber for a senior citizen. Then, in the middle of a sentence, he would walk away and go carry on a conversation with a light post or a wall or the wind. But when "Rootie" was out, Obadiah was always easy to spot in his baggy pants, striped suspenders, bow tie, and baseball cap — and he always, always had a polished chrome whistle. He was never violent, always unpredictable, and, more often than not, oblivious to life around him.

Like the old mule he could be sometimes, Obadiah trudged behind Zeke to the horseshoe pit, where the sights and sounds had escalated. One would have thought the crowd was watching a goal line stand in the Georgia-Alabama football game, not a horseshoe match. In reality, it was Pico playing to the crowd.

"You're up, my man," Pico said to Titus.

Titus pitched his shoe, the tension in his face quickly washed away when the shoe hit the stake.

"Dey you go, Brother!" Wallace shouted. "Dat be de whiskey-drenched mule skinner he-self on de old lamp post; dat be a leaner lookin' fuh a nudge." With his arms signaling a touchdown, he danced back toward his partner, like a windup bobble-headed doll. "Best not touch my shoe dey, Blood, or it becomes a ringer."

Cool as a matador before a bull, Gunny walked to the platform at the edge of the pit and brushed away the loose sand with his foot; then he sent a low side-arm shot toward the leaner. He nailed it at the bottom. The leaner flew end over end out of the pit, and Gunny's toss spun twice before it fell dead center around the stake.

"Well, I be go to hell," Wallace said as he walked back to his partner, hands deep in his pockets.

Gunny laughed. But then, having no time for revelry, he headed toward the house to check on Joetta. Obadiah walked alongside him.

"I hear'd dem be talk'um 'bout closin' de factory 'gen. Dis time it sounds like it be fuh real!"

Gunny responded as he walked, though he never looked at Obadiah. "Don't you spread dem rumors, Obadiah. That ain't goin' to happen. I talked to Mr. Drummond today. He said t'ings are fine. He told me to just keep runnin' de place like I been and eb'ryt'ing be fine." His voice rang with the confidence his heart lacked.

"Gunny, oonuh know I be a holy man 'en dem sprits dey tell 'um dat ain't so. Dey say dat dey be sump'n' deeper gwin down. Dey gimme uh cold feeling, real cold," Obadiah said, now from behind Gunny, unable to maintain his stride.

"Well, Obadiah, you better get a little closer to dem spirit friends of yours or lay off de spirits in dat can yuh 'cause I'm telling you dey ain't nothing going on. We just opened de new season and t'ings look good. So let's forget all dat. Give me a hand yuh. We need to gets dis food on dem plates so we can let eb'rybody eat."

"Sho' Gunny, 'cep'm' I be warnin' oonuh. Oonuh bettuh hab 'nodduh talk wid Mr. Drummond, h'yuh soon, real soon." Obadiah grabbed Gunny's arm with unusual strength and pulled Gunny around so he could look him in the eyes. "Dem cullud people h'yuh know oonuh be duh onliest kin git eenside dat man's head. Dese cullud peoples trusts oonuh." His stare alone was confirmation enough for Gunny.

But Obadiah didn't hold Gunny's eyes long. "One mo' t'ing." He looked up at the sky, paused, then finally pulled Gunny's attention back to the party. "I knows if'n us don't do somet'ing quick . . . us all goinna be soaked by dat storm wedduh."

Across the street, Igor, a basset hound–beagle mix that looked more like a brown and white Wisconsin dairy calf with short legs and long ears, began to bay. He was the unofficial neighborhood weather service, so he was the first to announce the weather—the same way every time. When he felt the weather, he wailed louder than the siren at the Lady's Island Volunteer Fire Station a mile closer to town, down Highway 802. Within minutes, a storm exchanged the usual thunder of Marine Harrier jets with a rumble, a crack, a flash of lightning, and a delayed ka-boom that rattled the entire island. The rain followed.

It was one of those percolator rains: one drop, then another drop, then two drops, then three. It came slow at first—and then the wind grabbed it and shook it and turned everything upside down. Trees and fences snagged foil and plastic wrappers dropped around the grill. The plastic clothesline stretched between two tall pines in the backyard vibrated like the hum of an old bass fiddle in a country jamboree.

Forced indoors by the rain and wind, the party continued, and so did the talk of the rumors. After about thirty minutes, Gunny was a victim in another storm: a verbal one.

"Gunny, what's dis I hears about closin' de plant?" Jameson Mendage asked over the din of the room, his question prompted by hours of courage from tall cans of

Colt 45 and a not-so-gentle elbow from his wife Sadie. "Is dat true?"

The topic had been an undercurrent in the conversations in the house until Jameson opened the dam. His words hushed the crowd for an instant before others chimed in, their tongues loosened by alcohol.

Someone yelled, "I heard dey was a survey team on de property dis mornin' lookin' to sell de place."

Micah turned away when Gunny scanned the room and found the only other person who knew of the incident.

"What's dat all 'bout, Gunny? What you goinna do about dat?" someone else asked.

Gunny looked around for Obadiah. "I can tell you I had a meeting with Mr. Drummond today and . . . "

"Dat's all bullshit, Gunny, and you know it. Drummond don't care 'bout us. He ain't a part of dis family. We all know dat. What you goinna do about it?"

"We needs to find out de truth," someone added from the back. "Why was dat survey team dey if he ain't fixin' to sell de factory? And when he do, what happens to all de ladies?"

"I'll dig into dis and show you it'll be OK," Gunny said. "Just relax." He wiped a curtain of sweat from his forehead.

The lights flickered, then went off a heartbeat later. In the darkness, Gunny continued, "I'll talk to Mr. Drummond again and get a commitment out of him."

"You expect us to believe him even if he do say he ain't goinna close de factory?"

Gunny knew the voice; it was Effie Boggs, one of the usual rabble-rousers.

"Y'all are going to believe what you want," Gunny said, with a lack of patience in his voice.

"What if we done pay him a visit at he house? What is to stop us from dat?" Wallace Pearsall asked, still angered over his loss at horseshoes.

"That's crazy, Brother," Titus said, then added, "Gunny, why don't you check his office and sees if you can find any proof. Dey is got to be somet'ing 'round. Dat way, we would know what to think."

Gunny hesitated. Snooping on his boss did not settle well with him. "OK, OK. I'll check his office tomorrow before he gets in. When I see him tomorrow, I'll tell him I need to talk to him again. Don't do anythin' stupid to piss him off. Let me work on dis. Just let me work on dis."

The lights came on and doused the conversation. Nobody had noticed the rain had stopped. Gunny was near the front door, soaked by perspiration from the ambush of questions, his back to the others in the room. He opened the door and walked outside.

The wind had died to a breeze. Thunder above the clouds rolled from left to right and back to the center again, and then it faded. The guests, beer cans in hand, filed out of the house like ants from their hill and took seats in the wet chairs. Their quiet remained heavy, like the air after the storm. In the end, the guests left earlier than they had in previous years. Whether it was the storm outside the house that drove them in or the storm inside the house that drove them out, everyone was gone before ten. Joetta and Gunny cleaned up after the party and went to bed. Gunny tried to sleep, but he could not. Once he was convinced Joetta was deep in sleep, he dressed and drove to the factory. It was a little before two, Saturday morning.

The light on the pole overlooking the parking area was out; Gunny had reported it to South Carolina Electric and Gas weeks earlier. With only a sliver of a moon covered by remnant passing clouds to guide him, Gunny relied on a GI flashlight. He entered the factory through the front door, the shortest path to the stairs to the mezzanine office. When he reached the top of the stairway, his ears caught the clang of metal on metal, then a scraping sound. His body tensed up. He flashed his light across the floor, but saw nothing. He moved up the stairs and hesitated at the door to the office. His ears did a double take. Then, a trash can lid hit the floor. He flashed his light toward the corner of the conveyor line and caught the mask of a raccoon as it jumped to the floor and out the narrow space between the sliding dock doors.

Inside Kip Drummond's office, Gunny inched the beam of his flashlight around the room, like a searchlight. Assorted photos and sports posters. A mounted prize-winning forty-two-inch cobia. A "jackalope" — a jackrabbit head with antlers — on the wall. Shrimp nets draped on furniture. A disassembled electric motor. Boxes from an old FedEx shipment. A small plastic basketball hoop with net hanging from the wall to the right of the desk, wads of paper beneath it.

With all the clutter, there was no need for Gunny to be concerned with how the items were arranged on the desk. He placed his flashlight on the side of the desk and began to work through stacks of files marked "Operations 1991" in wide letters. Inside, he found monthly reports Gunny had provided, month after month. He dug into a second stack marked "Business Outlooks," a file filled with articles from newspapers and magazines. He continued searching folder after folder for fifteen minutes. It was like horizontal dumpster diving: trash mixed with records mixed with bills. In Gunny's mind, it was a wonder the business survived at all under this guy.

He opened the large drawer on the bottom right side of the desk. It was jammed or weighted down with files. He pulled harder and yanked the drawer open. The dry metal of the salvaged Navy desk squealed a dreadful "finger tips on chalkboard" sound. Inside, He found a six pack of electrolyte-infused sports drinks and a bag of miniature candy bars.

On the other side of the desk, the bottom drawer was open and full of files, all dated back into the sixties. An open, empty FedEx box leaned against the drawer. Two large letters, TV, written with a wide felt-tipped pen, marked the outside of the box. Gunny did not think much of it at first, but then he noticed the documents inside were not repair slips for electronics repair. He pulled out the stack. Across the top of each document, the letterhead read "Taggett & Vystroon." They were formal documents from the firm mentioned on the survey work order that Gunny saw early Friday morning in the parking lot.

Gunny dumped the contents of the box on the desk; one document slid off the pile of other papers and fell to the floor. He picked it up, opened it, and stopped. Across the top, it read:

Ref. Letter of Intent

Taggett & Vystroon International
Subsidiary of Yatsuki LTD
One Liberty Square
55th Floor
Philadelphia, Pennsylvania 19103

I represent a syndicate of investors who are interested in purchasing the property described herein as the Lady's Island Oyster Factory located in Beaufort County, South Carolina. (See Annex B - Plats and Survey).

Gunny ignored the rest of the letter and read the signature line aloud:

Alexander T. Stringham
Partner, Taggett & Vystroon International, LLP

He recognized the signature was the same one on the surveyor's document from yesterday morning. He spent the next fifteen minutes going through the document; he scanned from Annex A through Annex F, then read through the letter one last time. The other materials in the FedEx box he had dumped were correspondence over a period of nearly eight months. The letters addressed the reluctance of the owner to sell, but then there was that "Letter of Intent" indicating an interest for the potential sale. Behind the letter in the file, he found scribbled notes for a reply and a simple chart which outlined different sales prices and profits. The last document in the folder was a draft of a press release about the sale. He sat, head down with hands in his lap, and exhaled in frustration. He found what he did not want to find.

He reassembled the packets and files he had dumped on the desk. The FedEx box slipped out of his hands and knocked over a few things on the desk before he could place the papers back inside the box, then place it back against the drawer where he had found it.

From outside the office, his ears picked up something. He froze. He listened, but he heard nothing. Damn raccoon is still at it. He brushed it off.

With flashlight in hand, he walked to the office door, stopped, and turned back to look at the desk. He debated whether or not to take the FedEx box he found and all the correspondence. He could use that to confront Drummond. He decided he would not.

He stepped out of the office. The dim beam of his flashlight covered the dock entrance, but all around he saw the dulled sepia tones of the work area. For years he had looked at these weather-beaten, rust-brown flaps of twisted corrugated metal overlying a skeleton of scaly iron beams and rotten timbers. But it all looked different to him now.

After he heard Gunny drive off, Obadiah Whyteson came out from hiding near a crate under the steps to the mezzanine. Obadiah had had the same intention as Gunny — to go through Drummond's office — but Gunny had beaten him to it. The noise was not the raccoon; it was Obadiah, who had watched Gunny's search through a crack in the door. Obadiah was quick to find the folder Gunny had placed back in the FedEx box. He removed a few sheets that interested him most; he had what he needed. Things were very different now.

CHAPTER 4

Storm clouds threatened on the Monday of the first full week of oyster season. By nine o'clock, the sun would flatten the blanket of humidity that covered the islands to make for another miserable steam bath inside the factory. The air was thick, and the bugs were thicker. Laughing gulls swooped down to scavenge for jagged shelled oysters that fell off wheelbarrows into the layer of pluff mud left on the dock.

Gunny Brewer and Micah rolled into the factory early after pulling crab traps at high tide. Gunny parked his truck under a humongous live oak toward the front of the lot. He never locked it, confident that nobody would mess with it, that nobody would want to, anyway.

Inside the factory, he unlocked the door to the retail sales area, hit the main breaker box switch to light up "the working end of the building," as he called it, and made a beeline straight to the loading dock.

A queasiness lurched in his stomach when he rolled open the monstrous bay door. In previous years, he would see flatboats stacked up alongside the dock like rush hour traffic in Times Square. Today, only two oyster pickers with scanty loads had showed to sell their catch. Gunny knew that many of the oyster fishers had moved on: they had switched to crabbing along the tidal creeks — a more lucrative business that demanded less physical effort. He flashed two hands of fingers twice to the boaters. "Twenty minutes. We be right with ya."

"Micah, give me a hand yuh," Gunny yelled. "I needs you to log in dem boats out back."

Micah grabbed the wheelbarrow in the canning stall and pushed it toward the dock.

"While I check t'ings inside, go 'head and have dem guys start fillin' in de log sheets. Only two out yuh today. Dey can save some time so we be ready when dem others showsup." He faked a solid body shot to Micah's gut as he left to walk back inside the building for his morning inspection.

Like a fighter pilot who checks his aircraft, Gunny performed a "walk-around" inspection before operations every day. He walked with a purpose as he weaved around conveyor belts to reposition empty shell-hopper buggies next to salt-stained wooden shucking stations that stretched the length of the building. Around the shucking tables, he checked the cartoon posters with OSHA safety tips, proud that they had not lost a day of work because of an accident or job-related injury in over fifteen years. He then inspected "the head" — the bathroom area for both men and women — to make sure that all the sinks and commodes functioned properly and were leak free, that all the trash was policed up, that there was soap in the dispensers. The ladies had a duty roster. They were to clean the areas on their assigned day and then initial the inspection sheet on the back of each door. It was not exactly the white-glove inspection he had practiced as a gyrene, but he cut the ladies no slack in keeping things in tip-top shape. He performed a few routine preoperations checks on the compressor in the packing area, wrote up the repair in his maintenance logbook, then flicked on the boilers at the end of the line to build and feed pressure to the steamers. Before today, Gunny's focus was the ground floor operations, but what he had learned during his search after the cookout caused him to return to "no-man's-land" on the mezzanine.

"Hey, Gunny. What brings you up here?" Kip Drummond glanced up as Gunny appeared in the doorway. Then, with his head back down, Kip continued to rifle through the folders on his desk. "How do things look downstairs? Got things in order?"

"De usual stuff, Mr. Drummond. We'll get there," Gunny answered. "Could I talk to you for a minute, Mr. Drummond?"

"Sure, sure. Come on in. Have a seat." He pushed a stack of papers to the side of his desk, then leaned over and picked up an open FedEx box. Gunny noticed the letters TV on the outside of it. After a pause, he continued: "I wanted to go over a few things with you, too."

Gunny, still a bit tentative on how to open his discussion, remained silent, standing just inside the door.

"Come on in," Kip said. "Go ahead, have a seat."

In daylight, the room looked more like a flea market than it did during his visit Friday night. In reality, it was an eclectic blend of Navy surplus goods, an old-fashioned corner five-and-dime, and a sportsman's cabin. A brown leather sofa and matching chair next to a large wooden crate that served as a coffee table. Mud-stained throw rugs strategically placed around the room covered weak wooden planks in need of replacement. In one corner were wooden bookshelves covered with old issues of Field and Stream, Runners World, and Sports Illustrated; they just collected dust, obvious purchases from a middle school magazine fund-raiser. In another corner was a pile of Styrofoam balls tied to faded, yellow nylon ropes brittle and crusted with dried seaweed; they waited to mark crab traps going somewhere. From the marsh mud outside the small window came the ever-present smell of salt and oysters—with a tinge of hydrogen sulfide, the smell of rotten eggs. Gunny took a seat on the front six inches of the chair, elbows on his knees.

Gunny waited briefly, then began, "Mr. Drummond, I . . ."

"OK, OK . . . give me just one more minute," Kip said as he scribbled a few lines and then fumbled for another folder. He wore a shamrock-green golf shirt with the logo "Kevin Barry's Irish Pub, Savannah, GA."

Gunny remained patient and kneaded his cap in his hands. Silently he questioned how a businessman like Drummond, with all his money, could ever make a business work if he could not even keep his office shipshape and squared away.

Finally, Kip looked up. "Sorry, I had to finish that." He bent down, pulled a folder from the bottom drawer, then looked up again. "Best I can determine, our operating expenses this year are going to jump by about 12 percent. The price of fuel for the steamers is probably going to hit us hard. Also, you say here in the maintenance log that we still need to get the major repair work done to belt four, I guess?"

"Yes sir, Mr. Drummond."

"And you have these repairs for the dock listed. Can't you and Micah fix the pilings?

"Oh no, Mr. Drummond. We need Byron Wittie and his boys to come by here and scrape dem pilings down. De buildup is darn thick. If one of de boats ties up and bangs into those pilings, dey could be some serious damage. We don't want dat."

"Right. Say, you want something to drink? Some water or Coke or something?" Kip asked as he pulled a warm sports drink from his desk drawer. He tapped his stubby pencil on the desk a few times, then shoved it behind his ear. But he kept his eyes on the papers.

"No sir, I'm fine."

Gunny ran his tongue under his upper lip; it made him less likely to blurt out something he might regret later.

"Then there is the issue of headcount and overhead," Kip said as he leaned back in his chair, his fingers interlaced behind his head. "If this year's predictions are right, we need to relook headcount. Probably have to drop a few people."

That one sentence set off lights, bells, sirens, and whistles of all kinds in Gunny's head. Kip had struck a nerve. Gunny remembered his purpose for the visit to the mezzanine office, but he had to address Drummond's statement. He fixed his eyes on the FedEx box.

"Dat would be kinda drastic, Mr. Drummond. Do you really think we need to go dat far? I mean dem ladies need de work. I can always find things for dem to do 'round here. If we have a slack day now and then, I have projects dat dem ladies can do."

"I am not talking about a slack day, Gunny," Kip replied, his face molded by tension. "Sounds like we are in for a tough season. We might have days when we have no boats deliver. How many boats did we have this morning?"

"Two, but we might—"

Kip interrupted. "We won't have any more. That's it for the day, and you know it. If those boats aren't in here by nine, we aren't likely to see them later. Last year, we would have had over a dozen boats in here before we even opened the dock door." He leaned forward in his chair. His eyes shot a silent salvo directly at his foreman.

"Look, Gunny, we can't just make up work for those women. If there is no work, there is no work. This isn't some sorta charity ward."

Kip shoved back from his desk, stood quickly, and walked to the window on the back wall. He ran his hands through his hair and watched the late day tide lift the waters of the Beaufort River above the fading green of the early-autumn marsh. Although muggy, the breath of air in his face allowed him to settle a bit.

Drummond's insensitive approach to the business infuriated Gunny. He turned his head toward the FedEx box; again, his tongue traced the teeth behind his upper lip. He refocused his stare onto a map of the Lowcountry in an enameled black frame just above Kip's right shoulder. He could see it was dated 1897. He reflected on images of his Gullah people, who once controlled all of St. Helena Island. Carpetbaggers had cheated and swindled his people out of their island; he was not going to let one more cheat them out of their jobs.

"Mr. Drummond, last week when I asked you 'bout dem surveyors who showed up Friday mornin', you said not to worry 'bout it. I ain't goin' to worry 'bout it, but tell me, what you are doin' with dem guys?"

Kip turned his head, "Nothing."

"Mr. Drummond, what about all dem letters back and forth 'tween you and dat company in Philadelphia?"

"What are you talking about?"

"Taggett & Vystroon. Dat company in Philadelphia."

"What did you hear about Taggett & Vystroon? Where did you hear it?"

"Mr. Drummond, I know dey are letters. I know dem said dey intend to buy dis business."

"They are not buying the business. I'm not selling the business. How many goddamn times do I have to tell you?" Kip slammed both hands on his desk.

Gunny jumped up and took a step toward the desk. "So why was dat survey team here?"

"No clue, and if you ever see them out here again, run their ass off the property." He dropped into his chair. "Gunny, we have a business to run."

"Mr. Drummond, what you have yuh is more den a business. It's a home, it's a family." Sweat streamed down Gunny's temple as he fidgeted with the hat in his hands, his tone bold and terse when he spoke. "Dese jobs ain't just a paycheck."

"Look, I pay them well. I pay better than any business in this town."

"Dese jobs ain't just work," Gunny said. "For eb'ry one of dem people, dem jobs is just about all dey have in life. Dey were born, live, and will die on St. Helena Island, and de whole time, dey done work yuh."

"Gunny, they chose this job. I didn't go looking for them."

"It's all dey got. Dey ain't got no place else to go or look. Dey ain't got nothin' more dey can do."

Gunny turned his shoulder and pointed to the office door and the steps down to the main floor. "If this factory goes away, you'll be killing them people."

"I told you, it's not going away."

"Yes sir. I'm tellin' you, if dis business closes, it would kill dem. Dey have no other jobs like dem where dey can provide for dey families. If dey lose dis job, dey would need two jobs, maybe three."

"Nonsense."

Gunny twisted back around and faced Kip. "If dis factory goes away, who is goin' to take care of dey little ones? Dey children and grandchildren and great-grandkids?" He moved closer to Kip and leaned on the desk.

"All dem ladies downstairs are scared. Dey be poor with nothin' 'cept de land dey live on, and dey only have dat 'cause it's been passed down through dey family since de Civil War. Dey don't have no big bank account. Dey don't have no big retirement savings. Dey live for dis building, for dis business. " Gunny headed for the door.

"Hey, look," Kip said. "I provide a business. I pay those women a decent wage for a decent day's work. What we have here is better than any business in this town, bar none. If they —"

The ex-Marine turned back and cut him off midsentence.

"Mr. Drummond, I've worked yuh for over a third of my life. My mother worked yuh for nearly fifty years. She left 'cause her health be so poor. She worked de fields and den worked in dis rundown building. It killed her. She had asthma so bad she could barely breathe. She died 'cause I could not take care of her, Mr. Drummond. You know how bad dat hurts me? My mother died 'cause I could not afford to take care of her. And all dem ladies downstairs right now are in de same boat. You take away dey jobs and dey are dead. And Mr. Drummond, you may be dead, too."

Kip locked on Gunny's stare, but he could not replicate Gunny's scorn. Neither flinched until Gunny pulled his cap down low on his head, walked out the door, and down the metal steps.

Kip listened to every foot that landed until the creaks fell silent. Numbed by the exchange, he remained frozen behind his desk, where he warped back in time to his days of due diligence. Before he was ever introduced to Milan "Gunny" Brewer, he watched him. One minute, Gunny was nose to nose with oyster pluckers on their flat-bottomed bateaux, arguing over spot pricing; the next minute, he was joking with one of the large female workers as they danced on the slimy concrete floor. The instant Kip heard the name, he knew he would keep Gunny around for a long time. There was something familiar in the name—Milan Garrett Brewer, something that Kip could not let go. Now he questioned his decision to keep Gunny, just as he questioned what to do with the business.

CHAPTER 5

G ood morning folks. Hope y'all had your second cup of coffee this morning and y'all are bright-eyed and bushy-tailed, rarin' to go. Welcome to Beaufort, the most historic city in the South. And thank you for choosing Indigo Buggy Tours. My name is O'Dell, and it is truly my pleasure to be your tour guide today."

The speaker was a white, twentysomething, lanky skeleton of a guy, audacious as a midway hustler at a state fair as he barked his spiel. Pumped full of Carolina sunshine and with the Lowcountry blend of Creole slur and a good-ole-boy drawl, he greeted the customers as they offered their tickets and boarded the surrey.

"On our tour today, we will compress some four hundred years and a good many of the ninety historical sites into fifty minutes of a living classroom as seen from the south end of a northbound horse."

He collected tickets as he chattered on. "My assistant today is Laddy, a fourteen-year-old Belgian draft horse who looks like Roy Roger's horse, Trigger, on steroids and, at times, behaves a bit like a teenager. Fortunate for us all, Laddy is our most experienced equine tour assistant. He will stay up front to 'lead' the tour. I will remain on the platform and guide the tour. But if, for some reason, I should fall off, Laddy here knows the way on his own, and he will ensure you have a chance to see all the historic homes on the tour, although he will probably not be able to tell you much about them."

As he turned to step up onto the carriage, a middle-aged man with blond hair and a Richard Nixon nose pulled on the back of O'Dell's faded blue T-shirt.

"Is this the Indigo Buggy Tour? How long does it take?" Dressed in tropical worsted-wool khakis and a seersucker shirt with broad pink and teal stripes, this was not the usual tourist.

"Yes sir, and the tour lasts about an hour. We are about ready here. The next one leaves in about two hours. You can buy your ticket for that tour over in the Visitor's Center two blocks down." O'Dell pointed to a small, white-block building down the street and next to the theater marquee.

Alex Stringham pulled a money clip from his pocket, then slipped a fifty-dollar bill into the hand of the lean tour guide. "I am sure this will cover the tour. Oh, and I have few extra questions to ask you at the end. Let's talk a little when we're done."

"Uh, sure. I need to grab some lunch before my next tour, but, yeah, I have a few minutes."

This was odd, for sure, but fixed in his routine, he followed Stringham onboard.

"OK, Laddy, step hop. Let's get on down the road. Come on, boy, step hop." He took his position on the step of the wagon as it started to roll.

"The house coming up here on the right is the Elliott House, also known as 'The Anchorage'; it was built in 1840 by George Elliott. After the War of Northern Aggression, as we sometimes call it around here, Admiral Beardsley bought this house. The Admiral was a whiskey drinker, and his wife was a teetotaler. If she caught him drinking, she would throw the whiskey out the window. He found a solution to this. He sent her off on a shopping trip and told her he was going to remodel the entire interior of the house while she was gone. He spent eighty thousand dollars remodeling the inside of the house, and adding some secret compartments to hide his whiskey. He actually died of sclerosis of the liver a few months later. It was not until 1980, when they did a major remodel of the house, that they found some of the hidden bottles of whiskey. The construction workers toasted Admiral Beardsley, drank the whiskey down, and donated the bottles to the Beaufort Museum. 'The Anchorage' has since become a popular eatery in the heart of the city."

As the carriage passed Harvey's Barber Shop, the smell of tonic, the hum of clippers, and the slap, slap of the straight razor on the sharpening strap piqued the attention of at least one younger tourist. A freckle-faced boy shimmied his way past the knees and elbows of the tourists and up the center aisle, then leaned around

O'Dell to take a picture of the shop, while the adults fanned the gnats from their eyes.

"Again, on your right is the Milton Maxey House, also known as 'The Secession House.' It is said that in this house, Robert Barnwell Rhett drafted the Ordinance of Secession, which laid the foundation for the Civil War."

His eyes wandered to the one and only cash-paying customer, who returned the stare, then turned to look at the house.

"Well, there is more history to Mr. Maxey. Behind his house, he built two small buildings, called 'cook houses,' where they cooked the meals. The walk between the 'cook house' and the main house is called 'the whistler's walk.' It was called that because servants were told to whistle when they brought the food across so the master knew they were not eating the food. Well, of course, the yard dogs learned quickly that when they heard whistles that meant food was moving through the yard, so they all came running. The servers were just as quick to learn. They started carrying fried balls of cornbread with them when they walked. They would throw these dough balls at the dogs and yell, 'Hush puppy, hush puppy.' And thus, the name for our Southern cornbread favorite."

"Another thing to note with the Maxey House and most all the others, the ceiling on the porch is painted that same color of blue. We call that haint blue. The Gullahs and some of the white people here believe ghosts or spirits or haints, as we call them, will not cross water. So, painting windows and doors and ceiling haint blue keeps the haints out."

The tour went up one shady street and down another as two coon dogs exchanged howls in a distant serenade of canine "howdy-do" and "I be fine." A mother in the middle of the buggy held up the hand of her sheepish daughter, who had her nose nestled in her mother's underarm.

"A question?" O'Dell asked.

A shy little girl gathered herself and, in a voice barely audible, asked with a very heavy New England accent, "What is that stuff hanging from the trees?" Question asked, she buried herself against her mother's side.

In an effort to comfort the youngster, O'Dell stepped up from the stairs of the platform in the front of the carriage and took a step toward her. He leaned toward her and whispered, loud enough for those around him to hear, "They say that a Spanish conquistador was chasing an Indian years ago and his long beard got caught in a branch. So the Indian jumped up in the tree, cut the beard off, and now we call that fuzzy stuff 'Spanish Moss.'"

She turned back at him and said, "Nuh uh!"

O'Dell rolled his eyes, shrugged his shoulders, and said, "Uh huh, that's what they say." The adults on the tour all had a good laugh. The little girl, tentative at first, joined in the laughter with them.

Pleasures of fatback popping in cast iron skillets and of biscuits baking in outdoor ovens tangoed with the sweet honeysuckle and magnolia that shared the air with pesky no-see-ums as the buggy inched its way down the route.

"Here's a little known fact you can tuck away. The tree we're passing under is a live oak, and it was the original 'pirate hanging tree.' Pirates would sail up the inland tidal basin, about twenty miles, all the way to this point. To ward off the pirates, the town leaders decided any pirate captured would be hung from that tree as a warning to other pirates. Records only reflect one hanging. When a branch of a century-old live oak dips down into the ground and then comes back up, it is called an 'Angel Oak' and can live to be five hundred years old. This one in the next yard is only one hundred years old."

As advertised, for fifty-five minutes, he waxed eloquent about the seven sovereignties which once flew flags over the Lowcountry islands and about the houses with names like "Tidewater," "Marshlands," "The Oaks," "Riverview," and "Tidalholm" — all of them classics in Southern architecture. When his passengers departed, they expressed their pleasure with kind words and their gratitude with bills they snuck into O'Dell's hand with a handshake.

"Y'all remember to stop over at 'Chocolates by the Bunch,' THE absolute best chocolate this side of Paris. Miss Denzlo Bunch is one of our sponsors. She will honor the coupon on the back of your ticket stub with a real nice discount."

The last rider to come off the carriage was also the last one on.

"Good tour, young man," Alex Stringham said as he stepped down onto the asphalt in the carriage park. "Very enlightening. Entertaining. You have a convincing presentation."

"Thank you, sir," O'Dell said, hitching the reins to the post.

"People around town say you have done your homework on the history of this place. Good research and market analysis are key to a successful business."

O'Dell listened with one ear as he moved to grab a bucket of water for his horse.

"So I hear you have been at this business a little over two years now."

"Yes sir," O'Dell said. He wiped his wet hands first across his forehead, then on his shirt.

"Also heard it wasn't going too well. Tough times. I heard you started this tour company right out of college and have burned through money faster than Sherman had burned from Atlanta to Savannah. Tough business. I might be able to help. A little cash infusion, so to speak."

O'Dell stopped to listen, with both ears, curious to what sort of business proposition Alex Stringham had in mind.

"I wonder if you could do a little research on the Lady's Island Oyster Factory for me?" Stringham asked. He pulled a folded sheet of paper from his pocket and opened it for O'Dell to see. "You get me the answers to the items on this list, I'll pay you twenty-five hundred dollars, cash. Have you ever heard of Doctor Buzzard?"

"Everybody in Beaufort has heard of the Root Doctor," O'Dell answered.

He took the list from Stringham and eyed it more closely. "These first three shouldn't be any problem. I can keep an eye on these folks and work some contacts at the bank. The third one, this hex thing, not sure. That one might take a little effort. How soon do you need the answers?"

"I need them within a week. As soon as you have the answers, call me."

Stringham handed him two business cards. "Use the private number written on the back. Leave a message with a number and a time when I can call you back. Write down your mailing address on the back of the other card. Also, you will need to fax copies of the documents on that list, so get copies; they don't need to be certified, just able to be faxed to me. I'll cover all your expenses if you need to pay for the documents."

Stringham reached into his pocket, pulled a one-hundred-dollar bill from his money clip, and handed it to O'Dell.

"When you finish with that fourth one there, I'll give you another seventy-five hundred dollars, cash. That's a deal that would help your business I would think. It's a win-win. You learn a little more history about root doctors and hoodoo while your business grows. Plus, what you discover may lead to an even bigger bonus on top of this."

O'Dell took the C-note from Stringham's hand.

"Do the leg work for the first three. For number four, ask around. You must know some Gullah people around here that practice hoodoo. They can answer some of that. If they charge you, just let me know. I will cover any expenses, too."

Stringham placed his hand on O'Dell's shoulder and squeezed his trapezius muscle with the caution: "But this is all strictly between us. We don't want folks to know; that might hurt your business." He squeezed O'Dell again, a little harder, and then patted his shoulder. "If you make it through all of these, I might have a couple chores for you worth a very hefty bonus. This little effort could be very good for your business."

Stringham shoved his money clip back in his pocket, slapped O'Dell hard on the back, and began to walk off. "Good tour, by the way. Good luck with the business, kid. I'll expect that call by the end of the week."

CHAPTER 6

After his squabble with Gunny, Kip sat at his desk like a paddle wheeler caught on a sandbar in the fog: he churned through folders and files, but the only thing he accomplished was to build up a lot of steam inside his head. He left the office at a quarter of six.

He headed across the bridge, as usual, but not the usual bridge. He crossed the Woods Memorial Bridge into town instead of the usual McTeer Bridge to Port Royal and home. His truck, slowed by the flow of evening traffic into town, seemed to know its way to the parking lot near the old Bank of Beaufort at the end of the bridge.

As he walked up the alley to Bay Street, he tossed pebbles into the air and watched the gulls swoop down to snatch them in midflight, then flick them back at him as if to say, "Check out your windshield, pal."

Three minutes later, at the corner of Bay and Scott Streets, he glanced at the cracked black chalkboard with "Today's Specials" printed on it in neon green and blue chalk: "Soup and Sandwich, $6.39. Fresh Shrimp and Grits, $8.95. Frogmore Stew (Bowl) $4.95. 'Catch of the Day' Cobia, $13.95." The entry to the building, marked by a white-washed wooden shingle with edges painted green and letters printed in black, "John Bull Tavern, 2d Floor," had no marquee, no window display with a full menu — not even a flashing Bud Lite sign.

Decades of coastal humidity had added a signature musty smell to the narrow, steep stairwell. A dim yellow halo from a bare bulb at the end of a frayed cord exposed the stares of Bull family portraits along the walls. As he approached the second level of the building, a deep-fat-fried Southern fragrance hooked his nose.

"Welcome to John Bull Tavern, Mr. Drummond."

Kip responded to the greeting with a nod as he passed the hostess stand, where he caught a whiff of perfume in the air. He looked back and guessed, "Katie?"

"No sir, Karen," the hostess replied with a toothy grin and a cute wrinkled nose. He smiled. He knew he had a fifty-fifty chance. The hostess stand was attended by Katie and Karen Creaseman, identical twins with long brown hair, dark brown eyes, shapely long legs, and 100-watt smiles.

Ancient globe lighting installed in 1930 did not allow the place to show itself very well, but it did add to the authentic look of this classic, historic waterfront venue. The original floral-patterned tin ceiling tiles survived major brutal renovations in the sixties and the disco-mania of the eighties. Black-painted pipes and electrical wiring crisscrossed the open air spaces between the photo-covered walls that stretched eighteen feet from bottom to top. The photos showed the tavern from pre–Civil War days to the War itself to the great hurricane of 1893 and, finally, to the Fire of 1907 that charred the original building and gave rise to the reconstruction of the second-floor tavern, which offered a better view of the Beaufort River as it snaked its way toward Port Royal Sound.

But without a doubt, the singular, most impressive fixture in the tavern was the bar: a massive island of solid oak imported from Plymouth, England, after the great fire. It was the last act of the tavern owner, William Rice, before he died. The bar was nearly twelve feet long and had wait stations on either end where two more patrons could squeeze in to stand. At the bottom were solid dark oak panels with carved shields of Plymouth's own Mayflower separated by posts with small lion heads and claw feet. Fluted columns on each end held the canopy above the bar, where glassware hung. Bottles on the wall behind the bar added a kaleidoscope of colors and shapes to highlight the mirrored sign with gold letters that read "John Bull Tavern."

"Man alive!" the bartender said as he wiped his hands on the towel tucked into his belt. "Spring tide on a full moon brings all kinds to the bar. Where the hell have you been?"

With hands the size of a first baseman's mitt, Jody Snow was a legend at the tavern. He was a barkeeper during the day, a Catholic deacon at night, and a retired Navy master chief for evermore.

Kip grinned at the sarcasm and added as he shook hands, "This dive offer any service?"

"Depends what kinda "service" you want there, matey," Chief replied with a pixielike smile and a wink. "Copy some numbers off the stall in the head, stop by Piggly Wiggly and pick up a six pack. You'd be good to go."

"Beer. Make it a Sam Adams, if you can pull yourself together to do a little bit of work there, Admiral," Kip said, his hand on the Boston lager tap.

"Master Chief to you, swabbie. I worked for a living!" Jody said with a furrowed brow. When he snatched a frosted mug from the cooler, Jody pumped his bicep, which made his grass-skirted tattoo, "Paige," perform a brief bump and grind.

Kip leaned his hip into the bar and looked out over the floor area to see who else had stumbled into the local watering hole. He spied the regulars: Father Tony Messimi, the Catholic priest from Saint Pete's; Kevin Williams, the owner of Fingered and Plucked, the small guitar shop on Carteret Street; and a few others—flattops with muscles, obvious Marines, decked out in Oakland Raiders football jerseys and prepared for Monday Night Football.

After his quick check of the floor, Kip turned back toward the bar and grabbed a stool. Jody slid Kip's mug across the bar, then wiped up the spillage.

"Drummond, you work too hard. I never see you down here."

"Gotta run a business," Kip told him. "Need to make living like the rest of you rich and famous people."

Jody laughed and continued to question Kip about life in general. The two of them spent time to get caught up on things: the usual small talk. Jody poured. Kip drank. They both spilled their guts on matters of the heart and soul.

At one point, with Kip's mug under the tap for the fourth or fifth time, Jody went to the end of the bar, where the young tour guide, O'Dell Foster, had slipped in next to a couple that looked to be in their late fifties. They were drunk as skunks and all over each other like teens at a drive-in. Partially concealed by the woman, who wore pearls, and the guy, who sported a gold chain around his neck, O'Dell flashed a congenial peace sign toward Kip and ordered a pitcher.

When Jody served the mug, he challenged Kip with a comment: "Rumor has it that you plan to sell that old factory of yours."

"Damn it," Kip fired back with a bit of a slur. "Where'd you hear that shit, Chief?" He took a deep breath, then chugged his fresh mug of beer, winced, then slid his mug back to Jody and nodded toward the tap. "Ah, can't always trust rumors, Jody. You know what they say. Ain't nothing sure in life except taxes and dying."

"Heard that from all sorts of folks. The word on the street is all those Gullah ladies down there at your place are worried stiff. It's like someone kicked the beehive and now they are all abuzz with gossip. Must have a mole or something snooping around." The bartender slapped the tap handle for the refill.

"Same old bullshit I hear every year when we get started," Kip said.

"Business is business, but if you close that place, I'd be a little concerned about how all of that would go down around here," Jody said. He slid the mug across to Kip and followed the trail of foam with a towel.

"What do ya mean?"

"You know damn well what I mean, Drummond. Not much of anything happens in the Gullah community that everybody else doesn't hear about."

Chief looked away. As he did, O'Dell Foster squelched his listening ear and bowed his head above the pitcher of beer. The cheers, jeers, and swearing from the Monday Night Football-ers huddled in the corner of the dining room had grown a little too rowdy.

"You guys wanna hold it down a bit back there?" Chief said as he acknowledged them with a sergeant at arms stare. The group responded with a chorus of boos and single-digit gestures toward the bar. It was well known around town that Chief Snow — aka "The Fridge" — was once the fleet boxing champ and held periodic "come to Jesus" sessions with guys.

"Just relax and enjoy the game, mates."

He turned back to Kip amid grumbles of "fuck you" and "asshole," but there was a definite reduction in the noise.

"Call it 'bullshit' if you want, but someone might just hex your sweet ass in a nanosecond if they find any truth in it."

Kip laughed, his nose in his beer. "You believe in that mumbo jumbo, Chief?"

"Ever hear of Sheriff McTeer and Doctor Buzzard?"

"Hard not to know about them around here."

"That root doctor stuff. They had it down. Those two would spar regularly in some sort of spirit world. They would drop a hex in a heartbeat."

"That's nuts. Why would anybody believe it?" Kip said.

"I was a skeptic at first, but there's been lot of proof over the years. Seriously. I saw this stuff down in the Dom Rep and Haiti back twenty years ago. I mean spooky. Some guy who got it on in port with some Haitian girl, then found a voodoo doll in his sea rack one night. All I know is this guy was sick for weeks, almost died, and damn sure never went back to that hooch again." Jody talked while he dried mugs and hung them from the pegs above the bar.

"Typical Navy guys playing games with their gullible newbies."

"I don't think so. There are all kinds out there, swear to God. Witches of all shapes, sizes, and degrees of ugly-stick. Hags, fortunetellers, seers, tarot readers, palm readers. . ."

Chief placed clean glasses on the peg above O'Dell at the end of the bar. "You probably include that stuff in your tours."

The cocksure entrepreneur youth acknowledged, "Hell yeah, I know about root doctors, hoodoo, witchcraft, conjuration, tarot, crystal balls, palm readers. All that dark side mojo, not that I've been listening, mind you." He walked to the middle of the bar, drained his pitcher into Kip's empty mug, and then slid the empty pitcher back to Chief with a high sign to fill it up again.

"I can tell you all sorts of stories about this place," he hiccupped. "Where do you want me to start? I can tell you about spells on the phosphate mining. Like the guy who ran the operation, D. T. Corbin—he once owned the house you live in, Mr. Drummond."

Kip's eyes opened wide.

O'Dell went on, "Yep, simple trivia like that. Or business facts, like how old man Mangino came here penniless from Italy and built up his oyster business to five plants. And the hex on the Polish workers he had who moved south, leaving him high and dry. That's when he hired the Gullahs about sixty years ago; they have been there since." O'Dell refreshed his mug and took a sip.

"You have all that historic minutia down," Kip said from within his alcoholic fog.

"All part of my business."

"How is that going for ya? A few others have tried that tour stuff and not made it work."

"Well, seems OK for now. Actually just picked up an interesting project that will add a little to the business," O'Dell said, loose lipped.

"What kinda project?" Kip asked.

"Oh, little stuff, research mostly," O'Dell said. "More trivia to add to my spiel. How's your business? I've been studying the history of that place a bit, too. You know, nosey history buff. Excuse me, Mr. Drummond. I need to make a quick phone call, designated driver, you know. I'll be right back."

Kip sat motionless at the bar, mesmerized by the bubbles floating in his beer. Satisfied the bubbles were a good thing, Kip leaned forward with both elbows on the bar, his eye lids half-closed.

"What were we talking about, Chief?" he asked. "Oh yeah, you ever used any of that hoodoo tarot shit, Chief?"

"Nope, but know lots who have, though. Guess it kinda depends on where my head was, what bothered me. Things bothering you so much, give it a shot; what the hell."

O'Dell heard Kip's question as he approached his stool at the bar. When the bartender finished with his answer, Kip turned to the kid.

"Tarot. Tell me what you know about tarot," Kip said, his tongue twisted around his words. "The Gullah pluckers down on the dock talk about it. They sounded scared shitless."

"Well, they're the real deal," O'Dell said. "Cards help sort out whatever troubled the mind."

"I'll be damned!" Kip yelled, shaking his hands above his head as he stared at the blurry ceiling tiles. "Those nuns in school had me believing prayer was the answer. Prayer solved everything. Hallelujah!"

Before O'Dell could answer, Jody rejoined the conversation. "Spoken like a die-hard, fish-eating Catholic. A regular. I see you out there, most every Sunday."

"I go to network. A business thing," Kip said with a smug look of self-gratitude.

Jody wiped the brass pull handles on the tap, then reached below to pour a bowl of goldfish crackers for Kip and offered another bowl to O'Dell.

"Yeah, but what if you had all this crazy shit in your head and couldn't sort it out? Would you go there?" Kip's thick tongue tripped over the words.

"Go where? Church?" Jody asked.

"Shit no. To the tarot reader."

"If that will make you feel good. Got nothing to lose."

"OK, then. Chief, pour me another Sam Adams while I go to the head."

"Aye, aye, Captain." The Chief saluted and watched Kip stagger around the end of the bar and through the heavy door marked with a brass plate inscribed with "HIS."

With the attention now on Kip, O'Dell placed a twenty-dollar bill under his half-empty pitcher and made his unannounced departure.

"Ask yourself in the morning if this is still such a good idea, Ke-mo-sah-bee," Kip muttered aloud in the men's room. With his forearm against the wall, he leaned over the urinal and uncorked his bladder for the first time in hours. "Must be the fumes from that urinal cake. Ah, naphthalene; it does the body good." He washed up, splashed some cool water on his face, pulled a half-dozen times on the endless cloth-towel dispenser by the sink, and never could get to the end of it.

As he left the men's room, Kip heard the familiar clang of the ship's bell at the bar.

"Yo, buy the house a round of drinks!" said a stocky, shaved-head Marine in a ripped Oakland Raiders jersey: Jack "The Assassin" Tatum. Number 32. His friends, still glued to Monday Night Football on the tube, exchanged chest butts and chanted, "Jocko, Jocko, Jocko." When he turned to flip his compadres the bird, he staggered into Kip. Instantly, at the suggestion of Sam Adams, Kip grabbed the silver and black jersey, pulled it up over the Marine's head, and shoved him through the restroom door. A brief calm fell upon the tavern. The only noise was the voice of the football commentator on the TV. Then, a muffled "asshole" echoed from the floor inside the men's room. Kip bowed to the applause of onlookers and returned to the bar.

"OK, dog breath." He winked at Chief. "I had a bit of a talking with my new best friend Samuel Adams while I was out. Guess I'll try some of that tarot medicine you prescribed with the kid. Speaking of which, where did he go?"

"Don't know. He just up and left. He paid for his beer, though. That's a first. He usually builds a tab that somebody else pays. This time he paid and even left a tip, thanks to Happy Hour prices!"

Chief handed Kip another frosted mug and slid a pitcher toward him. "Here, drink up and finish this one. The kid left it behind. It's paid for."

"So, big guy, now that you convinced me to place all my troubles in the cards, got any names for tarot readers in the area?" Kip asked while he filled his mug.

"Well, none off the top of my head. Let me go back in the kitchen. I'm sure Mr. Bill has a few." He was referring to Bill Erwin, the tattooed and pierced cook with the heaviest New England accent in the Lowcountry.

With Chief in the back, Kip noticed the rowdy foursome at the bend in the bar. The two girls, with makeup straight out of the Moulin Rouge, wore gray loose-fitting tank tops with "Carolina" embroidered in large red letters across the front and below that, in smaller red letters, "Gamecocks." The tops, strategically cut across the neckline, revealed their Carolina cleavage. The design modification worked on only one of the two—coincidentally, the well-endowed blonde: big hair, big tits, and big mouth. When she talked, she was loud, and when she laughed, it was a hideous nasal laugh.

"Hey, babe. Put a sock in it!" Kip shouted toward her.

"Creep," she replied, along with appropriate hand gestures unbecoming a Southern belle. It was obvious from their slurred speech that the two guys were interested in one thing and one thing only. It was time to stop drinking and get somewhere—anywhere—before they lost it all. The girls were loony with liquor and primed for the main event. Kip's chauvinistic slur offered the perfect excuse to pack up and head for the door.

Chief burst through the kitchen swinging doors, handed Kip a square stub of paper, then turned away to settle up with the loud-mouthed wench and her friends.

Kip froze when he saw the stub, his eyes glazed over.

"Madam Ayanda," Jody said. "Numbers and directions are on the back. Don't get your hopes up, Amigo; it's an old ticket. Not worth the paper it's on. Bill drives down to Savannah every week to buy a fistful of those lottery tickets and has never won a red cent."

When Kip never answered him, Jody turned around. "You OK there, General?" he asked as he walked toward the guy who had entertained him at the bar for the past five hours.

"Sure. Sure. Uh, you ever do that? Drive down there for tickets, I mean?" Kip asked, as he pulled himself out of some other displaced zone of reality.

"Nope. If you think all that hoodoo, tarot, root doctor stuff we talked about is hocus-pocus, talk to me about the lottery. There's some big time evil in that racket."

"Once again spoken like a true deacon, Mr. Jody," Kip said. He raised his mug to trace a sign of the cross in the space between him and the Chief.

"So let's see. How does that work?" Kip asked. "If your odds are one in two hundred million with one ticket, does that mean your odds are one in twenty million if you buy ten tickets?"

With heads only a foot apart, the two locked stares; then Kip's eyelids closed, and his head bobbed with a jerk. Embarrassed, Kip puffed a lungful of stale beer breath into Jody's eyes, then broke into a belly laugh. The sudden laughter awakened two marine recruits passed out nearby. The tabletop of empty beer bottles was a dead give away that they were experiencing their final preparations before the man-eating, head-shrinking aborigines at Parris Island put them through the Marine rite of passage.

Amid heehaws of laughter and nasal snorts that shot beer out of his nose, Kip stumbled as he tried to stand.

"Think it's about time you called it a night there, General. Here, try some of Mr. Bill's sludge before you hit the road." Chief poured remnants of coffee from the stainless steel carafe. "Reveille with the dog will be a tough one tomorrow."

"Bet your ass," Kip said. He sipped at the coffee. "Damn, does Bill filter this stuff through his dirty socks?"

"Hey, it'll wake most anybody up to get them home safely any night of the week."

"Yeah, reveille. You can bet Sparta will nudge my elbow at the usual time, and if I don't respond, he'll crawl into bed with me. Then the wife screams. Not a pretty sight, but guaranteed to get my ass up."

Chief pulled Kip's bar tab from the clip on the overhead frame. Kip chugged the half cup of coffee that remained, then grimaced. "Lord Jesus, save me. Man, that's nasty. Give Mr. Bill my compliments on his potion."

"Most definitely," Jody said with a slap to Kip's back. "Be careful on the drive home, Champ! The pigs will be moving around out there."

"Thanks for the warm and thoughtful counsel. I owe ya. Not sure what or how much, but I owe you. G'night, Chief."

Kip leaned on the wall as he slid his way down the dark staircase, nearly knocking the framed picture of John Bull himself off its hook. Through the intervention of his guardian angel, Kip found his truck, parked right where he had left it, the windshield now covered with gull droppings. He dropped his keys twice before he managed to fit one into the door lock.

As he drove west toward Port Royal, he passed the flashing yellow warning lights of the city street sweeper, parked with its brushes still spinning while the driver relieved himself on the lawn in front of the U.S. District Court House.

The only other conscious life Kip encountered on his ride home was Roddy Pinkerton—a friend, a fellow member of the Kiwanis, and the sole member of the Beaufort City Police Department on duty.

Roddy recognized Kip's truck as it rolled through the flashing red light onto Ribaut Road. He flashed the blue light atop his cruiser and pulled Kip to the side of the road. Surprised at how intoxicated Kip appeared, Roddy knew his friend was in no shape to be on the roads, but he also realized it would be a hassle to bust him. After instructing him to drive straight home, Roddy followed him, turned left onto Spanish Point Drive and around the loop to Kip's driveway, where he flashed his lights and then headed back on patrol.

Kip would not remember opening the door or falling asleep in his recliner. He would not remember that the time was just shy of midnight, the same time the mojo started on St. Helena Island. All he would remember was the bark when Sparta heard something, or someone, in the yard at the crack of dawn.

Chapter 7

When the sliver of moon dipped below the scalloped, tree-lined horizon, the pitch of night swallowed St. Helena Island. Starlight played peekaboo through clouds, while orphaned pockets of muggy air played hide-and-seek with occasional cooler breezes.

At the southwest corner of the island, in the small unmarked cemetery of The Chapel of Ease, O'Dell Foster huddled in silence with a stranger, one known only by reputation.

Slanted, worn, and stained limestone slabs with chiseled names and dates capped the pain, humiliation, hate, and vengeance laid on their souls' eternal rest beneath the sandy surface. For the souls of both the slaves and the freedmen residing there, this ground offered the first true peace they had known in the New Land, the final resting place for a Gullah people bitterly enslaved for centuries. Concealed by larger headstones, an irregular chunk of limestone lay close to the brick and tabby wall of the remote chapel destroyed by fire over a hundred years earlier. Lore among the residents held that the simple stone marked the grave of "Doctor Buzzard," arguably the most revered root doctor of all times. Known by the area residents as Stephaney Robinson, "Doctor Buzzard" was said to have passed his special powers inside his family, although for years some family members had vocally dispelled the rumor, swearing that he had passed his powers to a follower secretly known as "Doctor Flea."

The messenger and the root doctor exchanged no names and spoke very few words. Their business was brief, their timing critical. Layered necklaces of beads, bones, and feathers tangled outside a conjurer's hooded black robe. The root doctor reeked of sweat and the smell of blood. He smoothed a small space with the toe of his worn wing-tipped shoe, then etched a talismanic design that resembled the five pips on a die. In each corner, he placed a handful of sea salt, and in the center spot, he placed the screw cap for a small bottle and in it a single, short black candle, which he lit. The flame shone like a beacon, and seen from a distance, it cast eerie shadows on the stone markers around him and the messenger.

A screech owl perched in a tree outside the cemetery broke the silence with a distressed trill before Dr. Flea lifted a small painted bottle. "In dis bottle uh hab placed nine needles, nine pins, and nine rusty coffin nails to cause pain and harm, hair of de black cat and a black dog, which fight constantly, and vinegar and red pepper to make it all burn extra mo'. Us seal de jar wid de wax

fuh de candle, but first us mus' add de key element —
goofer dust. 'E time fuh."

He pulled back the salt-stained cuff of his robe and
reached toward the candle. From inside the robe's hood,
the voice said, "Goofer dust be dirt fum pun'top de
grabe collected jus' attuh middlenight. Ef us collect 'e too
early, 'e could provide good fortune fuh de pusson
affected by de spell." The conjurer checked his watch.
The trees whispered to the wind.

"We mus' wait two minutes mo'," he said. "Us
collect de dirt at de last stroke of middlenight.   Us
combine d'other ingredients while us wait."

The flame on the small candle cut the black of the
night. From his robe pocket, the conjuror pulled an old
red flannel bag and a handful of plastic storage bags.
From one of the plastic bags, he pulled out some dried
skin. "Dis one be de dried snake skin with 'e head
smashed, but attached," he explained.   Although the
light was weak, the diamond pattern on the snake skin
and the triangular head left no doubt to the messenger
that this was the skin of a rattlesnake, but without the
rattle. The conjuror placed the skin into a larger ziplock
plastic bag. From one of the smaller plastic bags, he
poured a yellow powder that smelled like sulfur into the
large ziplock bag with the snake skin. Out of a third bag,
he poured a red substance into the large ziplock bag.
"Red pepper," he said, as he mixed the powders into the
bag with the snake skin. He zipped the bag shut, then
eased himself to his knees; the messenger did the same.
The conjurer placed the plastic bag between them and

smashed it twenty-one times with a smooth, round rock he held in a deformed right hand.

"De 'tears uh God' be shakin'; 'e time fuh gone," he said, referring to the Spanish moss that hung above them.

From the red flannel bag, Dr. Flea pulled a small, rusted trowel with a wooden handle wrapped with black cloth tape. He bent forward toward the headstone, the inscribed name weathered beyond recognition. He brushed back the moss that straddled the stone. With the trowel, he scraped up sandy soil mixed with bits of twigs, acorn caps, and filings of grayish-silver moss until he filled the scooped blade; then he tipped the mix into the larger ziplock plastic bag containing the skin and the powders. He resealed it, shook it a few times to combine the contents, then hammered the bag twenty-one times with the smooth rock. The ground shook with each stroke; his silhouette on the gravestone resembled that of a caveman over his prey.

His movements were rushed. He opened the plastic bag and poured the contents into the colored bottle, leaving a portion of the hoodoo in the bag. He pulled a small box of wooden matches from a miniature saddle-bag purse, then poked a match into the flame of the shrinking candle. The match ignited, flared up, then tapered back. He stood the match on its end in the sand atop the grave and then quickly extinguished the candle. He twisted the cap onto the bottle before the molten wax could harden. He shook the bottle and heard the nails clinking against the glassy sides.

"Dis bottle holds de spell and de curse. Oonuh mus' position de castings of de spell properly. Only water can remove it. Oonuh mus' do 'zackly as uh say."

A fog crept in on the heels of a silent breeze that dropped a feather-light nest of Spanish moss on the root doctor's shoulder. He brushed it aside.

"Oonuh mus' begin wid de sprinkling of de powder at each of de four main corners of de house," he said. "Oonuh mus' carry de bottle with de powder in dis red flannel bag, de mojo, tied with de drawstring and carried from yo belt. Once de house be prepared, den dig a small hole under de walkway uh de most used entrance of de house. Bury de bottle upright so dat de cap be six inches from de surface; dat allow de foot track magic to ease upward to their feet as dey cross over it each and every time dey enter and leave de house." He paused; again the owl hooted further out. "All dis mus' leave no visible sign of de digging. When all be ready, walk away walking backwards for twenty-one steps, and sprinkle de last bits of de dust fum de mojo. Spread them like seeds over the footpaat. De ceremony mus' end jus' as de sun be rising, no earlier. Finally, go to de crossroads, away from de house, bury the mojo, and leave. Do not give no looks back."

The two parted on foot in opposite directions. The messenger, with the red flannel mojo upright in his hand and the detailed process fresh in his mind, returned to a rusted car, while Dr. Flea stashed his robe and chokers in a worn leather bag, walked back to his own rusted car, and drove away toward the southwest tip of the island.

The messenger drove nearly a quarter mile, turned onto Crossover Road and then onto Ernest Drive; then he turned on his headlights. When he lit his cigarette, there was a peculiar look in his eye before he tossed the smoking match into the rain-soaked oak leaves in the ditch.

The fog lingered and grew thicker throughout the night. O'Dell dozed on and off in his car, hidden in a thicket of blackberry bushes laden with the voracious plague of kudzu on a vacant lot well short of his destination. Each time he awoke, he checked his watch. He needed to wait for the window of time just before the sun.

When the time was right, as the morning skies lightened before the sun, he walked a quarter mile down the road to the drive to the darkened antebellum house which overlooked the river. Concealed by fog in the darkness before the dawn, O'Dell poured small piles of the powder from the mojo to mark the area. From under the roofline of the carport, he noticed the footpath from the carport to the side door, the obvious regular entrance for the family. The sound of the rusted trowel against the gritty sand beneath the walk broke the predawn silence. No crickets or locusts. None of the usual raccoon chatter. While he dug, bats left shadows in the predawn sky as they swooped back to their perch inside the gable vent at the southern end of the house. He placed the bottle, upright, into the hole and refilled the void with sand; then he covered the spot with a clump of Spanish moss.

As the morning sky lightened, O'Dell froze when he heard a dog bark from inside the house. No lights came on, but he knew the bark could arouse someone. Bent at the waist, he backed away from the house and dusted the path from the house to the carport with the seeds of the spell. Twenty-one steps, exactly as Dr Flea had prescribed. Urged on by the dog's bark and the thin morning light, he ran down the drive. From the road, through the fog, he saw the porch light come on and heard a figure at the door yell, "Sparta, stay here, boy!"

At an intersection of two back roads out on St. Helena Island, the tour guide, now the messenger, stopped briefly to scrape back shards of oyster shells on sandy soil to bury the remnants of the spell and the red flannel bag—his last deposit for the night. The hex was laid. One more question remained for O'Dell on the list from his generous benefactor, Alex Stringham.

CHAPTER 8

Four restless nights followed the night at the John Bull Tavern. Now, on the fifth night, still emotionally drained by the cerebral wrestling match with the others in the tavern, he found himself behind the wheel of his truck, driving a route over small bridges, which spliced together lily-pad plots of a causeway through the marsh, to St. Helena Island, where he would meet the tarot reader that Chief Snow and Mr. Bill had recommended.

The drive down Sea Island Parkway was a grass-free, strobelike psychedelic trip. The speedometer in his truck pegged at sixty, store fronts flashed by like colors on an Edvard Munch canvas. Their signs melted into citrus blends of yellow and orange, or smears of reds, whites, and blues: the truck stop with the "no name" gas; the red banner and check mark of the Winn-Dixie; the dilapidated wooden building with the hurricane-tested tin sign that flashed "Steamer Burgers"; the hardware store; the boat-and-bait shop; the "Golden Arches"; the Beaufort County Airport at Frogmore affectionately known as Frogmore International. When he reached the cordon of oaks crouched over the two lanes of Dr. Martin Luther King Junior Drive, the twilight turned into the dead of night. By the time he reached Land's End Road, he relied on his low beams and the interior cabin light. To keep it from blowing out the window, he placed the Georgia lottery ticket with chicken-scratch driving instructions on the passenger seat, under the corner of an old copy of Field and Stream. The local road map open on his lap fluttered and threatened to fly up in his face.

Land's End Road past the Penn Center. Two miles. Look for Kinte Drive. Take next right. Storyteller Road. Half mile, left at No Man Land Road. One mile, left at Wigfall Lane to the end. One house just as you make the turn, but you go to the end; that's the place.

He passed the Penn Center, a National Historic Landmark and well-known throughout the Lowcountry as the Civil War symbol of freedom, education, and prosperity for the Gullahs and the only significant checkpoint along the route.

The Crab Rangoon with sweet-and-sour sauce from lunch whirled in his stomach. His heart raced. His hands jittered so much that he dropped the directions. He began to talk out loud for companionship.

He turned off the dome light. "Now I can at least see the signs. Kinte. Storyteller. Kinte. Storyteller." With the radio off, he chanted and drove with high beams on, to spot street signs. "Kinte. Storyteller. How far out this godforsaken road is the damn turn?" Finally, the headlights washed over a dark green street sign bent down in the weeds, an obvious victim in a previous accident. He slowed to read the street name.

"Kinte Drive. Hot damn. OK, the next turn, with or without a sign, should be Storyteller Road."

There was not a soul around. No people walking. No headlights. No houses. No birds, bats, possum, raccoons. No signs of life except a distant nebula of lightning bugs over a field of withered tomato plants off to his left and another strange light at a distance further down the road. The only sound was the echo from inside his chest. He decreased his speed and flashed his lights from high beam to low beam and back to high beam, which spooked a black-crowned night heron about to spear its prey in the salt marsh inlet.

"Goddamn it, where's the sign?" He pounded the steering wheel. Two minutes later, he saw it, the tall bare pole with a green sign on top. "Storyteller Road," just as he expected.

With arms as solid as Jell-o, he made the right turn off Land's End Road. He felt a strange chill in the air. He looked back toward the light down the road he just left. For whatever reason, maybe the blackness, maybe the chill, maybe those jitters, he remembered the tale of the "Land's End Light," Beaufort's own Sleepy Hallow ghost. Was it a Confederate soldier or a Union soldier or a weary disgruntled slave guarding his land on St. Helena Island? He could not remember. One thing he knew for sure, he sensed someone or something was with him now, something more than the chirp of the crickets, which had appeared out of nowhere. He flipped the switch for the interior light and checked his directions.

He had no problems with the next signs. He turned onto No Man Land Road, and about a mile later, he made another left turn, onto Wigfall Lane, one of those roads covered with pine cones and a trove of archeological trash that would lead researchers to think they had discovered a "brave new society." Trash littered both berms of the road. "Super Size Me" cups. Burger wrappers. Fried chicken boxes. He rounded a bend, and through the trees, in the distance, he saw the faint glow of a solitary naked bulb, dim above a porch.

At the road's end, he parked his truck. He etched the house in his brain. It was typical for this end of the island: small, one-floor, an old slave quarters with single windows on either side of the door and a fireplace chimney on the end. The walls had a fresh coat of whitewash, but the windows and door remained covered with a leprosy of blisters, layers of "haint blue" paint: the hoodoo practice of warding off evil spirits. A screen door was propped open with a large Maxwell House coffee can filled with sand or dirt, or something. Moths danced in and out of the dim lure of a forty-watt bulb above the dry, bare wooden porch swing which hung crooked from rusted chains.

He hoisted himself out of his truck, dropping his keys when he bumped the door shut with his hip. He noticed his palms were sweaty and his hands still jittered. He wiped them on his shirt as he approached the house. He stretched to take the porch steps two at a time, and though he was good with dogs, the possibility of a dog no longer secured by the heavy chain across the top step concerned him. He rapped on the door and then did a full three-sixty scan with his eyes and ears for any signs of a dog. All clear, he wiped his hands on his shirt. When the door latch clicked, he fixed his eyes on the door knob. The porch light went off, and the door opened, without a creak.

A figure, silhouetted by a terraced altar of votive candles, appeared in the doorway. The candlelight blinded Kip as he peered in from the black hole of the porch. He was amazed that none of the light had seeped through any cracks around the door or windows of this shack.

"Mr. Drummond, I am so pleased to see you." The shadow in the doorway could not have been more than five feet tall and spoke in a high-pitched female voice without the usual accents, either Gullah or Southern. The hair on the shadow's head was not visible, but the shape suggested the hair was permed or set with tight curls: possibly a wig.

Kip froze, puzzled in a search for his response. "Pleased to meet you, too." Meet who? He had not yet seen the face of the body behind the voice, but he already began to question why he made the trip.

"Come in. Please relax," the shadow said. "I know this must be a new and strange feeling for you. There is no reason to be afraid. There is nothing here to harm you. At any point, if you feel you need to leave, do so.

Your time here is your time. I want you to feel perfectly comfortable."

Kip moved with caution; he still felt the chill despite sweaty palms and a rapid pulse. "Relax," she says, right. As he walked through the door, he realized this was no typical slave quarters. His escort led him first through a small room, maybe four by six, which served more as a hall than a foyer, then into an adjoining room. He paused before he entered it. The room was a shrine. Tiered surfaces with candles. Flowers and candles. Nothing more. There was no icon.

His escort moved past the candles and opened a narrow wooden door hidden behind a tapestry covered with images of black families near boats with cotton bales piled around them.

When his eyes adjusted to the dimness, Kip looked back at the wall of candles, then proceeded into the private room. His escort had disappeared. He found himself in the company of a black woman seated at a table with her back to him. In silence, she extended an arm with an open palm toward the empty seat across from her.

"Huccome oonuh cum 'fuh see me?" The voice was not the escort's; it was deep, and raspy with age.

Adrenaline charged through him like a finger in a light socket. "I . . . I . . . "

Kip was waylaid by the Gullah words. He struggled. Even though his own workers spoke Gullah, his ear was not trained for the conversational Gullah native to the Lowcountry.

The planks of the pine flooring creaked as Kip continued around the table and spied stains on the wood. Is that blood, or something left from the great storm? Regardless of what they were, they were reminders of the burdens faced by those who lived on this property through the years.

Kip sized up the room. Along the wall to the right was a sideboard washbasin table, which probably once stood in some plantation house. Decades of use in the slaves' quarters had stripped it of all the finish, but the beauty of the wood grain remained. Light from the shrine in the outer room continued to illuminate the table until the door quietly closed and the room darkened under the halos of two candles perched in wooden holders along the side walls. He peeked at the face of the person seated at the empty table, but the shadows made it difficult to see, and he dared not be caught in a stare. Her arm gesture withdrawn, she sat in silence, hands in her lap. He straddled the chair opposite the Reader, then took a seat in it.

The body with a voice lifted her head and sneered; her black eyes were hot coals that cut through him. She measured him for a response that never came. She bent forward, placed her hands flat on the table, and said with contempt, "Huccome oonuh cum 'fuh see me?"

Kip sat in her spell, unable to answer the question. Candlelight flickered. He stared at her eyes sunken deep into cheek bones, her face a reflection of the meals that never made it to her table. Her skin, worked and worn by the summer suns and winter winds in the fields, had leached the elastic from the flesh so that she looked like a head chiseled from black onyx. Shiny. Angular. Not soft and round. Creases crisscrossed with deep wrinkles from her forehead down through her cheeks. Shriveled folds of skin ran down her neck. Her hands had long, twiglike fingers with stretched black skin over swollen knuckles and nails that were long and dirty, cracked, not manicured—evidence of her labors of the day, probably of every day.

"Why have you come to see me?" another voice said. From the shadows of the corner, it was the voice that greeted him at the door, and it was translating the Reader's Gullah.

When the frail Reader leaned back in her seat, she loosened her spell on Kip. He cleared his throat and answered her question.

"I would like to know my future."

"Wuh oonuh wan'?"

"I want to know about my future. I want to know what to do," Kip said, now able to translate.

"Uh cyan' tell oonuh 'zacly wuh' tah du'um."

With each word from the Reader, Kip tuned his hearing a notch tighter—to a point where began to understand more, but not all, of what the mystic was saying.

"I don't expect you to tell me exactly what to do. A friend said you could help clear my head so I would be able to make decisions about the future; you would tell me what is going to happen."

The Reader's eyelids sagged, then drifted closed. She puckered her lips. She cocked her head to the right; then in slow motion, she dipped it until her chin rested on her chest. With a soft grunt, she pushed away from the table; her chair slid back a mere two inches, no more. She rose like silent smoke from a day-old fire. Kip looked on, unsure if he should help her. Is that it? Did I do something wrong? What did I say?

She uncurled from her seat. She leaned over the table until her knees locked; then she rolled her back upright, each vertebra popping above the one below until she could peel her chin off her chest, just enough to see the things above the floor. With her left hand on the table, she shuffled past Kip's shoulder, in the direction of the old washbasin table. Kip sat and watched, like an inmate watching the guard.

Atop the washbasin was a small box made of wood. It was about the size of a cigar box and held together with broken pieces of splintered wood. It showed its age like the furniture in the room.

As she shuffled closer to the stand, Kip heard the high-pitched, female voice from the shadow once again. "She needs you to ask your question."

Kip strained to find the person behind the voice. Though he was sure the voice was that of the escort who greeted him upon his arrival, he was puzzled why it remained in the room and why it remained in the shadows.

Candle flames danced as the Reader, dressed in a black robe that bunched on the floor, scuffed her feet across the stained pine. She picked up the old box and carried it as if it were made of glass. Once seated, she placed the box in her lap. She took a deep breath and tapped the table with her index finger. Another breath and another tap. Three times in the same spot. With each tap, the palsy in her hand became more pronounced. She repeated her breaths, her taps, again and again and again, until her taps traced the corners of a square. Finally, she tapped three times, directly in the middle of the square.

She caressed the box, her fingers moving slowly, like spider legs, over the top of it. Her body swayed in rhythmic cadence to a private incantation.

"Wid de o'pnin' ub de deck Uh mus' rech 'nside oonuh mind, oonuh head, oonuh haa't en' tell de tale been long time de reveal."

Soon after she started, the soft voice from the shadows followed with a translation. "With the opening of this deck, may I reach inside your soul, your mind, your heart, and tell the tale they long to reveal."

A minute or more later, the old woman stopped, her hands rested on the lid of the box, to conceal it from Kip. Her head straightened, stretched forward, and the phosphorescence of her eyes against the black features of her face telegraphed her thoughts.

"Wuh oonuh wan'?"

"I need to know what is happening with my life," Kip said in a monotone.

Candle flames bent toward the wooden box as she lifted the lid of it to reveal a multicolored cloth. Stripes of rainbow colors, each a half-inch wide. Lime green. Rose pink. Bright yellow. Sky blue. Deep purple. The cloth itself was a treasure, but what it held appeared even more precious to the Reader. She did not flip the box and drop the contents on the table or in her other hand. With the care of a diamond cutter, she lifted the bright cloth with its contents from the base of the wooden box, replaced the lid, and pushed the box to the edge of the table, her face wincing in pain. She pealed back the cloth like a bandage from a wound and exposed a deck of gritty cards. Spellbound, Kip refused to blink.

She placed the deck directly in front of her, in the space she had marked by tapping the table. The cards looked old — browned, cracked, worn, and torn. With her left hand, she lifted the top card as if she would pick up a single grain of sand from the beach, then slid it into the middle of the deck. With her right hand, she did the same with the bottom card. Then, again with her left hand, she divided the deck into three smaller stacks in front of her. With her right hand, she pushed the middle stack to the middle of the table.

Kip reached for the stack as she slid it toward him. She immediately covered the stack with her hands, but she did not pull it back.

"Oonuh mus' nebbuh tetch dese ca'ds."

Kip flinched. He pulled back his hand, placed his elbows on the table, then clenched his hands in a ball in front of his mouth. He drew a deep breath and exhaled through his laced fingers, mindful of the Reader's fingers as she turned up the top card from the tarot deck and placed it in the middle of the table. The image on the card was a falling stone tower of red bricks with a golden dome blown from its top by a bolt of lightning, the tower falling to the ground along with two bodies — a man and a woman — holding hands. The symbolism was lost on Kip; the Reader offered no explanation.

Kip edged forward in his chair; his fingers massaged his temples. The Reader continued. Perpendicular to and above the Tower card, she placed, first, another card, face up, with a picture of ten coins, and then four cards, encircling the two in the middle of the table. Her hands trembled; her palsy worsened. She positioned the cards, then tapped each one twice with her forefinger — as if to nail them in position. The new cards showed more coins and sticks. The last card showed a man, hands bound behind his back while he hung upside down, tied by one foot to a timber crossbar. Four more cards, strange cards, aligned in a column on Kip's right. The first card showed five wine cups. The next showed a wide-eyed skeleton, smiling and standing erect at the edge of a precipice; it held a single feathered arrow in its right hand and a tall bow in its left. The third showed a large coin or shield. And the card closest to the Reader was a surreal drawing of five characters: a bearded old man on hands and knees supporting a large wooden wheel, a blind-folded woman, and three childlike figures with the features of a donkey.

The imagery of the cards meant zilch to Kip, but each new card laid down sent an icy chill through his veins. His head, propped between two hands, pounded as he sat there. To him, all of this was one part séance and two parts circus. Why in the hell am I here? While he questioned his presence, he failed to notice movement from the shadows. When he looked up, Kip recognized the curled hair and shoulders silhouetted beneath the glow from the candles that sputtered along the wall. It was the younger girl who had met him at the door.

"OK, so what does all this mean?" he said, his voice trailing off in disgust.

The Reader pointed to the first card she dealt. "Dat Tow'uh," she said, "dat mean oonuh 'spect sump'n big gwine' happ'n sudd'n like."

Kip's hearing, somewhat suppressed by the spell in the room, found the Gullah more difficult than it had been earlier. He thought she said that something big could be expected suddenly, so he asked point blank, "Like what?"

The Reader raised her head and looked at him with scorn. Her eyes carved at him like daggers. She sneered, then redirected her focus to the spread of cards. Her taut black skin wrapped the thin bone of the forefinger she used to point to the cards.

"De coin pun'top de Tow'uh mean life bin berry good fa oonuh, mos' good nuf oonuh fa retire now."

Frustration nibbled at Kip's patience. "What? You said I should retire? So is the sudden change . . . retirement?" Her disjointed clues muttered in Gullah gave him nothing.

She coughed to clear her throat, but she did not speak. Instead, she unrolled her right hand onto the table, a gesture with an open palm toward her assistant, who stood in the dark alcove along the wall and behind the table.

"She tires quickly now," the assistant said as she entered the full light in the room. "For years I have listened and watched. She has taught me to read the cards and read her thoughts. I can interpret the cards and her thoughts."

With her entrance, Kip confirmed that the voice of the mysterious silhouette belonged to the girl who had greeted him at the door. She was much younger than the Reader. Her body was petite, but full. Her features were smooth, untouched by the stress of work in the fields. She locked eyes with Kip as she translated the cards on the table.

"Madam Ayanda has spread the cards to form a Celtic cross. The innermost cards in the center represent what is most important to you. The circle of cards closest to the cross is your life as it revolves around those matters most important to you."

Kip wrested his eyes from the young girl's stare. The Reader floated her left hand above the card with eight coins and back to the card of the Hanged Man. She raised her fingers to indicate something; then she placed her hand on the table to fully cover the burning Tower.

"The cards say you are holding a mysterious past, something that helped you enter business," the assistant said, emphatic in her interpretation. "If you continue to carry this secret from the past into your future, you must be careful. The Hanged Man suggests you must tell the truth, which will cause you to suffer, but you will gain."

"What the hell is that supposed to mean?" he said, the corners of his mouth curved down.

The nameless interpreter moved closer to the table, where he could see her hands. They were soft, clean, and manicured, not the hands of a field worker.

"The cards suggest there is a secret in your life, a hidden influence. That secret is at the root of your problem. It steers your thoughts and actions, but you wrestle with the secret. It clouds your decisions."

She stepped closer and tapped a card twice in the same manner Madam Ayanda had.

"The Five of Cups indicates you are emotionally sensitive. Your attachments in love are so-so. Emotionally, you emit a loss, losing something at some point, maybe soon. You are disappointed in yourself. Despite what you have achieved, something deeper than your success troubles you."

Kip slid back in his seat, surprised and confused. He folded his arms across his chest and scrunched his brow. He strained to process the explanation of the cards, until she tapped the card showing the skeleton. Then, it was as if her tap sent a jolt of electricity through the table, down the leg, across the plank, up through his chair, and into his attention. He leaned into the table.

"Death is a beginning," she said. "It is how you are born to those around you. What your mannerisms and actions, even your thoughts, say to those around you."

Kip rocked back in his chair, looked at the ceiling, blew a sigh of frustration, then looked at the interpreter. "What do you mean 'a beginning'? Death is the end in my book, and in every other book, for that matter." His question now seemed more like a rebuttal.

"Oonuh dun cross obuh. Dem de haant oonuh. Dey 'gwi bad mout' oonuh. Dey bex hex oonuh," Madam Ayanda said in a harsh rebuke, which Kip never grasped.

"She said you have already died and the ghost will haunt you. The hex is about you," the assistant said, her tone relaxed to help restore the calm. She paused a few seconds to let her words register with him. Then she lifted her fingers off the card and added, "The card can mean a transformation." She looked at Kip, his face still a portrait of total confusion. "To end one life and be born again. For life to come to you in another form. And the death does not necessarily mean that you yourself will end, but maybe someone, or something, close to you. The card could represent how others view you and how you project yourself to them. Or it might mean the general setting for life." She looked at Kip. He massaged his neck. She continued. "The next card, the ninth card, is the Ace of Coins which says life's treasures await you. A new beginning and a future you had never imagined, one that might be forced upon you."

She tipped the final card toward him, the one with the surreal image, but she did not allow it to leave the table. "The final outcome, the future, is out of your control. This card, the Wheel of Fortune, suggests your destiny may be out of your control. What will be, will be."

Kip threw his arms up and shook his head. "For Christ sakes, just tell me. "

The Reader snarled her indictment. "Uh done tell oonuh. Oonuh mus haa 'kee."

"She has told you. You just need to listen," the assistant said in translation. Then she appealed to him, her emphasis square between his eyes: "You need to understand, Mr. Drummond. These cards do not tell you the answers. You already have the answers. "The cards help you connect your feelings and perceptions between your heart and your mind."

The old woman leaned forward, and in a whisper lighter than air, she said, "Oonuh fetch-home t'ink 'bout dis. E time fuh gone."

"She said you need to leave and think about this. She says you need to go."

"No problem. Sure as hell won't get any answers out of you two."

As he stood, he caught the eye of the Reader first, then the eye of the assistant. "Ya know, I should have just trusted my gut. I don't think there is much connection between my gut and my heart or my mind, but my gut has kept me straight up to now."

The Reader's eyes reexamined the cards, her head bowed in silent concentration. Kip pushed his chair in, drummed his fingers near the battered small box on the table, turned, and walked out of the room. Before he reached the door, he hesitated and looked back. He saw the Reader still seated behind her cards. He gave her a wry look, shook his head, and turned to leave. He pulled back the wooden door.

When she heard the screen door open, Madam Ayanda said, "Open op fo oonuh way bek en' shayayre oonuh come fa be bye an bye."

The screen door closed hard with a rusty screech and a loud thwack against the door frame.

"Open your past and share your future, she says," the assistant shouted as Kip walked down the porch steps.

He searched for his truck in a night that was blacker now than when he had arrived. It remained invisible until the porch light came on. He opened the truck door and looked back toward the porch. This was the craziest goddamn thing I have ever done. What the hell was I thinking?

He stepped up into his truck, but before he closed the door, he looked back toward the house one last time. The Reader stood in the doorway, her assistant behind her, silhouetted by the altar of candles. He closed the truck door. When he cranked the engine, the truck coughed and wheezed, but it would not start. On his second try, it kicked over, and he started to drive off.

The assistant stepped forward to grab the Reader, who struggled for a breath, then leaned her slight figure against the haint blue door frame. As the truck lugged down the path toward the road, Kip heard Madam Ayanda one last time. "Oonuh see yo fr'en' at deh ribbuh puntop de boat." The only words he could make out were something about a friend on the boat. What friend? What boat? What in the hell was the woman talking about?

When he arrived home, late, only Sparta greeted him at the door — the usual practice. The dog joined him on the couch. The longer he thought about his visit, the more the tightness of his frustration gave way to the nausea he had on the drive out to the shack. He grabbed one hand with the other to stop the tremble. The eerie symbols and her words. The Skeleton. The Hanged Man. They made no sense. The secret she mentioned. He could think of only one thing. And she was right.

CHAPTER 9

A violent predawn downpour stomped giant footprints in the marsh and unleashed reeds in clumps to float like islands adrift with the tide on the Beaufort River. Fronds from the Palmetto trees littered roads and yards. Spanish moss dotted lawns like minibales of silver-green cotton. On St. Helena Island, the gale-force winds toppled the Pelican Roost, a century old oak and the uncommon resting place for dozens of local pelicans.

For Kip and his son, Chris, the remnants of the storm had little impact on their planned excursion. Since Kip forgot the trip planned for earlier in the week, he was determined not to let the storm cancel this one. This was their first outing in far too long. They planned to go out on a Lowcountry treasure hunt. Over the years, they had found bushels of stuff: buckles and buttons from the Civil War, a few Indian arrowheads, and shards of pottery from earlier times, never anything of real value. For Kip, the outing was a chance to be alone with his adopted son, a chance to groom their slight relationship, and an opportunity to address the endless prods from Sandi to be more involved with the family. The excursions were usually on foot, but today would be different. Kip promised they would search from kayaks, something Chris had never done.

"Chris, you about ready?" Kip said as he passed the boy's bedroom. "We need to watch the time, son. Tide is going out. We have about an hour and a half before the change. We want to make sure we're not too far downstream when the change hits, or we might not be able to paddle back."

"I'm ready," Chris said, still half asleep.

"It's going to be a hot one on the water. The storm cleaned things out. Did you smear on any sunscreen?"

"Yes sir," Chris said, his tone a poor cover for his lie. He rolled his eyes.

"OK, I'll take some extra. We can lather up more if we need it later. I'll get the kayaks unlocked." Kip grabbed his binoculars and a small mesh diving bag they routinely used to hold their loot. "Meet me down on the dock as soon as you're ready."

Before he could get out the door, Sandi appeared from upstairs in a pair of tight white shorts and a sports halter top, her usual tennis attire. She grabbed Kip's shirt tail and said, "Try to make this a good time. You owe it to Chris. You have been riding him pretty hard. Believe me, he knows how many times you cancelled on him before." She pecked him on the cheek, her lips light to the touch.

"I'll do my best," he said. "Look, I'm sorry I blew this last week. I need these trips, and I look forward to them more than Chris or you." He smiled and kissed her neck, then headed out the door.

As Kip walked across the lawn toward the kayaks, Sandi poked her head out the door. "And don't forget we have the LIARS party tonight," she said in her best sixth grade singsong voice, her reminder that she would attend the party to uphold her end of their deal. Kip blew her a kiss and continued to prepare the two kayaks.

He unlocked the kayaks from the storage rack. Although they were not heavy, they were awkward to hoist over head. Before he lifted the first kayak, he made a quick visual check of the marsh to note the direction and strength of the breeze lingering after the storm. The tide was in their favor. He dropped the first kayak in the water pointed into the tide, then he noticed that the osprey nest, which had been on top of the neighbor's dock piling, was now crunched against the downstream side of Kip's dock, a victim of the earlier winds and the swift tide.

Chris, still groggy, sauntered down the stairs dressed for the day—baggy swimming trunks that looked like a potato sack with holes for his prepubescent skinny legs and a bright red T-shirt with "Buccaneers" in bold, royal blue letters across his bony chest. He grabbed a handful of small powdered doughnuts and crammed them into his mouth, then inhaled the powdered sugar. He gagged, coughed, swilled some cold milk, and swallowed the soggy mix. He wiped his mouth with his forearm on his way out the back door. He took his time, in no hurry to spend the morning alone with his stepfather. After Sparta cleared the kitchen floor of doughnut crumbs, he followed Chris down to the dock.

"Sparta, go back up to the house, boy," Kip said. "Go on! No room on this adventure for you." In previous expeditions, when they walked the land, Sparta went along. At times, he proved invaluable for digging on command.

"Go on! Get back up to the house where it's cool." Sparta went only as far as to the edge of the lawn, where he lay down and watched the seafaring duo shove off in the two kayaks.

"Is your life jacket snug?" Kip asked as he paddled closer to Chris. "I didn't check it."

"It feels OK, pretty tight."

"Well, better too tight than too loose. You'll get used to it."

They paddled away from the dock and moved side by side out toward the middle of the water.

"Now remember, stay centered in the shell," Kip said. "Don't reach too far with your shoulder. Don't lean far out to the side. Just let the current move you along for now. You just try to steer with your paddle. Remember, you need to dip the oar on the side opposite of the direction you want to move."

"OK, Dad, I know what to do," Chris said. "I'm not six years old." He dipped his paddle deep and pushed away from Kip.

"Hey, hey. I thought we would move with the water and head over to Oyster Cove," Kip said as he paddled to catch the boy. "With the low tide, there's a good chance the storm churned up some new things for us to find. From the kayaks, we can check out some of the sandbars and marsh mud we can't get to from the island. How's that sound?"

Chris simply nodded, then squinted from the sun's reflection off the water as he studied the marshes in the distance.

As they edged along, Kip scanned the surface for signs of curious dolphins or submerged alligators, while Chris pushed hard to paddle faster than Kip. He paddled a good distance ahead. Then, challenged by a few shallows where he had to back himself out without Kip's help, he took a right fork into a shallow basin surrounded by marsh alive with the usual crabs and oysters and littered with a variety shells and flotsam—including the rusted remains of a Sesame Street metal lunchbox. Kip pulled up alongside Chris just as a broad-winged pelican began a belly-to-belly aerobatic glide against its reflection on the mirrored surface of the tidal river.

"Can we do something? Can we stop and check here?" Chris said, his boredom too much to contain.

"Sure."

Kip slipped his kayak sideways, to be closer to the muddy bank. He knew that marsh mud is like quick sand: it can suck you in and swallow you up in a flash.

"OK," he said. "Let me scrape the surface mud back a little more, and we can sift through things here. Use the small trowel there on the kayak. Don't use your hand. There are probably dozens of small oyster shells in that mud; they will cut through your fingers like razor blades."

After Kip pushed back a layer of mud with his paddle, he slipped to the side to let Chris get closer. With the trowel, Chris began to scoop and sift. Unlike their hunts on land, where they could see their finds first, here Chris had to dump a scoop of the soupy black slop into a small sifter box and shake it in the water. Eventually, he could lift the box and see what he had dug up. Kip moved to a point on the other side of the pool, a safe distance away, and started digging for himself.

After thirty minutes of sifting and exposure to the late-morning sun, Chris shouted, "Hey, I think I might have something."

Kip pulled two deep strokes and moved back alongside the boy. Chris handed him the sifter box. Inside was the usual collection of small oyster-shell fragments and marsh vegetation, but among the sharp chips and slimy grass there was a round, flat object. He opened the clasp on the box and removed a small coin — about the size of a quarter. It was darkened by the elements in the mud, but not covered by barnacles or wrapped in a free-form mass of oyster shells. Kip rubbed it across his swimming trunks as Chris leaned further toward him to see what it was. Kip was able to clean some of crud off, but not enough to identify the coin as old or new. About the only thing he could tell for certain was that the coin appeared to be made of copper.

"What do you think it is?" the boy asked.

From the sun and the glare off the water, Kip squinted. "Hard to tell, Chris. There is still too much gunk all over it. We'll have to clean it up a bit when we get home. One thing for sure, it's the first coin we've ever found."

Reluctant to show any emotion, which would have pleased his stepfather, the preteen masked his excitement. But the discovery did encourage him to dredge deeper and faster. Yet the deeper he dug, the less he found. Eventually, he wasn't even getting shells. He paddled farther, and came to the pool at the end of the tributary, but his results remained the same: nothing but shells, and only a few of those.

"Can we move somewhere else? I'm tired of this place. I can't find anything," he said, disgusted over his fruitless efforts.

"Sure, but we need to watch the time, son. We don't want to paddle against the tide after it changes."

The sun was directly overhead now, and the winds — not brisk, just steady and hot — were signs of a front headed their way. An open kayak on the river at high noon is like a broiler unit in a forced-convection oven: their exposed arms were burnt red, even though Kip's were covered with sunscreen.

But elements be damned: the rush from the first find encouraged them to ignore the sun and the heat.

Kip pointed back upstream. "Chris, why don't we go back out of here and take the other fork in the creek and see what we can find."

"Whatever," he said, quick to move out. Patience was not a virtue for this twelve-year-old. If he had to spend the day out here with Kip, he knew he had to move around, or Kip would paddle from place to place while Chris followed. His kayak waddling like a duck, Chris paddled faster, dipping deeper into the water to pull ahead of Kip to find a new hunt site.

At the end of the other fork in the stream, Chris plunged his kayak into a mound of marsh grass left by the storm, close to the bank, where downed trees offered a natural timber bridge to a wooded lot. A hummingbird-sized deer fly whizzed by him. Initially, Chris was too preoccupied shadowboxing with the fly to remember why he was here. But after he settled a bit, he dug his trowel into the mound and flung out mud everywhere. His first divots were thick, and full of shards of marsh periwinkle and of wrack from spartina grass, but he found no treasures of interest. Kip snuck inquisitive glances at the boy as he eyed the marsh for a spot that had promise.

A Harley on one of the nearby streets squelched the white noise of the locusts and the marsh wrens. The breeze had died, so the only movement of the water was the ripples from the mud dumped from the sifters.

After fifteen minutes of fruitless digging, Chris shouted, "Hey, I think I found another coin!"

Kip emptied his sifter, stroked his way across the water, and pulled alongside Chris. By the time he got to him, Chris had already opened the box and pulled out a fist-sized wad of barnacle and shells.

"Well, it definitely looks like a coin," Kip said. "But in all those shells, I can't really tell. Don't want to break it open out here. Put it in the mesh bag. We'll take a look when we get home. Who knows, these might be two great additions to our collection."

He was referring to an old plastic laundry basket in the carport with all their interesting finds, which would, someday, become their unique trophies in a shadow box display for the rec room.

"Keep it up," he said. "And we might stumble upon the Gullah Treasure."

"The what?" Chris said.

"The Gullah Treasure. It's one of the old Gullah stories the people down at the factory talk about from time to time. I'll tell you about it later. We need to finish up our digging and get ready to work our way back up the river."

"I want to try one more spot, over there where that big tree is in the water; then we can head home," Chris said.

"That works for me. About fifteen more minutes of slack tide is all we can spare."

Chris looked like a windmill as he paddled toward the downed tree. His approach spooked a snowy egret with spaghetti-like legs hidden in the reeds directly in front of him; the feathered rocket launched straight up into the air with a squawk, then swooped down toward the boy. The bird's sudden movement startled Chris. When he ducked to avoid its flight, he lost his balance and tipped the kayak onto its side. At low tide along the edge of the marsh where he was, the water level was quite low. Chris fought to get his kayak upright, but in frustration he jettisoned the kayak and landed in the water.

"Chris, hang on to the kayak and float," Kip said as he paddled hard toward Chris. "Don't put your feet in the mud."

It was too late. Chris had planted himself in the mud, the water just above his shoulders.

"I can't get my feet out," Chris said, as he struggled. The more he tugged, the more the mud sucked him down. The water inched closer to his chin. With every attempt, another oyster shell sliced at his foot or ankle. His wide eyes reflected the panic, fear, and pain that shot through him like a jolt from a high voltage wire.

"Chris, don't fight it," Kip said. "Just hang on. I'll be right there."

Chris listened to Kip and remained motionless, with a firm grip on his kayak. But he had not realized that his spill had awakened a cottonmouth in the sun atop the downed tree right next to him. Flushed from its nest by the heavy rains earlier that morning, the pit viper was in the water directly in front of Chris. Although not normally aggressive, when startled, the water moccasin is known to attack.

"There's a snake in the water," Chris said, his panic renewed. "He's swimming right at me." Once again, he wrestled to free his feet. The waterline inched up over his chin. "I'm stuck. The mud keeps pulling me in. I can't move. Help. Quick, help me."

The boy's scream broke the quiet of the marsh. Kip reached deep with the paddle blade, then twisted his torso and dipped the other blade in a frantic effort to reach his son. Something snapped in his shoulder and shot a familiar pain down his arm. His rowing career had ended with the same sensation; the injury, dormant and untested for years, was quick to haunt him, but he worked through the pain to get to Chris. As he approached, he saw the snake's head and although the body was partially submerged as it made its serpentine movement toward Chris, Kip noted the olive-and-black markings along the four-foot body. The cottonmouth was on an attack run to strike the boy as he struggled to free himself or drown.

Kip dipped his paddle deep to whip the front tip of his kayak sharply to the left. He grunted with the pain in his shoulder.

"Lean back, quick." Kip said, as he lifted his paddle directly overhead.

With his head inches above the water, Chris leaned back. His kayak smacked into his shoulder blades. From the corner of his eye, he detected movement and covered his face with his left arm. Kip slammed the edge of the paddle blade into the back of the snake. The splash went straight into his eyes. Kip wiped his face and surveyed the area for the snake: nothing. Chris reached his kayak to stay above water, though his feet remained trapped in the mud.

"Do you see it? Do you see the snake? Did you get him?" Chris asked, unsure of what danger remained in the water. He looked around for the snake, then toward Kip.

"Just stay calm," Kip said, as his eyes scanned the water. Without warning, with reflexes fast enough to grab a fly in midflight, he twisted to his right, lifted the paddle, and sliced it into the water toward the backside of Chris's kayak. His hurried attempt pushed the snake under water. Kip raised the paddle for another shot, not quite as fast as he did the time before, since his shoulder would not allow it.

They both spotted the snake when it resurfaced between them, too close for another swing. Then they saw the brownish-red slick of blood. Kip's second swing had been on the mark. The spoon-shaped blade of his paddle had sliced through the water, cut through the skin, and crushed the skeleton just beyond the head. Kip dipped his open-faced paddle into the water and catapulted the dying snake toward the bank—for the great blue heron to feast on.

The recovery was simple, sweet, and silent. With Kip's help, Chris squirmed and kicked to free himself from the mud. Once Chris was back in his kayak, Kip helped him check the sifter one last time before they stowed it in the hatch. Before they left the spot, they checked the mesh bag of flotsam and trinkets. Chris made sure his two special finds were still in the bag. With everything accounted for, they began their slow paddle toward home. The incoming tide allowed them to drift leisurely with long strokes. It was awhile before either said anything. Once they were out of the marsh and back in the river, Chris asked about the Gullah Treasure Kip had mentioned earlier. The pain in Kip's shoulder slowed the pace of his row as he told the version of the legend he had heard over and over again at the oyster factory. Like musak, it added mere background noise to the splash of paddles; Chris, now a sun-burned pink and exhausted from his ordeal with the snake, did not listen.

Sparta met them as they paddled in toward the dock. As soon as they had secured the kayaks, Chris hobbled to the house; the pain from his lacerated feet brought tears and muffled grunts. Kip offered to help him, but when the boy pushed him away, Kip took the mesh bag to the carport to work on the two finds Chris had made. The copper coin was easy to clean. It turned out to be "phosphate currency" issued to locals by the Marine and River Phosphate Mining and Manufacturing Company back in the late 1800s. Kip remembered what O'Dell Foster had told him about phosphate mining in the Sea Islands until the great hurricane of 1893 destroyed the equipment and the industry moved to Florida.

The second coin was a bigger challenge. He told Chris he had to send it to his friend Jamie Gentry in Charleston. Jamie worked at the Isle of Palms Marina during the week, and on weekends he ran The Goldfish, for custom-chartered excursions for treasure hunters. If anybody could clean up the blob, Jamie could.

Kip lingered awhile in the carport, where he nursed the pain in his shoulder while Sparta lay next to his feet. He was glad Chris had found a few things of interest, but he felt the incident with the snake had sucked much of the excitement out of Chris. Kip hoped his son would be there next to him, anxious to see what the mesh bag offered: an adventurous boy, twelve going on twenty, standing by his side, anxious to share high fives and to joke about the great time he'd had with his dad.

But that's not the way it was to be. (Kip himself had wanted to be like his own father, but he had continued to fall short the whole time his father was alive). Even the story about the Gullah Treasure did not seem to interest Chris at all.

And now Kip had to face Sandi, who would use the events of the day to reinforce his failure.

CHAPTER 10

The tempest of words erupted the instant they left the driveway. Sandi launched into a hissy fit about how Kip finally took Chris out on a treasure hunt for the first time in months, not having lived true to his promise of taking him once a month. And how could he let her son slash his feet and ankles in a bed of oysters? And why did he allow him to go even near a snake. Her argument flowed down a laundry list of neglect. Then she circled back to the present and rolled through a litany of "honey dos" he failed to complete. She fired salvo after salvo and ratcheted up her volume with each new item of her list. Kip waffled through one hollow excuse after the other; Sandi did not buy any of them. She stared out the side window as she listened.

As they pulled into the driveway and onto the grass parking pad next to the other vehicles of the LIARS who had arrived earlier, Kip pieced together Sandi's tantrum.

"This has nothing to do with me, does it?" he asked. "This has nothing to do with Chris or us, either. It's just that you didn't want to come to this party at all and you are hell-bent on making this night as painful as you can. That's what this is all about, isn't it?"

Sandi opened the door to the truck. As she did so, she tipped her head down and looked at Kip out of the side of her eyes. "Bastard! Just remember, we have a deal. That's why I am here." She slammed the door and walked away. Her actions did not go unnoticed.

"That's a penalty. Unnecessary roughness," Marga Snelling said with two shrill toots from the tin whistle around her neck. The fun-loving matron of the LIARS, dressed like a true NFL official with her zebra-striped shirt and Phyllis Diller hair, pulled a yellow cloth from her back pocket and tossed it in the air toward Sandi. "Better tone it down over there, sweetie," she said as she greeted her newest guest with a hug. "I still need two people to lead the parade."

Regardless of the theme, when Marga threw a party, as a veteran of the silver screen and related Hollywood falderal, she always had a parade—her special patriotic, off- Broadway, not-so-impromptu formation marching around the pool with flags, banners, songs, music, and fireworks.

Kip turned to unload things as the two women walked off in the direction of the bar.

"Que pasa, amigo?" Bill Malcolm said as he walked up behind Kip.

"Oh, hey, Bill," Kip said, absent his usual party spirit.

"Woe, what gives?" Bill asked. "That didn't sound like the guy who would be leading us in his usual Zulu Warrior dance here in thirty minutes or less."

"Sandi is just a pain in the ass."

"Uh, she is a woman, yes? QED. Pain in the ass. Why is she upset?"

"The business is—"

"Oh, that business thing we talked about on the phone last week. What did you decide to do?"

"I decided to go see a tarot reader. She—"

"Are you nuts? What in the hell—"

Marga blasted another long toot on her whistle. "Delay of game!" she hollered. "You two jabronis knock off the chatter out there and bring the goods over here!" she said.

"Hey, let me buy you a drink, and we can talk some more about this," Bill said to Kip, and he sipped the last drops of his martini. They each grabbed a few bags of ice from the back of Kip's truck and headed toward the bar.

There was no better nonstadium venue for a tailgate party than Casa Snelling. Marga's husband, Cray, dropped the tailgate on his oxidized blue Ford F-150 and parked his battleship-sized Cadillac Fleetwood Brougham across from it, trunk popped with coolers, ice buckets, and a complete portable bar. Plopped randomly around the bar were tables draped with white cotton cloths and a centerpiece made from honest-to-goodness Georgia football helmets—thanks to Cray's annual sizable donation to the University of Georgia football program—stuffed with Chrysanthemums. The eating area was neatly positioned beyond the tailgate in an area marked by two rows of potted shrubs, symbolic of playing "Between the Hedges," a Georgia Bulldog and Southeastern Conference tradition.

As Kip and Bill Malcolm approached the bar, they were surprised to see O'Dell Foster as bartender.

"Well, hey there, O'Dell," Bill said with the good ol' boy pat on the back. "Doing a little moonlighting, eh? How's that tour business of yours going?"

"Doing just fine, sir. Just trying to help Bonney with Mrs. Snelling's party, that's all," O'Dell said, as he nodded toward the caterer's white van.

"Hey there, Mr. Drummond," O'Dell said with a smile. "Uh, if y'all need anything, Bheki can help you. I'll be right back."

Bill took matters into his own hands; he began creating his own patented martini. Kip looked down into the trunk full of liquor and placed his order. "How about a Rare Breed and a splash of water," he said. "Light on the water."

The petite black caterer wore a chef's jacket on top of baggy red pants with silver football helmets printed on them. She went directly to the bottle, poured the drink, added a demisplash of water, and handed it to Kip.

"Here's your drink, Mr. Drummond," she said, then turned to help O'Dell unload bags of ice. Her voice sounded familiar to Kip.

"So you didn't listen to me. You went to the tarot reader," Bill said, twirling the ice in his drink.

Kip motioned for them both to step to the side, away from the others. "I don't know. Just a wild hair. Probably the dumbest thing I've ever done."

"So what do you think? She tell you anything?"

"She went through a bunch of hoodoo mumbo jumbo. She honestly scared the shit out of me. She talked about death and a hanged man and meeting somebody on a boat."

"Did she hit on anything? I mean is she for real?"

"Well, one thing she said did sorta make sense. She said the cards were telling her that I have been wrestling with a secret, something that was at the root of my business."

"So? Do you have some secret? What is it?"

"Well, that was the eerie part. I sorta do, I guess, but nothing big. Not anything I need to talk about."

"Come on. It will make you feel better," Bill said, with a pat on Kip's back.

"Hey, Bill," Melinda Malcolm called, and she motioned for Bill to join her over by the bar. "Marga wants us to do the kabobs. Come give me a hand."

Bill hoisted his drink toward Melinda, then turned back to Kip. "You still owe me an answer, but I need to go make sure she doesn't char those babies. Part of that QED thing I mentioned earlier." When Bill left, Sandi walked up to Kip.

"Would you go get the pies out of the truck like I asked you to when we got here? Take them over to the dessert table." Without any further discussion, she walked off.

QED!

Drink in hand, Kip walked down the pine-straw-covered drive toward his truck. From a distance, he noticed something tucked under his windshield wiper. He walked to the front of the truck and pulled a worn playing card from under the wiper blade. He looked at the other vehicles; none of them had cards. He assumed everyone else had pulled their cards and this card was another one of Marga's party games. In the twilight, Kip could read the face on the card. It was the five of spades. What the hell is this? He looked around, but only as a reaction. Who put this thing here? He folded the card over and placed it inside the pocket of his water boy costume and under the belt of water bottles strapped around his waist. He balanced two pies on one arm and carried his drink in his other hand back to the dessert table in the casita without being ambushed by any of his liquored-up friends.

Just outside the casita at the far end of the pool, the movers and shakers of the LIARS swapped profundities of small-town business development and ogled Bonney, the vixen caterer Marga had hired for the party.

"So, Harvey, have you and the rest of the county council decided to lower my taxes yet?" Dave Dowdell asked.

"Hey, Dave. Not yet. How is Seamanse Inn doing these? I need to stop by."

"Better give Dave some time," Barney Thayer said. "Dave hasn't figured out how to make Southern grits; still makes them Ohio-style."

"Spoken like a true Professor," Dave said, as he shook hands with the other two. "Up to no good again, I see. The dreaded curse of the useless PhD in history. Told you before, you should have majored in partying like I did. Helps build social skills early." He squeezed Barney's neck.

"History, my dear fellow, is the common-man's guide to the universe. It tells him where he has been and, therefore, what to avoid in the future," Barney quipped, with Shakespearian flare.

Barney went on: "'History is a mighty dramos, enacted upon the theatre of times, with suns for lamps and eternity for a background.' Thomas Carlyle."

Barney took a sip of his drink and held up his hand to acknowledge the claps and hoots from his listeners. Dave twisted his prematurely white handlebar moustache, then seized the opportunity to cap the debate.

"'History is a pack of lies about events that never happened told by people who weren't there.' George Santayana."

"Here, here." Claps grew to an applause, whistles, hoots, and cheers for their Yankee transplant. He tottered as be bent over in a deep bow.

"Looks like you've been working the chorus line with your old buddies Johnnie Walker or Jack Daniels again," Barney said as he reached to steady his proprietor friend.

When he righted himself, Dave raised his glass. "May bad fortune follow you all the days of your life."

After a brief pause, he continued, "And never catch up with you." He chugged the remnants of his cocktail, bit into the lime wedge, and wiped the citrus pulp from his hairy upper lip.

"Did Doc Rakofsky say you can drink again, Dave?" Barney asked. He knew Dave was in treatment for the effects of Agent Orange.

"Tonic is good medicine. Pirates used it to fight scurvy. You can't tell me that somewhere in all that pirate do-da you teach that you don't mention scurvy? " Dave asked.

"Talk about it all the time. Scurvy and exotic diseases seem to be the second biggest hit in the class — right after the Gullah treasure piece," Barney said, eager to explain.

"Hey Barney," Kip interrupted. "Speaking of pirates, Chris and I kayaked around Port Royal this morning. We found the usual river litter and marsh trash. Most of the barnacled doodads we chucked into a mesh bag and took with us. Chris actually had a couple of interesting finds."

"Oh yeah? Like what?" Barney asked.

"Not sure. At Oyster Cove, Chris scooped up a coin stuck in an oyster cluster. Looks like a token from the old phosphate dredging operations. It says, 'Bulow Store,' and it has the name 'William L. Bradley' on it. The date on it is 1879."

"Could be. That guy partnered with the Marine and River Phosphate Company back before the Great Storm of 1893," the Professor said.

"Probably not much value in the coin, but it was cool for Chris to make the find. He stashed it away in his room somewhere. The other coin was a weird shape, not very round. We noticed an edge sticking out of one of the oyster blobs we tossed into our bag. It could be a piece of metal off one of the docks built down in the cove after the phosphate business shut down. I tried to clean it up, but I only got far enough to realize it was probably just another coin."

"Need help to figure out what it is?" Barney said, enticed by academic interest. He moved closer to Kip.

"I sent it to a friend of mine on Isle of Palms. He is one of those treasure hunter guys who combs the beach with a metal detector. He has more junk from the bottom of the ocean, and a story for each piece. I figured if anybody could identify this thing, he could."

"You trust this guy with it?" Barney asked, his eyebrows pinched beneath his wrinkled brow.

"Hell, it could be something out of a Cracker Jack box for all I know. I'd pay him to lie just to get a smile out of that kid and get Sandi off my case. Jamie is an old friend; I trust him."

As the party grew, other LIARS joined the group to slosh drinks and exchange polite insults. Kip fumbled with the playing card in his pocket until it got the best of him.

"Hey, did Marga put one of these on any of your windshields?" he said as he pulled out the five of spades for the group to see. "Is this one of her game ideas?"

Heads shook. None of them had a card on their windshield. Nobody knew anything about any game.

"I found this earlier, not long after I arrived. No idea how it got there."

"No clue partner," Dave said; then he hollered over to the bar, "Mr. Cray, what's the latest on the game?"

"The Dawgs won," Cray said, as he headed toward the costumed group, his limp more pronounced, an obvious side effect of his three-finger bourbons.

Bill Malcolm took the diversion as an opportunity to pull Kip aside. "So what's with the card?"

"Not sure. One interesting thing though . . . " Kip pulled the card out again, " . . . is the design on the back. This is the same design that was on the back of the tarot cards the Reader used." Bill Malcolm's eyes opened wide.

"Weird. Think this is a sign from her? Oh, and what was that secret she pulled out of you?"

"Well, she did not pull it out of me, but somehow she knew." Liquored and loose, Kip struck a deal. "I've never told this to a soul around here, so don't let this get out. Don't mention it to anyone, especially to Sandi."

"My lips are sealed."

"Years ago I, uh, won a bundle of money and used it to buy the factory."

"You gotta to be shittin' me. Why?"

"I can't answer that. I'd been looking at the place, then got that money and . . . I paid a portion of the winnings to keep it totally quiet and bought the business."

Before Bill Malcolm could push for more details, a tipsy Marga Snelling waddled up on boney pigeon legs, her white double-knit athletic shorts stretched over her seventysomething paunch, and blasted out another warning on the whistle. Kip shoved the card back in his pocket.

"How dumb of me, she said. "I almost forgot we need to have the parade before dessert. Joan, you and Harvey have the honor of being Grand Marshals since y'all are the two longest living residents of Lady's Island." She pushed Bill and Kip into a line of others near the bar. "On your feet everybody. Chop, chop. Once around the pool, marching with Sousa."

"Marga, how many times have I done this?" Harvey said, to contest the selection to lead the parade. His costume, if one could call it that, was modest. In his words, he came as a Southern football fan, dressed in Dockers, Sperry Topsiders, and a Ralph Lauren polo shirt. He was never one to rock the boat—a middle-of-the road conservative: timid and unwilling to expose himself to potential criticism.

"Harvey, you know we love ya, shugah. Besides with that costume . . . " Marga sighed, as she eyeballed Harvey up and down. "Just get out there and strut your stuff. We'll be right behind y'all. Grab the flag, Harvey. I'll strike up the band; then you're on, Hon."

Grand Marshall Harvey whispered something under his breath, snatched the flag pole, and unfurled Old Glory in an unceremonious huff unbecoming of a public servant. Sandi took the opportunity to powder her nose in the guest bathroom, the perfect excuse to miss the zany spectacle to follow.

"Positions everyone. Stage right, behind Harvey. Come on, Joan. Don't let the Grand Marshall get carried away with the pace. We need to keep moving until the music stops.   Sorta like musical chairs, remember?" Marga pranced around with short steps while she clapped her hands like a nun backstage at a grade school Christmas pageant. She flipped the switch on the poolside boom box and unleashed John Phillip Sousa's full military band—horns, fifes, and percussion—blaring "Stars and Stripes Forever."

Harvey Elliott hoisted the flag high and strutted around more like a drum major than a color guard. Like patriotic ducklings, the guests in their ala carte football attire high-stepped smartly behind him, while Cray closed in the ranks from a distance. Marga was quick to note that some of the guests were either rhythmically challenged or beyond the legal limits of consumption; regardless of their plea, they were unable to maintain a cadence to the march. The partiers snaked their way around the pool and across the lawn. Some rendered rigid military salutes, hands knifelike against their brow, while others flapped their arms feverishly, conducting the music of the imaginary band inside the stereo.

"'So be kind to your web-footed friends, for a duck may be somebody's mother.'" Marga belted out the old Mitch Miller theme as they marched. In the background, rolls of thunder drummed in the distance as an interlude to the fifes and flutes. The storm breeze off the marsh stretched the flag stripes to horizontal.

When the final note of the march sounded, Harvey ended the parade near the dessert table. "Come and get it," he said, as he planted the flag pole.

"Better grab some food and head for cover. Feels like Hurricane Danielle kicked up her heels and is headed this way after all," Jane Thayer said, as she stripped out of her costume: "Cocky" the University of South Carolina mascot complete with the oversized gamecock papier-mâché head. She stumbled as she walked through the buffet line, when someone stepped on her costumed foam bird foot.

Gusts ahead of the front dropped the temperature by twenty degrees in less than half an hour. The women, wrapped in beach towels, began the clean up. Throughout the parade and cleanup, Kip thought about what Bill Malcolm had said about the card as a sign from the Reader and tried to figure how the card had ended up on his truck windshield. Anyone off the street could have put it there, but the likely candidates were there at the party. Other than the LIARS, there were three suspects. He discounted the caterer, Bonney Reade: she was strictly business, but socially connected to Marga and Cray. O'Dell Foster did seem a bit aloof, given his earlier friendly chat at the John Bull Tavern. Then Kip thought of the other female caterer. Her voice was familiar. He pulled the card from his pocket and recalled where he had heard the voice. She was the Reader's assistant.

"Excuse me. May I talk to you a minute?" Kip asked the young black woman as she scurried to pack trays and chafing dishes in the van. They stepped to the far side of the van, out of view from the partiers.

"I believe we've met before," Kip said, without a mention of where, though he was sure. "What can you tell me about this card? I found it on my car tonight. I think you might know how it got there."

"Yes, Mr. Drummond. I put it there. I was not sure if I would have a chance to talk to you, so I left it as a sign. You need to see Madam Ayanda. Soon. The cards say you are in danger. The hex is bad."

"Look, the last time I was out there, you two got nowhere with my question."

Strobe like flashes of lightening accented the 3D coarseness of tree bark and the delicate weightlessness of the Spanish moss.

"Madam Ayanda wants to help. Trust her," Bheki said.

"Bheki, party's over sweetie," Bonney Reade said when she saw her with Kip. "Let's get this van loaded and hit the road before the storm rolls in."

"I need to go, Mr. Drummond. Trust her." Bheki rushed back to the serving area to gather the last of the silver. Kip stood, alone, in the dark.

"Joan and I need to go by the shop and board up the windows," Harvey Elliott announced. "Not sure I want to wait until the morning. Thanks for the good times, folks."

"Probably a good idea," Barney said. "I checked with the maintenance on-call supervisor down on campus. He pulled the latest weather off the university wire. They now predict the storm to hit right at Mink Island on the Carolinas border. Winds and heavy rain may make it this far south. I need to drop Jane off and run by the security office myself."

Since Seamanse Inn was just across the bridge in town, Dave and Bev Dowdell agreed to stay behind to help to pack up the last of the furniture. As the rain began, Kip and Sandi ran to the truck. Before Kip could back the truck out onto Lucy Creek Drive, Sandi was back into her tirade, now fueled by her own words: "The ridiculous, classless, drunken display over the previous five hours." Kip tuned her out. He was more concerned about the winds that pushed the truck around like a rubber duck in a whirlpool.

"It's a sad day," Sandi said, "when the most interesting person at the party is a young guy who gives tours of this crazy city. O'Dell Foster is sure enamored with you and your crazy business. He told me how you two chummed it up at the John Bull, which you never mentioned to me. He asked a million questions about how you managed to run that place. I hope I convinced him you were selling the place."

When Sandi realized Kip had not heard a word she said, she clammed up, slouched deep in her seat with her arms crossed, and stared straight ahead into the rain as it splattered on the windshield.

As soon as the truck stopped in the carport, Sandi was out the door and into the house. Kip lingered. He pulled the card from his pocket. Although he had cause to doubt the Reader, what her assistant had said at the LIARS party made him uneasy. Almost as if he had visited the Reader again, his stomach quaked and sent out a wave of nervous ripples. He fumbled with the card and put it away. He knew he had to make time for a visit. He also knew the timing of the visit would create a new conflict at home.

CHAPTER 11

The weekend storms had passed. Life around the factory returned to the two sacred Monday rituals. First, the gospel spirituals that reverberated under the metal roof of the factory to deaden the clank of the conveyor, the hiss of the boiler kettle, and the thump-snap of the banding machine returned. And, second, the plebeian debates over the emphatic and inflammable sermon Reverend Twines had delivered from the pulpit at Brick Baptist Church. Known as the oldest church on St. Helena Island, Brick Baptist was the house of worship for every righteous Gullah. Week after week, one would have thought the Holy Spirit himself had descended upon the congregation to enlighten every soul present, each in a different tongue, because every single Gullah had a different view of the sermon.

"I knows sure as I be standin' yuh, Mr. Gunny, dat Reverend Twines, he didn't mean no harm when he talk 'bout Miss Eleanor," Loretta Travis said as she all but pinned Gunny against the wall by the water fountain.

"Was like he just hit the replay on her grandbaby's funeral—baskets of white daisies and yellow jessamine, the wreath with 'Littlest Angel' on it, and dat tattered sock doll her call Shadrack pun'top dat pine box casket. When dat girl die, she left a hole as big as Daufuskie Island inside Miss Eleanor."

"OK, Loretta, sounds bad, but let it go," Gunny said.

"Let it go? Let it go? Mr. Gunny, I can't just let it go. Why, soon as she came out the church, Miss Eleanor, she almost fainted. I saw Obadiah Whyteson take her to he car, and dey sat dey, he just thumpin' he Bible, preachin' and all, and she just rock back and forth holdin' her stomach, both of dem sweat clean through dey clothes." Loretta Travis eased up for a second to look around. Nobody was within earshot.

"OK, I'll talk to Miss Eleanor and—" Gunny said, and she cut him off.

"You can talk to her 'cause I know you done help her with money in de past when she needed to pay dem medical bills for her grandbaby after she kicked dat no good son of hers, Cudjoe, out de house," she said. "We's all in bad shape, Mr. Gunny, and we trust you will see us out dis." She whipped her head in a pronounced nod to punctuate the end of the discussion, then just walked off.

Kip Drummond returned late from lunch and the monthly Chamber of Commerce meeting at Plum's Restaurant. The grilled Reuben, the fries, and the sweet tea settled in his stomach as he watched heat devils skip their calypso on the asphalt while he sat in traffic by the swing bridge which connected Beaufort to Lady's Island.

Gunny saw Kip come in and allowed him a few minutes before he worked his way toward the staircase to the mezzanine to confront him.

"Kip, you old shark bait, where the hell you been?" the voice on the answering machine said. It was Jamie Gentry, Kip's longtime friend and treasure hunter from the Isle of Palms in Charleston. "That factory of yours got some kind of hold on you. You still married to that babe that looks like that fox from Top Gun? When are you going to bring that chick back up here for a little moonlight cruise? Gotcha all set right here at the Isle anytime." Jamie had an eye for women and was none too shy about what he liked about Sandi. Kip knew Sandi would rather swim with sharks than be caught onboard the same boat with Jamie.

"I guess you found a little time for some local treasure hunting," Jamie went on. "From the looks of the barnacle ball you sent me, you didn't find that in your garden. And I am not sure where you did find it, but it might be worth a trip back over there with a good shovel. I could be wrong, but after I chiseled that blob for about fifty minutes, I was able to get the coin out. I cleaned it up nice and good — good enough to see some markings on it anyway. If my research is right, what you got there is a silver coin from Mexico that dates back into the 1500s. Man, you did it up big there, fella. The book says it's a Mexico Felipe II 8 Reales (no date), and it lists for somewhere between five hundred and eight hundred bucks. Give me a holler with some chart specifics on the location. I'll shut this place down one day this week and head your way for some honest-to-goodness treasure hunting."

The machine voice assured him there were no more messages, and the machine clicked off. Kip laughed.

When he returned Jamie's call, the answering machine picked up, "Ahoy, Matey, you've reached The Goldfish. This is the Skipper talkin', but I ain't in. I am out with my crew diggin' up pieces of eight. If you want to join the crew, leave a message, and I'll be sure to get back to you as soon as we tie up again."

After the beep, Kip left a message with the chart coordinates and invited Jamie to pull away on Thursday to do some treasure hunting around Beaufort.

No sooner had he hung up the phone when Gunny appeared in the doorway.

"Can you spare a few minutes, Mr. Drummond?" Gunny asked.

"Sure, Gunny," Kip said. Always time for you. How are things down on the floor today? Get all the first week snafus worked out yet? So what's up?"

The edges of Gunny's thick, black lips curled to a wrinkled frown between prominent cheekbones above a pointed chin. He fumbled with his hat. "Mr. Drummond, can you explain dis to me?" He threw a single sheet of lined paper onto Kip's cluttered desk. Kip stared at Gunny, then reached for the paper.

"Where did you get this?"

"Mr. Drummond, I think I asked you to explain it."

"Wait, this looks like . . . "

"It looks like notes in your sloppy handwriting, and it says you agree to sell dis business," Gunny said with a bull-like huff.

Kip dropped the paper and pushed back from his desk.

"Where did you get this, Gunny?"

"Where I got it don't make no difference. Let's just say a little bird gave it to me."

"Where did you get this paper?" Kip pounded his desk. Gunny remained silent.

"Look, Gunny, if you took this out of my office, that's theft, for one. Second, if you are trying to sabotage the business or blackmail me, you are flat out wrong."

"I asked you before about sellin' dis business, and you flat denied it. You told me you wasn't. So how do you explain dis letter?"

"Gunny, I told you I had talked to people. I have received offers. I have not made a decision."

"Dat letter sure sounds to me like you decided."

"It's a draft letter. I never wrote it final, and I have never signed it, and I have not sent any agreement. Now, how did you get this paper?"

"Do you expect me to believe dat?"

"You believe what you want. I am telling you, I have not agreed to any sale, but shit like this, you undermining the business, sneaking around my office, stealing records and personal documents, that has me concerned whether or not I can trust you with this business."

"Well, the rumors must be true, den."

Kip swiveled his chair to take his eyes away from Gunny's stare. "I heard all kinds of rumors. I heard we were ready to expand with another cannery over in Blufton. I heard we were going to open a seafood restaurant here at this place. Ya want to know the best rumor, the most outrageous rumor I heard?" Kip asked. "Hell, I've even heard you plan to leave this job. Ain't that some shit." Kip chewed out the words, his accusation just short of firing Gunny on the spot. "Now that isn't true, is it Gunny? You wouldn't leave, would ya?" Kip leaned back in his chair, his best poker face a weak disguise.

"Look, Gunny," Kip said, "this town thrives on bullshit gossip and dumb-ass rumors."

Gunny's rage burned bright red beneath the pigment of his skin. Sweat trickled down his back and off his arms. He stared as he listened. He fought the urge to jump across the desk, grab Kip by the collar, slam him up against the wall and say, "Yeah, you're absolutely right. I'm out of here." Gunny flicked his head up as if someone had kicked him from behind.

"What about de letter?" Gunny asked.

"OK, I wrote it," Kip said, his voice stern once again. "It is a draft. Unsigned, and nothing has come of it. Nothing is decided." He swiveled back toward the desk and fumbled with a newspaper, an excuse not to look up at Gunny.

"With all the construction up and down the coast, the golf courses going in, and the pollution in the waters

around here, the oyster beds are taking some big hits.
Fewer oyster pickers are in the water. Newspaper says
the Bluffton Co-op folded because the industry has
moved to Louisiana."

"All dat may be true, Mr. Drummond, but them
ladies downstairs, dey be scared Mr. Drummond. You
ain't bein' honest with me, and you ain't bein' honest
with dem." Gunny wiped his brow with his cap.

Kip tossed the newspaper down on the desk and
cocked his head toward Gunny. "Gunny, this business is
my life," Kip said, though his tone lacked conviction.
"Everything I have I put into this business."

"Dat may be true, as you see it, Mr. Drummond, but
you gots to understand, you ain't de only one who put
eb'ryt'ing into dis business," Gunny said. He slapped the
back of the chair with his cap. "I told you before. Maybe
you ain't listenin' to me, Mr. Drummond. Ya see, dis
business don't belong to you. It don't belong to me,
neither. It belongs to dem ladies downstairs." He folded
his arms across his chest. "And most of dem has children
and grandchildren to feed and care for. Like with Ethyl
Ramey. She has two daughters livin' with her. They each
have three kids and are livin' in her tiny three-bedroom
house over on Haigh Creek. Without dis job, how is she
goin' to care for her babies?"

"Look, they set their life, not me."

Gunny turned back toward the desk, the veins in his
neck squirming like snakes under his skin.

"See, Mr. Drummond, every penny dey make goes to
family. Dey sold just 'bout all dey land to survive. Land

dat been in dey family since de Civil War. Dey wear hand-me-down clothes from de thrift stores. Dey eat off food stamps."

"So do a lot of other people in this town," Kip said, smug and short.

"You ask dem, dey never say dey be poor 'cause de Lord had given dem family and dey be together and dey pray together, and if you close dis business, dey will die together."

"Come on, Gunny." Kip turned away, his head shaking, then jerked back. "This whole damn building could be gone in a flash with one of the storms that roll through here. I mean, shit happens! They gotta be prepared for these kinds of things. This is life."

"Dey can accept Mother Nature, but dey won't 'cept someone who sells dem out after all dey put into dis business." Gunny stepped around the chair.

"Look, Gunny," Kip said, "their job is to shuck oysters—nothing more, nothing less. I pay an honest day's wage for an honest day's work. Each of them planned their own life like I planned mine. If they couldn't plan their lives to survive, then why is that my problem?"

"One big difference, Mr. Drummond. It all comes back to money. You got plenty, and dey ain't never had any at all."

"What's to say I always had money?" Kip lost his patience in a prolonged shout that drowned Gunny. "What do you expect me to do? March down the damn stairs, stand up on one of those tables down there, and sound off like some blue light sale announcement? 'Attention ladies, there ain't no sale today. Nothing is on sale today, so stop all the gossip and rumors and get back to work. Is that what you want me to do? Would they understand that?"

Kip walked around to the front of the desk, but he stopped well short of Gunny. The black foreman never blinked. He cocked his head back, his lips pursed tightly to hold his tongue pressed hard against his front teeth. Kip stared. His pulse raced. His hands tingled.

Gunny shifted from one leg to the other. Kip backed off. He walked back to his chair and wiped his face with a shaky hand, then he looked at Gunny and spoke in a tone that was soft and pensive.

"I appreciate what you are doing for those women by coming up here and talking to me, Gunny. I really do," Kip said, calm and confident, but with his arms folded across his chest. "But do you really want to do something good for them? Do you really want to help them — I mean really help them? If you do, I first would forget about this piece of paper you brought up here, and then I would tell the ladies to knock off all the rumors and gossip. Just flat work. Just come in, sing their songs, hum a merry tune, and get the work done. When they do that, everybody is happy. You are happy. I am happy. And they are happy. Everything works out just fine. The business will be just fine."

Kip extended his arm to suggest that Gunny go back downstairs. "Look, Gunny, I really didn't think this would take quite this long. I have another appointment that I am already late for, so maybe we should just drop this conversation." Kip grabbed the knob and pushed the door open.

Gunny nailed Kip with his eyes. "If you want to sell dis business, let me buy it." He pulled his cap visor low on his brow and walked out.

When the ladies noticed him on the steps, they nudged and whispered to each other. The singing stopped, which was never a good thing. The footsteps on the metal staircase answered their questions. When he reached the floor, he tilted his head, chin held high, and acknowledged the hopeful stares as a flood of impassive denial spread table by table. Without a word, Gunny moved across the floor and out the large dock doors.

Kip watched his foreman walk down the steps, then closed the door. He picked up the draft letter Gunny had tossed on the desk. He quickly skipped over how Gunny had gotten it and then checked his files. Other documents were missing. He wondered if Gunny had those and what he might do with them.

Gunny walked to his truck and picked up the folder from the seat. He had no idea who left the folder in his truck, but he knew it was now empty.

Chapter 12

Jamie Gentry posted the "Captain Is Out" sign on the door of his small charter office on Thursday morning, loaded metal detectors and other gear in an old, wooden army ammo crate stenciled on the sides with "M-406, 40mm HE, 48 rounds" (an M79 Grenade Launcher), and headed to Beaufort in search of more silver coins, the type Kip sent him to identify.

With a thin moustache and short-cropped hair, a holdover from his days with Kip in the army, Jamie wore a fourteen-pocket fly fishing vest with an assortment of small necessities, such as his stainless steel hip flask topped off with Kentucky's best Wild Turkey bourbon. On the floor of his car, passenger's side, was an old, mangled steel thermos which Celeste, his current bed partner, had filled with black coffee, and a second metal thermos wrapped in OD hundred-mile-an-hour tape filled with his own ragtime Bloody Mary concoction.

Morning coffee was more like a transfusion for Jamie. His thermos lasted nearly the entire drive to Beaufort. It brought new life to his body while the radio twanged country rock to his soul. By the time he hit Ribaut Road in Beaufort, he was ready for his tomato elixir and fought the urge to unscrew his coffee thermos to recycle some of his coffee. He decided to hold off until he hit 32° 24' 04.35" North, 80° 40' 49.59" West, the coordinates where Kip said he and Chris had found the coin. He parked on a side street close to the marsh, prepared his gear, and took a healthy swig of bloody Mary. Then he trudged through the mud, walked into the water, and got right to work.

"Hey, there, Jacques Cousteau. Find anything that looks like pieces of eight out there?" Kip yelled from the bank of the Beaufort River, about thirty feet from where Jamie stood, sweeping just under the surface of the water with his metal detector. Jamie did not see Kip walk up and the click-click in the earphones he wore with the detector muffled Kip's shout.

"If it ain't Blackbeard himself," Jamie said, as he pulled the earphones down around his neck. "Ain't found nothing but a few more of those coins from the phosphate company. You sure you found that other coin around here, or do you just want a complimentary scan of this marsh?" Jamie said. He stumbled in the mud as he moved to the bank where Kip waited. Every step through the pluff mud came with a slurp of suction that threatened to pull off each boot. When he reached the bank, Kip helped pull him out of the mud and onto solid ground.

"Been quite awhile since I last saw you, old man," Kip said. "Is that all you under that vest? You've developed a serious case of the 'Dunlop Disease': your belly done lopped over your belt."

"It's called the good life," Jamie said, while they shook hands. "If you didn't work so damn hard, you, too, could experience life with a brew or two." Jamie reached around to the snap link on his hip and hoisted the thermos. "Care for a little pick-me-up?" Jamie unscrewed the cap and extended it to Kip.

"Chonga!" Kip cried. He cringed and swallowed. "Go a tad lighter on the hot sauce next time, Jamie. Man, oh man. That's third degree burns all the way down."

"When I'm out on the boat with a charter, it's all business; I work my ass off. On little excursions like this, I like to relax a little." He laughed. He pulled the flask from his vest and tipped it high for a three count.

"Been out there long?" Kip asked, somewhat throaty, still recovering from his shock from the thermos.

"By the looks of the tide, guess I been out there a couple of hours. Got here well after high tide. Tide is just about done going out. Perfect time for me to be picking through the oysters and rocks for things. Wanna join me? I'm sure I can find some extra gear in my truck."

"I'll pass for now. How much longer are you going to be out there?

"An hour, maybe a little more."

"Can I buy you some supper when you're done? We can sit down, catch up. I'd invite you over to the house, but you remember how Sandi is; she's not real keen on unannounced dinner guests." What Kip really meant was he didn't want to let Jamie anywhere near Sandi. If he did, Sandi would give him hell for weeks for bringing "that uncouth, social ingrate, filthy loser" into her house. Kip knew better. "We could grab a beer or two and something to eat somewhere."

"When I'm done here, I'll be pretty ripe, after wading around in rubber boots in this sun and mud all day. I can handle a bar, a beer, and a burger, then I need to head back north. I have a charter over the weekend and need to get The Goldfish set up for another hunt."

"Let's meet at the 11th Street Dockside down the road in Port Royal at six. I'll draw you a map. The bar is good, the food is better, and it's laid-back. We can watch the sun set and sip suds. Does that give you enough time to finish your little scavenger hunt there, maestro?"

"Hey, it's my business to find stuff, and one of the easiest things for me to find is a bar. Isn't it obvious? I'll be there, and you bring your wallet. You owe me for the last assay I did. Speaking of which, where exactly did you find that old coin?"

Kip pointed to a spot where he first saw Jamie. "Right about where you were when I got here."

"All right then, governor. Back in the mud."

After they shook hands, Kip patted Jamie on the back and walked back toward the road. Jamie wiped his brow, reached down, and took another man-sized swig from the flask; then, he noticed the police cruiser and the officer by his Jeep.

"Hey, what's that guy doing by my rig?" Jamie yelled to Kip.

"Looks like he is writing you a welcome note from the Beaufort Police Department. Can't park on the grass like that, Skipper. I'll go talk to him about parole or bail or something. You go find some treasure. Looks like you might need it."

Kip left a rough sketch map under Jamie's wiper next to the traffic ticket the police officer had left, then drove directly to Dockside; he didn't bother to go back to work. Likewise, he never bothered to stop by the house, which was only three minutes away. He didn't even bother to call.

The 11th Street Dockside was an aging, white clapboard building with a slight lean. Over the years, the pilings that supported the pier side had settled in the mud to give the walls and floor a noticeable slant, which caused patrons, regulars, and tourists alike to stagger about like drunken sailors. Pine floors were covered with grit tracked in from the crushed-shell parking lot. Dark inside, night and day, the only sunlight filtered through the screened porch, which overlooked the water. People forgave the basic décor of the place after their first whiff: the blended spices in boiled shrimp and crab pots, the fresh sweetness of melted butter under their nose, and the cracklin', deep-fried oils of the melt in-your-mouth hush puppies — the best in the world. The Dockside was a great place for down-home cooking and a great place to meet a friend for a cold long-neck Bud.

"Ain't that a kick in the ass," Jamie said, pulling the barrel-backed chair out and falling into it. His yellow T-shirt that must have fit him at some point had a picture of a trawler flying a skull and crossbones flag with a treasure chest in the middle and black letters that read, The Goldfish, and in much smaller print, "Treasure Hunting." "I been out there all day, doing my environmental best to clean up the junk in your river, and you sit here sucking suds."

Kip laughed.

"Worse yet, you ain't even bought me a drink! So much for hospitality."

Kip clanged together the necks of two empty Sam Adams bottles held over his head. The waitress, standing beneath a driftwood sign which read, "Don't mess with the Mother Shucker," winked with a nod and headed to the bar.

"Well, I was going to wait, but hell, you never showed. I thought you skipped town."

"I should have. Damn police, anyway. Hell, then you told me I had been looking in the wrong spot all goddamn afternoon; I moved upstream."

Kip had picked a spot in the corner of the screened porch, but he made a quick, squint-eyed scan to ensure Jamie had not offended anyone with his swearing. Fortunately, most people migrated toward the window to look out over the weathered dock, the Battery Creek inlet, and the emerald-green marsh beyond.

"Hell, I found a clump of oysters and barnacles, the usual stuff, but when I plucked them up and whacked them with my hammer, I found three of those coins you sent me," Jamie said, quieter than before. "Not the tokens. These look like the silver coins. I need to clean them up a bit more, but initial survey says, 'Bingo'! I spent the last hour and a half trying to find the rest of them."

"Hell, that's good news," Kip said with a hearty slap to Jamie's back. "That means the beers are on you, right?"

"No way, Jose." Jamie paused to admire the waitress, a young oriental girl with jet-black hair, who had brought their beers.

Kip prodded, "What do you mean you spent an hour and a half looking for 'the rest of them'?"

"Now come on, son, you know that shit don't grow on trees, and it ain't like oysters. It doesn't multiply underwater. Where there's one, there are others. It's not like some guy just emptied his pockets there one day, ya know." Jamie guzzled about half his beer, slouched deeper in his chair, and talked louder.

"Look, I've been over just about every known shipwreck and dive site off the coast of South Carolina, and a good bit of North Carolina."

He chugged the last of his beer, grabbed Kip's bottle, stood up, and gently tapped the bottles together. "That is the way you get a drink around here, right?" Jamie asked.

When Jamie stood up, Kip read the back of his shrunken T-shirt. It said, "Come see my chest."

Kip burst out with a laugh, which attracted eyeballs all around. "Nice shirt, Jamie! Great marketing tool."

"You should check it out on some of the chicks who go out on the boat. I make sure I have smaller sizes for them! Yeah," he smirked, "they look even better when they are wet! Where was I? Oh, you can't begin to imagine how much gold and silver is out there at the bottom of the ocean. Tons of it, and it ain't been found. Plus, Blackbeard, God rest his soul, stashed booty all up and down the coast, inland, not in wrecks. I spend weekends looking for it in deep water, and it's probably all right under my feet."

"You really believe that stuff, don't you? If it was ever there, people would have found it by now, don't you think? Oh, by the way, nice earring, Jamie."

"It adds a certain pirate flair and authenticity to my business," Jamie said, twisting the single gold hoop in his left ear. "Besides, they say it's like acupuncture and improves my sight. At my age, I need all the help I can get."

Jamie looked up from the table about the time the young waitress brought the beer. She smiled. He slapped a ten-dollar bill on the tray, and said, "Thanks," with a wink, which would be his best, but futile, attempt at a quick pick up for the night.

"You got to remember, my business is to take people out in a boat to look for treasure. Most are satisfied with finding a buckle or a button from some Civil War blockade runner, or thrilled to see underwater remnants of some unknown paddle wheeler that sank in the 1800s. For me, I am interested in finding coins. No lying about it. I'm going for the gold! Silver will do on a bad day.

And, my friend, there is plenty of it out there." Jamie clinked his bottle against Kip's, then proceeded to chug it. "When I am not on the boat or fixing other boats, I am reading history."

"Reading history?" Kip said, surprised.

"Pirate history."

Jamie's exuberance apparently carried across the room to a few seated at the bar. They gave him a queer look and continued to talk.

"I use it all the time when I take folks out. You know, a little up-selling goes a long way with people, gets them excited. First time they go out, they see a button or two. Sell them on the idea of gold, and they keep coming back, so I need to have places to take them, or at least a good story to tell them. I memorized all sorts of bullshit trivia about gold and pirates and treasure. For example, your little town of Beaufort and the Lowcountry in general has not always been the quiet little coastal tourist stop. Did you know that, Buckaroo?"

Kip returned a weak shake of his head.

"There was a time when it was considered a hub along the great trade route between the New Colonies and Europe. Mines opened in South America, Central America, and Mexico. Metals slowly began to move back to Spain by boat. The pirates caught on quickly and began traveling the shipping lanes and trolled the coves of the Lowcountry islands for ships filled with precious cargo."

Jamie was on a roll. For Kip, after four beers, Jamie could entertain him with almost any yarn—with his

Southern accent, his gnarly pirate jargon, and his penchant for storytelling. Kip flagged the waitress for another round, as Jamie chattered on, encouraged by his buddy's nods.

"Agriculture on the islands flourished. Cotton and indigo sprang up and sprawled out. The plantation owners couldn't find enough laborers. Their scrawny, fellow countrymen wouldn't leave Europe to sail here to farm the fields or dig in the mines for very modest wages. Likewise, landowners would not part with or share their land in their new world. So they looked to the Dark Continent — Africa."

"Do you really use this stuff on your boat?" Kip asked.

"You bet your sweet ass I do, amigo. I usually just babble on with some Cliff Notes version. Sometimes people stop and ask for details, not often, but I do need to keep it all kinda fresh." He took a long slug of beer, leaned back in his chair, and continued.

"In Sierra Leone, after warring chieftains conquered other tribes, they'd sell their 'bad subjects' to Portuguese and Spanish slave traders. Mariners would sail to Africa, fill their ships with slaves, sometimes in the hundreds, and sail to Spanish America, where they would sell them for muskets, food, and items of worth. And the rest of the story is history."

"What do you mean history?" Kip asked, curious about the shift in the subject. "I thought you were talking about pirate treasure, not slave trade."

"Well, let me drain off some of this beer, and I'll tell you. Where's the head — uh, the little boy's room — to you fancy businessman types?" Jamie asked, as he pushed away from the table.

Kip cocked his arm with a hitch-hiker motion and pointed to the darkened hall behind him. Jamie stood and steadied himself, sauntered toward the bar and, rang the antique brass ship's bell, which hung above the cash register.

"Drinks for everyone in the bar!" Jamie yelled. The applause from around the room was spontaneous. With a bow, Jamie slipped into the darkness, then stood at the urinal in the restroom for a full two minutes to relieve himself.

Rejoining Kip and fresh beer in hand, he continued with his lesson in pirate history.

"Ah, much better; pressure is off. OK, so you want to know what all of that has to do with pirate treasure? Well, I did a little research on your coin, the one you sent me. Seems a Sir John Hawkins, a Brit, bagged a Spanish ship with coins from Mexico, and rather than share all the silver with the British Crown, he buried it around here. The coin you sent was the type that might have been in that load." Jamie was confident in his research.

"So you are saying there could be treasure buried here? In Beaufort?" Kip asked.

"Could be," Jamie replied. "Records say he looted the Spanish ship, then dropped the stuff in a deep port near Hilton Head. Port Royal is the deepest in the area, so why not?" Parched from his recitation of pirate lore, he inhaled deeply, exhaled hard, then emptied an entire bottle of beer and rattled the bar with a belch loud enough to wake Davy Jones from his locker.

"Argh! Not many like that around these days," he said, while others around him sat open-jawed in amazement.

"They found that Spanish shipwreck last year in the Little Bahamas. No treasure on it. I heard some around here call it the Legend about the Gullah Treasure. Some say the treasure was found years ago. Some say the Union Army took it with them. Some say that the treasure is guarded by hoodoo, that the root doctors in the Lowcountry protect it. Some say your Sheriff McTeer was on to it before Doctor Buzzard slapped some hoodoo on his ass — and poof, the sheriff was gone! And that, my dear sir, is 'the rest of the story.'"

"Bravo, Captain. I can't believe you can spiel that BS. You sound like some hick professor. Must be impressive on the boat."

"Hell, no. You think a bunch of drunk, sunburned people that pay to go on a treasure hunt really give a shit about all that? Nah! It does sorta sink in when I hit them with 'not sure if it has been found or not.' Then they just say, 'Where is Port Royal?' and 'Is it buried or sunken?' Hell, I don't know and 'frankly, my dear, I don't give a damn.' All I know is that I need to refine my notes after today. Those coins have promise."

"Come on, Jamie," Kip said. "You mean the Gullah Treasure? For real? Give me a break. I've heard that legend for years. Every time I hear it, it changes, but you've convinced me. I'm going home and dig up my yard." Kip was ready to leave.

"Woe, Ke-mo-sah-bee. Stories, man, just stories. It's part of my business. Say, are we goinna eat anything or what? I need to get my fat ass back on the road at some point."

"Sure, dinner is on me. What are you up for?" Kip asked, smelling hot grease everywhere.

"Burgers, beer, and babes. If you can talk that sweet little waitress thing over there into joining us, then we have ourselves a party."

Kip blew off Jamie's comments and rambled through the menu. The two of them managed another beer over the course of the next hour and a half, and then Jamie hit the long road back toward Charleston. For Kip, the drive home was short. He received an earful when he walked in the door. He explained to Sandi that Jamie was in town and that he was sure his only option was to take him out for dinner. Sandi rolled her eyes, picked up a book, stretched out, and sank deep into the pillows on the couch to read. Kip headed back to the door, pulled the leash from the hook, and took an excited Sparta out for one last tour of the neighborhood before bed. While the dog sniffed for earlier canine visitors, Kip thought of how he would share Jamie's stories with Chris, especially the part about the coin they found and the Gullah legend.

CHAPTER 13

For four days after the party, Kip listened to Sandi's frequent tirades about the LIARS' ribald antics, and for four nights, nightmares filled with tarot cards and the thought of a hex kept him awake. His morning runs with Sparta allowed the only quiet time. He agonized over how to tell Sandi he could not go to Charleston. He sure as hell could not mention he planned to use that time to revisit the Reader.

Despite his mental torment, on Thursday, he challenged Sparta to a race — past the azaleas, the crepe myrtle, and the magnolia tree, then down the drive and through the patches of sunlight that knifed through the humongous oaks draped in Spanish moss. Kip held enough in reserve for a short sprint to the two-story, white columned front porch, while Sparta loped to catch up, his tongue flapped outside his jowls like a limp wind sock. A classic tortoise-and-hare finish.

The silvery coolness of the dew on the lawn tempted Kip to plop down to stretch, but he knew the sand gnats would get the best of him if he did. He scratched Sparta behind his ears, then took the dog inside. Sparta tanked up at his water bowl, before assuming his postrun position near the air duct, which oozed cool air faster than he could pant. Ensconced in his small office, Kip closed the door, cranked up his head phones, and suspended himself in a psychedelic cocoon of Iron Butterfly. The seventeen-minute dose of "In-A-Gadda-Da-Vida" just might help purge any lactic acid buildup and hopefully leave him free of aches or stiffness.

Cooled, loose, and limber, Kip left Sparta in the office to lick his paws. Still soaked in sweat, Kip shuffled barefoot down the hall to the kitchen, aglow in a fireball of morning sun. He stopped at the fridge to fill a glass with ice water and flicked on the coffee maker his Aunt Tantsie gave him and Sandi for a wedding gift. With six years of daily use, it sputtered and hissed like an overheated Model T Ford, but it brewed unbelievably good coffee. He boosted himself to the second floor, two steps at a time with his glass of water in hand, and sauntered into the bathroom, where he found Sandi. Still in her light blue chemise trimmed in lace, she was contorted with arms overhead in a yogalike pose, prepared to brush her hair. She saw Kip's reflection in the mirror as he entered.

"How was your run?" she asked.

"All published world records remain intact; nothing special happened today," he said, winded from his sprint up the steps. Unlike most Southern gentlemen, who go to seed after they reach thirty, Kip was still well-developed, a phenomenon he attributed to a daily regimen of running, push-ups, and an occasional pull-up from a pipe he installed in the rafters in the carport. As he struggled to pull his sweat-soaked T-shirt over his head, Sandi shifted slightly to get out of his way, but she left behind a whiff of her perfume.

Kip had entered Sandi's personal world. The bathroom was Sandi's design and the creation of Autry, Simpson, and Wendell, the Charleston-based architectural firm that had converted the original, dark, nineteenth-century bathroom into the glitzy and glamorous modernized interior even far and above the panache of The Battery along Charleston's waterfront. She spared no expense. This residential spa was like no other. Polished blue granite counter tops sparkled like lapis lazuli. A sandstone tile floor was heated and cooled to bring refreshing seasonal changes for soothing feet. Mirrors, mirrors, and more mirrors covered the spa, with adjustable lighting to reduce wrinkles and bulges. In the corner beneath windows that overlooked the marshy banks of the Beaufort River sat a stone Jacuzzi with a teak deck large enough for two; it had been christened as such when they moved in, but even so, it had provided lonely solace for Sandi ever since.

Sandi had not yet created her daily look. She needed very little makeup to be presentable, but she was rarely seen outside her bedroom suite without her gentle application of liner, mascara, and a touch of lip gloss on her Marilyn Monroe lips. Deep red. Always deep red. Armani. Always Armani.

Kip peeled off his running shorts just as Sandi leaned away from him, lowering her head to fluff her hair a bit before she brushed it. The semisheer chemise contoured her hips and slid up her torso to expose the hint of her cheek at the top of her long, athletic leg. She was tanned and toned. Her body was full. In public, her curves invited unblinking stares from scores of fantasizing men and desirous women.

Kip's instinctive glance at Sandi sent a jolt through his veins and triggered a sensitive tingle that stiffened between his legs. The chilly first blast of the shower doused the spark before it caught fire. He stood with his head back; the water warmed as it slowly rained down on him. Kip's only addition to the bathroom had been a corner shower with a natural design: exposed rock on three sides. Three shower heads at various heights from the floor offered a range of aqua mood therapy — from a springlike mist to a mountain midsummer's spray to large monsoon drops delivered in a range from slow motion to pulsating jets.

Seated on the large stone bench, even the white noise of the shower could not calm him. Surrounded by the whoosh of water, he rehearsed what he planned to say to Sandi when he went down for breakfast. His heart fluttered, like the time he met Sandi, but now for a very different reason. Deep in thought, Kip was unaware of much else around him.

"Don't forget Chris's scrimmage tonight, Kip" Sandi said. Her tap on the shower door pulled him out of his thoughts, still dazed. He did not understand her. He cranked off the water, leaned out the door, leaving a puddle where he dripped. "What?"

"I said, don't forget Chris has a scrimmage tonight, and you need to be there."

"Yeah. Sure. I have that on my calendar at the office. I'll check, but count on it. I'll just meet you there."

She pushed the bathroom door closed. He lathered, rinsed, and stood with his back to the water that lulled him like the call of a siren, until he noticed the water had turned from steamy to icy. He hopped out of the shower, dried, and slipped on a faded dark blue polo shirt with the familiar "Virginia Crew" embroidered under an orange letter V.

"Ah, the luxurious aroma of fresh-brewed coffee," Kip said, as he came down the stairs, uneasy about when to launch his announcement.

"Would you like some?" Sandi asked, her attention drawn to the hummingbirds that jitterbugged around the feeder outside the window.

"I'd love a cup," Kip said, with a nervous, dry mouth. "Any English muffins left?"

"Well, I might be able to find one. Seems someone has raided the stash I snuck in from Twice Baked Bread yesterday. How do you two find these things?" Sandi said. She checked the stainless rolltop bread box, then a brown bag on the counter, and finally the fridge.

"Me? Had to be Chris. Remember, I work all day," he said, seated on a stool at the breakfast bar, where he rifled through the newspaper.

"And most of the night and weekends," Sandi added, with an exasperated harrumph, unable to find the muffins. She straightened her shirt across the front and placed her hands on her hips. "Of course, that string of consecutive nights at the office ends today with the scrimmage; then, tomorrow we're going to Charleston, remember." She turned to the pantry and found the muffins in a ziplock bag.

"Sure," Kip said, his mind already engaged in a completely different conversation. Sandi dug her ruby-red enameled nails into the sides of the English muffin, separated the top from the bottom, and placed them in the toaster to brown the potholed sides. When the toaster bell chimed, she paved both halves with butter and served the order. "One burn the British with a little shimmy and a shake," she hollered, with an exaggerated Southern accent, and down the kitchen counter, she slid the white china plate with its buttered, toasted English muffin, jelly on the side. Kip snagged the plate before it flew off the end.

"Haven't lost your touch after all these years, but the accent has got to go," he said, with a groan. "You sound like Daisy Duke from the Dukes of Hazard."

"Well, ah declare. What's a poor lil ole girl like me goinna do with you?" she laughed, then curtseyed and posed, fingers laced beneath her chin. Although her pose was old-fashioned, everything about her was as forward as tomorrow. Her sporty, tight, white tennis shorts and her two-button yellow top were eye-catching, especially when accompanied by her seductive, ice-blue stare. With no further reaction from Kip, she abandoned her obvious invitation, turned sharply toward him, and said, "Why don't you come up and see me sometime?" —just like Mae West.

Kip was not ready for morning humor. He smeared the strawberry jam on his muffin. He was already behind schedule when Sandi turned back toward him and said, "OK, for Friday, I am planning to wear my little black dress. Do you think that will do? I mean it is the Mills House, and it will be hot outside. Maybe I should wear the chiffon halter top dress. You know, the one you like so much with the pastel flowers, no back and the low, plunging neckline. After all, it will be our night."

Kip picked up on her emphasis of "will" and her inflection on the "our" in her statement.

"Whichever you feel more comfortable in," he said, avoiding her eyes. "You will be the center of attraction, regardless." He kept his eyes in the newspaper.

"Four?"

"Yeah, something about some other corporate guy in from Italy for one night."

"OK, I'll think about it. I have an appointment to have my hair and nails done at Dominque's today."

Kip looked up over the paper. "Sandi, I can't go Friday!"

"What?" she exclaimed, agape, the butter dish in a million pieces on the floor.

"Well, there . . . " he stammered, "there is something I need to do for work; I have to do it before the weekend, and the only time I have is tomorrow night. I just can't spend the time to go to Charleston with those bastards. I'm just not up for their gang tactics. Every day they call and—"

"Thomas Drummond, what do you mean you 'can't go'?" she interrupted, her cheeks lobster pink. "Don't you realize how much I have looked forward to this one night vacation?"

"I said I can't go," he said again, without additional explanation.

She tossed her half-empty mug in the sink and approached him from the opposite side of the counter. He tried to look away, but knew it was best to face her. He lowered the paper and looked at her, but not at her eyes. He glanced at her face only briefly.

"Look, I'll make it up to you. We can plan another weekend."

"Oh, sure. Like all the other weekends you promised to take off. Just like the weekends you promised to take Chris out."

"Hey, if it means that much to you, let's just set a date now, and we can plan on it."

"What do you mean 'if it means that much' to me? Doesn't it mean that much to you? Apparently not." Sandi sniffled. "And what about the sale? This would be the perfect time to hash all that out right there with those guys, Kip. I mean if you need to go off for some private caucus and leave me at the bar for awhile, that's perfectly all right with me. I think I can ward off the big, bad business wolves with their cheap pickup lines."

"They wouldn't make it that simple," Kip said.

"So why can't you go? Tell me. Tell me, why can't you go?"

"Something came up, and I need to tend to it right now."

"What is it? Tell me," Sandi said. "Is this another one of your secrets? Another lame secret so you won't have to go? We had a deal. I would go to that ridiculous LIARS party, and you would take me to Charleston. That was the deal. No more secrets, Kip. Tell me!" She had fire in her eyes. When Kip did not respond, she broke off her stare and walked back toward the window, her back toward him.

"Oh, I had it all planned," she moaned as she sobbed. "The dress, the perfume, the mood, the music, the excitement." She ran her fingers through her perfectly coiffed hair as she paced.

Then, like a cat with its tail on fire, she spun back around and pounced with a scream, "Goddamn it, Kip. We had a deal. You promised you would pull yourself away from that filthy fucking office of yours and give me a little attention for a change. You probably don't even realize how long it's been since you did that, do you Mr. Big Shot? Well, I'll tell you, asshole. Never. Not since a month after we were married have you bothered to do anything for me. To treat me like the woman. A woman needs more than a broken promise, Kip." She turned back toward the sink and continued to sob.

"Hey, look, I know—"

"You know what? How precious that business is? For what? For all the poor little ladies that work down there?

For the old guy, Gunny? For your miserable fucking, inflated ego? Give me a break!" He watched her chest rise and fall rapidly. "There is more to life than work and certainly more to love than one night, and you cannot even give me that? What could be so damned important that you would break your promise to me? Huh? What is so secret? Like not telling me about going to the Tavern? Some other secret? Like that five of spades you pulled out at the party? What was that all about? Another one of your secrets? Big poker game with the boys? What about me, Kip? What about me? You bring me to this miserable one-horse town, build this big place, then leave me stranded here for life, a prisoner in my own house." She rolled her eyes and shrugged. "I don't know what more I can do to get your attention. I'm not some old hag. What am I missing here, Kip? What is so damn important that you can't go? Tell me? Why should I have to be the one to suffer? Why persecute me?" She turned her back and walked away, prepared to launch into a second tirade if his answer was the least bit weak.

Kip pushed away from the counter and stood up. He wet his lips. He knew she would never buy the idea of the tarot thing. Hell, he was not totally convinced himself, but he had set his mind to go through with it, to go back to see the Reader and ask about the card on the windshield, and more. He had to do it before the weekend. He never really wanted to go to Charleston in the first place. He had promised Sandi earlier just to get her off his back.

"Damn it, it's just something I have to do," he said. He slammed the folded paper on the counter; his eyes burnt a hole in her back.

Sandi turned abruptly, stood akimbo, and said, "OK, well, I'll tell you what." She dabbed tears that flowed with her sobs. "You do that, Mr. Big Shot businessman puke. You do whatever is so goddamn important. I am going to Charleston. I am going to have the time of my life compliments of Taggett & Vystroon, real businessmen who can somehow mix business with a little pleasure now and then, something you can never seem to do." Fighting back tears, calmly, almost matter-of-factly, she said, "I'm going to Charleston to just relax and forget the miserable past five years."

Sandi stomped around the end of the counter, her face raw from rubbing tears. As she climbed the stairs to the second floor bedrooms, she hesitated midway. With volume open full throttle, she leaned over the handrail and decked him, verbally, "Hell, with you, Kip. And you'd better not be late for Chris's scrimmage tonight!" Her voice left no doubt. She waited for a split-second to dare him to respond, then bolted to their bedroom. Kip never felt the urge to leave his place in the kitchen. He knew enough to let her work through this in her own way.

All the commotion awakened Sparta. He nosed his way out of Kip's office, paws clicking down the hall as he watched Sandi head upstairs. He walked over and wiped his muzzle up and down Kip's leg. In return, Kip rubbed the dog's ears and said, "How about if you go outside for awhile and catch a few rays there, buddy? I don't think you want to be here right about now."

Kip opened the door by the carport. Sparta bounded down the stairs and over to a giant magnolia tree close to the road. He balanced on three legs and gave the trunk a good watering, then returned to the foot of the steps, where he took up a full layout position on the pine straw walk between the house and the carport. Kip sat on the floor, back against the door. He could hear Sandi bawling, sobbing, sniffling, and cursing for fifteen minutes. In a corner of his heart, he felt sorry for Sandi, but in his head, an image of the five of spades appeared over and over again. He thought through what he planned to say to the Reader: what to ask about the hex and what she knew of his secret — the part he did not tell Bill Malcolm.

CHAPTER 14

The truck coughed and coasted to a stop. The moon provided a soft light, the only light for the last quarter mile of his drive. Kip felt the familiar nausea when he stepped onto the porch and the shack and saw a handwritten note tacked to the blistered screen door:

The cards say you would come back, Mr. Drummond, even though you do not believe.

Five of spades, the card of the great evil, disinterest.

The card says there is evil in you, Mr. Drummond.

The card says you lie.

Your disinterest soon will cost you separation, violence, and loss.

Your question is not about the five of spades.

Your question is about your secret, the one that drives you, controls you.

Believe what I speak, Mr. Drummond.

I see danger for you.

Cards say you will see a friend on a boat on the river. Beware for that danger.

Believe the cards I read, Mr. Drummond. They say what will happen if you do not change. The cards are your warning. Your decisions are your future.

Do not doubt, Mr. Drummond. Believe.

The cards will tell me when you ready. I will not see you until then.

BU

His clammy skin took a chill, though there was no wind as he walked to his truck. He reread the note, and listened. Odd. Not a whisper.

"Sandra, it has been a most enjoyable evening," Alex Stringham said, the veneer of his pearly whites flashing next to the dimple in his cheek. "I truly am so sorry Thomas could not join us this evening. Pardon us, but Armando, Mazan, and I need to confer on a few details. Please assure Thomas that it is our commitment at Taggett & Vystroon to create terms for an agreement that works for all parties. We will contact Mr. Drummond in the morning to assess efforts to satisfy his recent additions to the paperwork. If you and Antonio will excuse us."

Alex nodded to Antonio and pushed back from the table, wine glass in hand. "Antonio, I am sorry to leave you alone with the South's most beautiful lady, mio amico, but some of us have work that beckons before we rest. We trust your work will be ready for review tomorrow, so please enjoy your night in the 'Holy City,' historic Charleston."

As the three businessmen rose to leave, Antonio also stood, dabbed his lips with his napkin, and shook hands.

In sequence, the trio made their way around the table to extend goodnights and farewells. Sandi Drummond extended her hand. In true Italian style, Armando kissed the back of her slender hand and said softly, "Potere le stelle e la luna nei cieli brillano su lei la bella signora. Oh, scusilo. I said, 'May the stars and moon in the skies shine on you, beautiful lady.'"

Sandi, charmed by the unexpected flattery, acknowledged the comment with a demure smile toward Armando Ventresca, along with his associates.

As the trio from Taggett & Vystroon walked through the arched doorway and out of the Barbadoes Room, Alex slid in between the other two and threw his arms over their shoulders. When they reached the door to the dining room, he said, "Ok, Mando, after all your talk about Italian women versus American women, let's see if your boy Antonio can seal his end of this deal. You two yahoos have not been able to!"

Mazan gave Alex a sharp jab to the lower ribcage with his elbow. "OK, wise ass. It takes three to tango here. I didn't see your footwork close the deal, either."

They exchanged barbs as they continued to the First Shot Lounge, adjacent to the dining room, where they sipped Remy Martin Extra, puffed on thick cigars, and discussed the strategy to close the deal.

Antonio took his seat across from Sandi with a leering Casanova grin. The wait staff was quick to clear the empty cups from the places vacated by the others. As they clanged china and silverware, the pianist provided a medley of show tunes by Andrew Lloyd Webber. Antonio chuckled from across the table.

"Tempo per amore," he said under his breath.

"Excuse me?" Sandi asked, intrigued by the Italian.

Antonio measured his words, carefully wrapped in a heavy Italian accent. "I am so sorry. I said, 'I just love this.' Here we are. Two strangers abandoned in a new country, a strange city. Abandoned by friends. Are all Americans like that? Always work? Never relax?"

"Well, some probably think that, but actually our situation is not quite that bad." Her finger unconsciously traced the rim of the china water goblet until it gave off an eerie tone. Her eyes opened wide, her red lips curled into a diminutive smile. Her fingers slid down the stem of the goblet and back up. "Remember, I grew up here in Charleston. I know the city rather well, if you'd like a brief tour." She continued to stroke the glass.

"Splendido. I would love it. The night is young. The weather is perfetto." He labored for words to form his reply. "It would be an honor for me to have such a beautiful escort and hostess."

"Thank you." Her face turned a rosy pink.

"I noticed the carriage out front. Possibly we could enjoy a ride, with a tour and a bottle of champagne as you show me the 'tesori unici,' uh . . . the unique treasures of Charleston?"

Across the table, they locked stares. Their movements relaxed. The noise in the dining room faded to white. Sandi fluttered her long lashes and closed her eyes in a flash of fantasy, until a waiter appeared.

"Pardon me. Would either of you care for more coffee?" he asked, the silver pot at the ready.

"No, thank you. I believe we will be leaving now," Sandi said.

Antonio placed his unfolded napkin on the table. The waiter helped Antonio with his chair; Antonio offered the same for his elegant tablemate, breathing deeply the flowery subtleness of her perfume. Sandi reached for her small puckered velvet clutch purse. As she pushed back her chair, the weight of the purse in her lap caused the folds of her simple but stylish black chiffon dress to gather, then drop to the top of her tanned thigh. She looked up and caught Antonio's gaze. She smiled. His eyes lingered with pleasure before he looked at her with a suggestive grin, like a boy caught with his hand in a cookie jar. She stepped out and away from the table.

"Shall we go to enjoy the night?" His dark chocolate eyes suggested much more.

"Why, yes," she said, with a flirtatious pause. "Let's do just that."

As they walked toward the doorway, Antonio placed his right hand on Sandi's lower back. She had forgotten how the simplest of gestures could warm her insides. She could not remember the last time she had been treated with such gentlemanly attention. For the first time in years, she felt wanted. Startled by the pure pleasure and his gentle touch, Sandi turned her head toward Antonio, who had motioned to the maître d' to come forward.

"Please excuse me while I freshen up," Sandi said, with a wink and playful smile. I'll only be a minute." As she walked away, Antonio nodded. She sensed his eyes on her as she walked. The spiked heals added a jaunty sway to her movement, a subtle rhythmic bounce that flicked the transparent material in the skirt and exposed the tan on the backs of her upper legs. Like a magnet, with every step she turned heads of men and women alike.

The maître d' watched Sandi walk off, then turned to Antonio. "May I be of service, sir?" he asked.

"Signor, please bring a bottle of chilled champagne to the carriage in front of the hotel."

"I am so sorry, sir, but we are not permitted to serve outside the hotel," he replied, his tone most apologetic, and most put on.

With eyebrows raised, Antonio cocked his head, speechless. He turned away from the man in the tuxedo and grumbled in Italian, his hand gestures paralyzed in frustration, then turned back toward the maître d'. "Oh, my apologies, scatto," he said. He rubbed his palms together to avoid what could become a scene. "Then, please have the sommelier select his best champagne and meet us at the hotel entrance in five minutes with two flutes and an ice bucket. Have the concierge call for the carriage and have the driver spotted at the front door in six minutes. Have a second bottle of champagne delivered to the Presidential Suite. Send the bill to Signor Alex Stringham."

His voice was deep, stern, and direct, his eyes wide and dripping with anger. Delivered with the same Italian accent, this was a different message, one the maître d' easily translated. Like a queen bee, he buzzed back to his station, snapping his fingers to summon the sommelier; he strained his eyes above the top of his glasses to follow his Italian guest before he looked down to dial the concierge on the house phone.

Antonio stood with one hand in his pocket, the other combed through his thick, black hair. He was impressed with the luxury in the Southern hotel. Fresh flowers atop the oval table bordered high-backed Georgian winged chairs. Tall white pillars flanked the two stairways to the upper floors. One stairway displayed the Stars and Stripes of the U.S. flag, and the other proudly displayed the blue cloth with the palmetto and the crescent moon of the South Carolina state flag.

Antonio fidgeted while the crowd milled about, a mix of self-important guests: undersized, oversized, and supersized. Some, in suits, wafted aimlessly between the grand foyer and the lounges. Others, a group of Citadel revelers decked out with bulldog ball caps and buttons, staggered from the courtyard through the lobby, lured like moths to the street lamps and an early start to Saturday's tailgate party before the game. "Last one to Big John's buys," one of the loud-mouthed, more intoxicated partiers challenged, referring to the classic watering hole for alums over the ages. Near the refined marquee entrance way, one unattached young Turk in jeans and a yellow T-shirt that read "Hog's Breath

Saloon, Key West, Florida" — obviously a personal fashion statement — bemoaned the lack of entertainment in the area and shouted back toward the Bellman, "Tell the valet to keep his fucking mitts off the bags in the front seat," which garnered the stares and quiet comments of several passersby in the lobby.

Antonio walked to the other side of the great room. He checked his watch. He straightened his tie. Out of nowhere appeared his escort for the evening: shapely legs in longs strides; one foot in front of the other; every bit as stunning as a model on a runway walk. She smiled, slid around him, and clutched his right arm tightly with both of her arms, all in stride.

"Shall we tour the fantastic city of my birth?" She shared a twinkle in her eyes and a radiant smile.

"I would be delighted, mia bella," Antonio said, with his hand on hers.

As they approached the front door, they heard the jingle of the harness when the carriage stopped beneath the muted glow from the street lamps. A salty breeze carried the whoop-whoop whine of a distant emergency vehicle siren and the laughter of vacationers along the street.

Antonio offered his hand to assist Sandi up the two steps into the carriage. When she stretched for the first step, a gust blew her skirt to the top of her leg.

"Oh!" Startled by her accidental display, she hopped up and seated herself with a laugh. She patted the leather seat next to her, "Join me."

After securing the ice bucket, two champagne flutes, and the bottle of the hotel's finest, Veuve Clicquot Demi Sec, presented by the sommelier, he took a seat beside her.

For an hour, the carriage meandered through and around the Battery, the historic waterfront of Charleston. They shared stories of themselves and their families—from their childhood to the present. The champagne decreased Sandi's listening skills and increased her laughter as she shared embellished tales of the Queen City. Antonio stumbled to make conversation in English.

When the carriage reins went slack in front of the Mills House, Antonio offered to escort Sandi to her suite. At her door, she fumbled with her key; Antonio reached out and slid the key out of her hand. "Allow me," he said. When Sandi danced through the threshold into the room, she immediately spotted a sweating champagne chiller.

"Compliments of Mr. Alex Stringham," she said, and placed the note card back on the tray. "How thoughtful. Stay, Antonio. Please stay. Open the bottle, and we can toast Alex and the Queen City."

Antonio was quick to oblige her. He pulled the bubbly from the polished silver bath and wrapped it in the monogrammed white serving towel. Sandi giggled as he removed the wire bail from the cork. The cork steady in one muscular hand, Antonio turned the bottle with the other to release a whisper of a hiss; the cork popped.

"Ah, why didn't you shoot that cork clear across the room?" Sandi asked. She hoisted the two empty flutes.

"I am quite sure the management would not appreciate this demi-sec on their Seirafian rug," he answered, trying to top off the flutes as they bobbed a-rhythmically in Sandi's hands.

"For someone from the world's finest wine country, you sure have problems pouring a thirsty lady a much-needed glass of sparkling wine."

"It is not our custom in Italia to pour delicate wine into moving vessels," he said with a bit of a laugh, then reached to steady the glass. Her hand was soft and warm in his grip. "Much easier this way."

Her eyes rotated slowly from the glass up to his eyes; her thoughts moved with them. Her lips moved even slower, but they managed to mutter with a trace of a slur, "You are so nice! Just like all the movies. Charming. Handsome. Tanned. Athletic. A real gentleman. What makes you so nice?"

"You bring out the best in me, Signora." He stepped back, smiled to hold her gaze, and in a mix of languages, offered a salute. "A voi, a toast. May the business deal be a completo successo and all you ever wanted nella vita come to you."

"To the deal," she echoed, with a scrunch of her nose pixielike.

They clinked glasses and sipped.

She leaned forward, stretched on her toes, and gently planted a kiss on Antonio's cheek, then nuzzled his neck. Intoxicated by the spicy scent of his cologne, she traced her nose under his chin, then kissed him above the button on his open collared shirt. She looked up. Without a word, his dark eyes called her.

"Actually, much of what I wish for is here right now. You have given me what I really want." She kissed his neck. "I want to be cared for." She kissed his cheek. "I want to be caressed." She kissed his lips, an elongated kiss. "I want to be enjoyed." She pulled away, her eyes still closed. When they opened, a broad smile blossomed on her face. She pushed away and began to spin around in front of him.

"Oh, what a wonderful night. What a gloriously wonderful night." She twirled, round and round. Her dress lifted. She spun like a top. Antonio leaned back in laughter. Then, like a top, she began to wobble a bit until Antonio reached forward to steady her. With his hands loose around her waist, she continued to turn. As he gently tightened his grip, her torso slowed its rotation until she came to a complete stop. Her eyes closed again; she breathed heavily through her mouth at first; then, closing her mouth, she breathed deeply through her nose, while the room continued to spin. With each deep breath, she could feel his warm and tender hands, one on her lower belly and the other on her lower back. As she swayed, she waited for him to do something she had missed for so long. He broke the silence.

"I should go now. You have documents to sign and more work at the breakfast meeting tomorrow with Mazan, Armando, and Alex. Beauty, like yours, needs rest."

"Beauty needs company. Besides, I can sign the papers, and you can deliver them for me. That way, I can sleep in. Wait there. I'll get the documents and things. Once they are signed, we can have another toast to the success you mentioned earlier. Maybe there is more to this deal."

She twirled, tapped him on the nose with a finger, and paraded to the bedroom area, holding her champagne in one hand and flicking her skirt with the other.

Antonio sensed he had been successful to this point. His persuasive efforts were certain to earn the ten grand that had been promised him if she signed the paperwork. He sipped his champagne and moved to the window on the far wall that overlooked the main entrance. He pulled back the drapes and gazed east down Queen Street toward the black of the ocean three blocks away. He spotted harbor lights, boats returning from their twilight sail, and specks of passersby walking along the waterfront, relaxing with a purpose. He saw the alumni partiers from earlier in the evening as they made their way back to the hotel, now more exuberant and more inebriated than before. He took his eyes off the street to find a place for his empty glass. As he turned back toward the window, he noticed the lights in the suite had dimmed. The reflection in the window pane inches from his nose explained why. Sandi had emerged from the bedroom, her thin, black cocktail dress replaced by a cream-colored bathrobe, monogrammed, loosely wrapped, and sliding off one shoulder. She sashayed

toward him, one foot in front of the other in a sassy sort
of way. The evening glitter of pearls rested silky smooth
around her neck. In one hand, she held a small valise; in
the other, she carried her champagne glass. Draped over
her bent forearm was another terrycloth robe. Antonio
did not turn. He tried to regain focus out the window on
the street below, but he failed to shake the reflection of
the moment before.

"Well, since I was kind enough to offer you the tour
of my city," she said in a businesslike voice doused in
alcohol, "maybe you would be so kind as to walk me
through these papers so I don't spend the entire night
reading the fine print. Just point out the key parts so I
can sign them; then we can have that toast to the deal."

Antonio turned. He faked surprise and remained
speechless. She tossed the valise aside; it landed on the
floor near the sofa. She drained the remnants of her
champagne flute and placed it on the end table.

"But now I feel so underdressed with you there in
your Firado Uomo suit," she mocked. "Don't you think
you would feel much better while you helped a friend if
you weren't so dolled up? You tend to make a poor girl
feel so casual and inferior," she added, with a theatrical
pout on her face. Her movement was slow and seductive
as she closed the space between them.

Floors below them, the ruckus on the street grew
louder. The concierge was in discussion with the
merrymakers in the Citadel attire. "Come inside," he
said, to avert a scene on the street outside the hotel.

Sandi stopped toe-to-toe with Antonio. Her fragrance engulfed him. She placed her left hand on his chest and began to unbutton his shirt, top to bottom, one button after the other. Her perfume mesmerized him and drew him closer to her. He buried his nose in her hair as her hands moved lower on the open shirt. Without looking down, she tugged and pulled out his shirttail, unbuttoned the last buttons, then parted the opening like a curtain. Her bulky robe slipped off her shoulder. Antonio lifted his hands to hold her: bare skin with tan lines from what must have been a "next-to-nothing" bikini top. Aroused, but true to his gentlemanly ways, he pulled the robe back over her shoulder and closed it around her chest. He held her shoulders tightly. "We have papers to review."

Sandi, numbed by the two hours of free flowing demi-sec, ignored his comment. It was obvious he meant to distract her. She looked at his face; her tired eyes in search of love, her fingers slid along his smooth, stiff leather belt. She fumbled with the buckle momentarily, then flicked open the prong. Pressed against him, she opened it, and with both hands, she unbuttoned his trousers. Her fingers found the pull on his zipper. She inched it down slowly over each tooth to the end of the tape. She turned her head slightly, kissed his chest, and began to bend her knees, lower and lower, kissing his chest, then navel, then lower on his stomach. As she moved, she pulled his trousers to his feet. She knelt on the floor, forehead resting against his silk boxers, her eyes closed. She hesitated. Sighed. Each breath was deeper and more audible. Sandi rubbed her head against his thigh, then dipped lower to untie his shoes.

Antonio could feel her warm breath through the thin cloth. He placed his hands on her back and watched her slow-motion shadow on the ceiling. The tingle of excitement continued to arouse him. He bent over and clutched the sides of Sandi's head.

"You American women are so bold . . . but pleasing. I wish to thank you for your tour tonight. As you requested, I will gladly assist in going over the paperwork with you. Allow me to 'Slip into something a little more comfortable' as you say, while you lay out the papers on the coffee table."

"But . . . I'm, I'm not finished!" she said, her voice stuttered, caught off guard by the sudden change in the mood.

"I think I can handle this from here. Please, work on the papers. I will be back in a minuto."

Sandi's smile evaporated. She knelt with a confused and dejected look on her face while Antonio pulled his trousers back to his waist, zipped them, lifted the extra robe off her shoulder, and sauntered to the bedroom, his shirt still unbuttoned.

The pub-induced repartee of the crowd out on the street had died down; only the chime of the elevator down the hall broke the black hole of silence. Sandi, still on all fours, crawled to the end table and hoisted herself to her feet, where she tottered, then abandoned a thought to follow Antonio. Instead, she grabbed the opened bottle of champagne, refilled the two champagne flutes, promptly chugged one, and refilled it.

Antonio appeared from the bedroom. His robe, like hers, was loose. His chest was muscular, chiseled, and blanketed with a thick mat of black hair. Since he was dark-skinned and broad-shouldered, even his walk was sexy as he approached her with his hands in the robe pockets. Caught with her refilled glass in hand, Antonio joked, "In Italia, they say drinking alone is not good for you."

"I was thirsty, and I had no idea how long you would be," she said, with a serious tone in her voice as she looked away to sneak another sip. "Besides, what's a poor girl to do?" She turned back toward him and laughed. Antonio laughed with her. He shook his finger at her and said, "Naughty, naughty girl. I thought this was a casual business meeting."

Sandi offered him his champagne and jabbered, "Indeed it is. I'll drink to that. Business it is. Real business. First-class business. One of us is selling, one of us is buying, and both get what they truly want. A deal can't get any better than that." She gestured, her glass raised in a silent toast, then downed the contents and poured herself another until it spilled over the rim and onto the rug. As she took a seat, she spilled more on the sofa, placed her glass on the rug by her foot, then patted the sofa cushion next to hers. "Per favore, please sit. We have work." She leaned forward and took another healthy, prolonged sip.

She opened the valise next to her and pulled out a batch of legal papers about an inch thick. Colored tabs throughout the stack. Text highlighted in neon yellow with paper clips sticking out to mark specific pages. Yellow tabs with red letters that read "Initial" and red arrows with black letters read "Sign Here." Removable "date & sign" labels on several pages. An embossed seal on the final page. It was all there. Enough legalese to keep a second-year law student busy for a day or two. Sandi pulled and signed papers before Antonio had a chance to examine what they were or explain anything about them. As she signed, he returned them to the small leather satchel. In the end, Sandi followed the tabs on the pages and signed forms, documents, and letters laid out on the table; she did so without a single word.

With her signature on the last form, Sandi slammed her pen on the table, raised her arms, and sang out, "Ta-da! Ok, a deal is a deal! Time for that toast."

She reached for the bottle of champagne as Antonio stuffed the last of the papers into the valise. In the excitement of the moment—finishing the paperwork—Sandi jumped up quickly, too quickly. Her legs were rubbery. She reached out to stop the room from spinning; instead, her eyes rolled back and she felt herself drop in a slow-motion tailspin onto the sofa.

Antonio leaned over, took the chilled bottle from her hand, and held it ever so slightly against her forehead and along her cheeks. She flinched, embarrassed, and bounced back onto her feet, still woozy.

"Must be all the excitement, the paperwork, and all," she said, her free-spirited self once again. "Come on, we have a toast to drink. Pour that French elixir. Or was it California?   Wherever. Let's have a toast." Antonio obliged her, topping off both glasses with the smidge left in the bottle.

"Signora bella, to your future and all that you desire. May this decision be the start of a new life." He grinned and raised his glass toward her.

Sandi's face drained to a surprised pallor. With a thick tongue, she over enunciated her response, "And may we always remember this magical night and the life that started here. Cheers!"

With her eyes on his, she sipped, but her sip lasted much longer than his. She emptied her glass. When she finished, she gently tossed her glass over her shoulder, then snatched his from his hand. Spilling a small amount, she belted down the remainder and tossed his glass into the chair behind her.

"Can you reach the bottle behind you there?" Sandi asked, pointing toward the champagne. Antonio looked at her, amazed at her capacity, then turned at the waist and bent forward to reach for the bottle. With his weight shifted, Sandi drove her shoulder into him like a linebacker. Antonio fell, off balance, onto the sofa behind him, and Sandi's momentum carried her forward. She landed on top of him. She leaned back, untied the loose knot in the belt of her robe, and allowed the heavy folds of cloth to slide off her shoulders. As it dropped, she arched her back and stretched her arms behind her. The robe fell and exposed the fullness of her perfectly shaped breasts. Neither uttered a word; their eyes, rapt in mutual thoughts, never strayed from the other's breathless stare. She welcomed the lustful intentions she read through his eyes, which warmed her breasts and made them swell. Her nipples hardened even more. Antonio remained still as her hands, at rest on top of his robe, began to unravel his twisted belt. She could feel him through the robe. Excited, his warm hands inched up her legs still covered by the bottom of her robe. She trembled. Her breathing slowed, though her heart raced faster than hummingbird wings.

When she had untangled Antonio's belt, she pushed his robe aside and undraped his chest. Her hands slid to his waist as she peeked with delight. Her breathing quickened; she sipped little breaths. From her first step onto the carriage on Market Street, she knew she needed to see him this way. It wasn't this way with her Kip. It had not been for a long, long time.

His robe was caught under her leg as she straddled him. With one foot on the ground, she lifted herself enough to free his robe. One side fell to the floor; she brushed back the other and then began to fondle him. Velvet-soft hands with perfectly manicured nails painted red. Hot, firm, pleasureful. She held him with both hands and gently inched her thighs further back on the sofa, then dropped her chin, arched forward, and placed her mouth on him, gently scraping his thin, sensitive skin with her teeth as she bobbed ever so slightly, lips and tongue engaged. For Antonio, the relaxing effects of the champagne gave way to a volcanic pressure, which sucked its power from all his extremities. He leaned his head on the back of the sofa. His fingers combed through her hair and down her delicate neck. He enjoyed every stroke. He wanted more from the night. She was his assignment. He had been sent to do more.

He tucked a lock of blonde hair behind her ear, then slowly lifted her head off him. Her long lashes flicked up; her ice-blue eyes locked on his once again. With a featherlike touch, his warm hands lifted her; the robe fell free, left to drape the sofa. She nibbled on his ear and nuzzled into his neck as he carried her to the bedroom. As she lay there, the passion in his eyes explored her body to appreciate her total beauty. He discarded his robe and leaned forward, his lips locked on her as he rolled onto the bed; his body melted into hers.

Sandi pressed forward, then pulled back and exhaled; her head fell back onto the pillow. "I have wanted you all evening," she said, straight-faced. She made the trip to spite Kip. To enjoy a get-away. To relax. She had not come to look for love or lust or passion, but it felt good. It was pleasure. The champagne had dissolved her bond of chastity and fidelity. Her body was hungry for sex. Hot and hard. She rolled back toward Antonio, her lips mashed against his, her tongue thrust as deep as it would go, exploring and tasting the desire. They kissed with animal-like fervor: carnal rapture stoked fires of lust. Antonio lay close, his hand on her thigh. His fingertips began a slow, intimate, erotic search for the tender notch between her thighs—wet, hot, and aching for his touch. She moaned, her body writhing, contorted, and frozen in that breathless moment she had nearly forgotten.

When Antonio pulled his lips away, Sandi gasped. She panted and sighed as he teased her nipple with his teeth and traced her areola with the very tip of his tongue. She arched her back and pushed harder against his hand that was lost between her legs. She strained a moan of ecstasy, reached across his back, and dragged her nails from his shoulder to his head. She pulled him harder onto her body as it quaked from the prolonged arousal, rigid with the spasms and limp with their relief. Arms outstretched, she clutched at the satin sheets. Antonio eased himself on top of her, their bodies lathered in passion. She spread her legs further apart and squirmed feverishly to align herself as he entered her. Her hips lifted from the bed and pushed toward him. "Deeper. Harder," she screamed, then eked out a solitary chuckle, and then a groan, before all her senses went numb; the euphoric tremor transported her, then numbed her again. As she lay there, helpless, unable to breathe, a strobelike flash of memory recalled this same feeling in her distant past. Breathlessly, she whispered, "Oh, oh yes," in slow, breathless submission. Shivers of the lust rippled through her body. The pain was pleasure, and it was heavenly.

The smell of sex hung heavy, unmoved in the air beneath the high ceiling. Her hair clung to her cheek as Antonio nibbled on her lips before another feast of pleasure. Again, and again, through the night, he pushed wildly to satisfy her. She begged him to quench the denial she had lived with for five years. Every cell in her body tingled to his touch. Only once did she think of Kip. The vision of his face at the height of one of many orgasms brought a pleasurable smile to her face, followed by a subdued demonic laugh, before her body surrendered to the hot love Antonio pumped in her. She never thought of Kip again that night, and she never heard Antonio leave the next morning.

CHAPTER 16

The squared red numbers blinked once before the alarm on the clock resounded. It was Saturday, thank God. Across the Lowcountry marshes, the day dawned full of humidity and sand gnats, but not a single ray of October sun could wedge through the circus parade of elephant-like gray clouds that drifted in from the stormy Atlantic. The forecast called for showers, heavy at times, beginning later in the morning. Kip was prepared to get his run in and hoped the rains would hold off until after Chris's pee wee league football game. Regardless, he would be the dedicated dad and sit through whatever the showers threw at them. He owed that to Chris, and Sandi would expect it.

Kip turned off the alarm and noticed the tarot reader's note next to the clock on the nightstand. He read it, and read it again; then he dressed for his run. Ordinarily, Sparta would nudge him to hurry; after all, the dog had priorities: chasing squirrels, treeing raccoons, rolling armadillos. But today, Sparta was a no-show. It wasn't like Sparta to spend the night outside the house. There were neither phone messages from Sandi nor a note from Chris. Kip decided to take a solo run, an unusual chance for him to work on his speed.

Up and down Bay Street, smells of cinnamon buns fresh out of the oven enriched the breeze. Early risers rocked in porch swings. A few spread out the Beaufort Gazette on park benches near the Oak Tree on The Bluff. An older man with bug-eyes walked with his look-alike Boston Terrier on a leash in one hand and a coffee mug in the other. When Kip reached Carteret Street, the turnaround point, the rain started. Two brief downpours came in volleys, like buckshot. Wind gusts slapped wrought iron gates shut and choreographed a square dance of do-si-dos and an allemande that dropped foliage into pools of water that looked like murky, bubbling tar pits.

For the distance, Kip ran his personal best time. Without the usual rambunctious escapades from Sparta, he wasn't too surprised. As he walked into the house, the sweet, coconut fragrance of the potted miniature gardenias overwhelmed him. He purchased them the day before, as a late summer "welcome home" truce offering for Sandi. He checked the answering machine. He was surprised that she had not called to say she was headed home and to remind him about Chris's game. He expected her up early and on the road back in time for the pregame tailgate party with pancakes made on the Coleman camper stove, freshly brewed coffee, à la Dyson's Deli, and Naked Screwdrivers, aka OJ. The shopping in Charleston the day before had probably exhausted her, and she had seized the opportunity to lie around in bed and enjoy the morning.

He walked to the kitchen, washed his hands, fired up the coffee maker, and grabbed a handful of grapes before his postrun stretch. As he walked down the hall, he picked up one of the many tennis balls Sparta had fetched and gnawed. This one had no felt cover at all. He dribbled while he walked, his footsteps and the thump of the ball echoing off the slatted wooden ceiling in the hall. He pulled at his rain drenched T-shirt, one of his favorites; it read "Beaufort Water Festival 1987 Honorary Commodore." He was the first unanimous selection ever. The Beaufort mayor commissioned him when the festival opened. His citation read: "For saving the Lady's Island Oyster Factory—Beaufort's most historic business and the livelihood of the faithful and loyal workers."

Kip finished his stretches and sat down at his desk to read a fax he had received. It was the lab report about the coin he had sent to Jamie Gentry in Charleston. As he started to read, the phone rang.

"Hello." The caller ID on the telephone display window read, "Lady's Island Oyster Factory."

"Mr. Drummond?" It was Gunny.

"Hey, Gunny."

"Sir, this is Gunny Brewer down at de factory."

"Gunny, didn't expect you'd be calling from down there. I figured you'd be out on the water somewhere. Getting to be just about low tide. Better get those shrimp while you can; they won't be there all day. Don't tell me you let that rainsquall this morning keep you out of the water?"

"No, sir. Dem shrimp can wait. Mr. Drummond, sir, I need you to come down yuh to de factory," Gunny said, his voice anxious and concerned.

"Well, I was just headed out to watch Chris play football. Today's the big game against the kids from Hilton Head. I was hoping to see Chris leave a few Dolphins in his dust."

"Sir, I need you to come down to de factory, now. Your dog is down yuh."

"Sparta? Over at the factory?" Kip said. What in the hell is he doing down there? He knew Shelby lived not too far from there, so if Chris took Sparta with him, there would be a chance Sparta could end up at the factory. But why would he leave Chris?

"Well, if he is there, just leave him in my office. He's used to being in there alone. He won't do anything but sleep on the couch. I'll stop by after the game and pick him up. He'll be fine."

"No, sir, I mean you need to come and get de dog now! We can't do nothin' with him." Gunny's tone was direct, insistent.

"OK. Sure. I just got back from my run. Let me clean up, and I'll swing by. I might miss the kickoff. I'll see y'all in a bit."

"Thank you, Mr. Drummond. Hurry, if you can." Gunny hung up.

Kip stared at the receiver, then placed it back into the cradle. He walked out to the kitchen and poured fresh coffee into his chipped, orange UVA mug and headed upstairs for a quick shave and shower. He threw on some baggy gray gym shorts and his Beaufort Buccaneers Booster T-shirt. The oyster factory sponsored the Buccaneers, so the back of the T-shirt was plastered with a cartoon oyster logo and "Lady's Island Oyster Factory." He gulped down the dregs of his coffee, jumped in his truck, and headed toward Lady's Island with Mick Jagger as copilot and "Satisfaction" his woe of the day.

Despite the usual chaos of pee wee football—kids that run into each other, kids that run the wrong way, kids that trip over their own feet—one sure thing about the games was they always started on time. Chris played offense as a wide receiver, away from the rough-and-tumble interior line action, which was much closer to where the glory was. His only real contact came during kickoffs. So when he lined up to receive the kickoff, he looked to the sidelines. But he did not see Kip. Chris took it in stride, disappointed again. When Kip did make it to the games, he was often late because he always had one more thing to wrap up at the office. It looked as if today would be the same. Chris could not find either Kip or Sandi over where the parents congregated and watched. He assumed Kip was late and Sandi was not back from Charleston.

There was a crunch of oyster shells under the tires as Kip parked his truck in the lot adjacent to the factory.

Although there was not a sign for designated parking, Kip always parked in the shade of some short palmettos and scrub oaks. But there was no sun to worry about today. Charcoal-gray storm clouds billowed westward above the marsh.; the rain threatened to return.

The factory was quiet. Gunny had a couple of the ladies in the office to stack orders that needed to go out. They hesitated to look at Kip and did not offer any greetings. The weekend crew was always in and out before Kip made his Saturday appearance to catch up on the office work. Maybe they were startled to see him in the factory this early on a Saturday morning. He nodded.

"Do you know where Gunny is?" he asked. They did not speak; they only gestured with a tilt of the head that he was out on the dock.

They watched him as he moved through the packing area, past the conveyors, and out the back door toward the dock, where Gunny stood beneath the threatening sky. There was still no sign of Sparta.

"Hey, Gunny, will you have these folks out of here before the rain?" Kip asked, with a nod over Gunny's shoulder toward the marsh. "It doesn't look good out there."

Kip scanned the area for Sparta.

Gunny was reserved, not his usual self. Even after their recent disagreements, Gunny had remained professional and carried on as he had prior to their sessions. Today, he was different. His shoulders slumped. He wore a dour expression painted on his face. He was quiet. Kip noticed.

"OK, so what's up with my ferocious pup? What did you do with him? I'll get him out of your hair and let your folks finish up so you can get out of here."

Gunny did not speak. He stood, tight-jawed.

"Mr. Drummond, de dog is over yuh," he said, as he moved toward a pleasure boat tied up overnight, unannounced, at the far end of the platform. Kip followed.

The splintered railroad ties and shredded tires hanging from the iron dock cleats did not offer much support for the twenty-five-foot Irwin sailboat. On most days, the dock wall would be the temporary tie-down point for the local fishermen scows and flat-bottomed bateaux loaded with oysters plucked from the local waters.

"Where did this baby come from?" Kip asked, as he followed. Gunny did not respond.

The clouds thickened, as predicted. Winds slapped the snap shackles of the halyard against the metal mast as Kip and Gunny passed the Carpe Diem. Gunny continued toward the aft end of the boat, where he stopped and pointed up above the captain's wheel. Kip followed Gunny's hand. He looked above the cockpit, where he saw his best friend spread across a blood-soaked, faded blue bimini. Each of Sparta's legs was tied to a different corner of the stainless-steel tubular frame. His eyes were wide-open, the lids pulled back and secured with large fish hooks. His tongue, almost white, hung out the side of his mouth. The dog had been castrated and dismembered: his ribcage cracked, his chest spread wide-open. He was completely disemboweled. From his neck to his tail, only his big, stilled heart remained, plucked and placed low in the carcass where the stomach once churned. Flies clung to the wet skin, while gusts jerked and twisted the remains in an eerie animation.

Kip went limp. He turned away, dropped to his knees, and retched. His pulse quickened; his breathing became rapid and shallow. He remained on all fours, his eyes closed. His stomach gurgled for minutes as he fought to stave off another attack. When he felt he could stand, he forced himself upright on rubbery legs.

"When did you find him?" Kip muttered, his gut still queasy. He wiped his brow, then continued to slide his hand over the top of his head and back to the top of his neck, where he squeezed a knot of tension.

"I saw him 'bout an hour ago. I called your house but got no answer. I didn't want to leave a message."

"Any idea who the boat belongs to?"

"No sir, not a clue. Never seen it before 'round yuh, but I doubt dem folks have any idea 'bout any of dis."

Kip rubbed his forehead with his hand, then raked his fingers through his hair. "Who would have done this to my dog? And why? Why Sparta?" He pulled at his hair as he staggered, unsteady on his feet against storm winds that brought a steady, light rain out of the northeast.

The ladies inside watched from the shadows just inside the dock doors. They shared mixed emotions: grief for the dog and satisfied bewilderment for the haughty Mr. Drummond, now dissolved in a pitiful heap.

"Mr. Drummond, sir," Gunny said. "I know this ain't de right time, and you probably don't want to hear no more, but dey is something else. I don't know who did this or why, and you can bet that I will find out, Mr. Drummond, but dey is something else I got to show you."

Kip blocked out Gunny's voice. He continued to stumble around until Gunny squeezed the back of Kip's neck. Gunny pointed toward the stern and walked to the back of the boat. The rains, pooled on the bimini, dripped into a crimson-colored puddle. Gunny pointed down to the deck near the puddle, where there was a hastily drawn design in black paint.

"That sign be evil. It is a hex, a hoodoo five-spot, a jinx," Gunny said.

The sign was a square with a mark in each corner and one in the center. It looked like the five of spades.

"Whoever did dis put a hex on you, Mr. Drummond. A death wish. Dat dog got caught up in dat spell. Dis might only be de beginnin'. De ladies are afraid to go near dat dog. Dey say we shouldn't go near de dog. Dat's why I said you had to get him. Dey ain't nothin' we can do. We can wash away dat sign, but dat won't wash away de hex."

Kip stood there, transfixed by the painted design and the blood-stained surface of the boat. He did not chance a glance at Sparta. Emotions blurred his concentration; his grief battled rage. He wanted to get even, but with whom? What Gunny had said began to register. The trio from Taggett & Vystroon had warned that they were tired of playing games, that he needed to do things their way or "things" would happen. Then he did not show for the meeting in Charleston. And the tarot reader. Her words now made sense. Her note even said, "You will see your friend on the river upon the boat." She knew; the cards had told her.

The clouds burst. The rain was no longer the light shower that had fallen earlier. The winds curled the surface of the river into tiny whitecaps of foam. Curtains of water pushed horizontal by gusts strafed the dock. Kip borrowed a large pocket knife from Gunny and cut the dog free from the gruesome display on the unclaimed boat. He collapsed to the deck and cradled the stiff remains of his dog in his lap. His tears masked by the torrential rains, Kip sat there, undisturbed, for nearly a half hour, until Gunny came to help him. They wrapped the butchered carcass in a shrimp net and laid it in the bed of Kip's truck for the final ride home.

CHAPTER 17

For over an hour, Kip lumbered through the wind and the sheets of rain to bury his best friend in a special spot near the carport—the spot where Sparta had always waited for Kip. He allowed the tears. His thoughts never drifted far from the images of the runs they shared, and the images always ended with their final meeting on a boat on the river. He turned the last scoop of sandy slop onto the grave, threw the shovel against the side of the carport, and dragged himself inside.

The rain, like grapeshot, pelted the glass doors to the back deck. Kip collapsed in the sunroom wicker chair, unable to lift his arms. He slumped deep in the seat as blood stains appeared on his soaked gray shorts like those of the Shroud of Turin, and pools of rainwater formed around the chair. As he dozed off, he heard the familiar click-clack of dog claws on the wooden floor in the hall, silenced by thunder that rocked the house. He opened his eyes when lightning flashed. As if a great light had flashed in his head, he remembered he had promised Chris he would be in the stands to watch his game. He realized the game, if played at all, was over now and there was no sign of Chris; he should have called to let Kip know where he was.

Kip moved to one of the stools along the kitchen counter. His body ached all over. His head pounded. He pulled out the Buccaneers team roster to call the other team parents. After the customary exchanges ("How are things?" "Sorry I missed the game." "How did they do?" How is Trevor?" "How is Shelby?" "How is TJ?"), Kip asked if they had seen Chris or knew where he was.

"Last time I saw him," Coach McCafferey said, "he was walking off the field carrying his helmet. Everybody scrambled pretty quick to get out of that storm. Some of those gusts just came out of nowhere. I am not sure where Chris went from there, but if I hear anything I'll let you know."

Coach McCafferey said he checked the field before he left and all the boys were gone, so he assumed Chris went home with someone from the team.

After calls to everyone on the roster, Kip found no one who had offered a ride and no one knew where Chris was. Kip realized he had been pretty hard on the kid after his last game. And he promised to be at the game today. But where would Chris go? Why did he not call? And where was his mother?

Flickers of lightning turned the midafternoon skies from moonless midnight into still life grays and browns filtered through a curtain of rain. Thunder rattled the house, but it did not jolt Kip as much as the grisly thoughts of the Reader's words and Gunny's suggestion that Sparta's death might only be the beginning of the hex.

Through the kitchen window, he watched the slanting, driving rain. Death in the cards. Had something happened to Chris? Once again, the house shook with another thunderous quake, but this time, it wasn't the weather. It was the door.

"God, it's like a hurricane out there," Sandi said, as she shook her pink umbrella and placed it in the corner inside the door.

"Where the hell have you been?" Kip lifted himself off the stool. "You were supposed to be home hours ago."

"Did you not notice that it's raining cats and dogs? I could barely see the road, for Christ sake."

A long, deep rumble of thunder rolled through the house. "Did Chris call you?" Kip asked.

"When? Last night? I didn't have any calls. I was in the room all night," she said, truthfully. "I went to dinner with your group from Taggett & Vystroon, went back to my room to relax, signed some papers, had a drink, and went to bed. I didn't get a call from Chris — or from you, for that matter. Today? When was he going to call? I have been in the damn car all day."

Sandi was busy with the snaps on her jacket when Kip stepped forward, the palms of his hands pressed on his head just above his ears. "Chris is missing."

"What?" Sandi whispered in shock.

Kip turned and walked away from Sandi, his hands still pressed on his head.

"What do you mean 'missing'?" she asked, as she jammed her wet rain gear on the hook just inside the door.

"Nobody has seen him since the game," he said, as he paced.

"You were at the game, weren't you?"

"No, I didn't make it. I—"

Sandi interrupted before he could finish. "You 'didn't make it.' What do you mean you 'didn't make it'?"

Kip did not respond. Sandi marched to Kip, and spun him around, her nose just below his chin.

"So, where were—"

"Sparta's dead," Kip choked out.

"What?" Sandi asked, with a wrinkled brow, bewildered that Kip had changed the subject from their son to his dog.

His jaw locked, he repeated, "I said Sparta is dead. They butchered him."

He walked away from her and stood in front of the wall of glass that faced the river. Lightning exposed the horizontal rain.

"He was missing last night when I came home." He went to the sink, poured himself a glass of water, and took up a seat on the stool again.

"Kip, I'm sorry," she said. "I'm sorry I yelled. I . . . I didn't know. I don't know what else to say." She walked toward him, and, briefly, she slid her palm across his back. But then, dropping her hand, she continued to walk toward the window over the sink.

"Oh, God. So what do we do about Chris? What are they saying about the weather? It's already dark."

Kip sat on the stool with his head in his hands.

"I've called everyone. He is not at anyone's house."

"The coach?"

"He hasn't seen him since the game."

"Have you called the police?"

"They can't do anything until he has been missing for twenty-four hours."

"Even in this storm? Hell, it's like a hurricane out there, Kip."

Kip came off the stool. "No, I hadn't noticed. I was standing out in it for three hours, burying my dog."

"OK, sorry." Sandi hesitated; then, as only a mother can do, she raised the unthinkable. "Would someone have taken Chris? I mean, what if someone has him? And why?"

The cards. The Reader. The hex sign. Kip said, "No, that's not it. We need to find him."

Together they laid out a frantic search plan, not interested in getting the community or police involved just yet. They compiled a list of places where Chris might be, not to include the houses of his teammates. Kip would drive a route and stop at places from their list. The usual places: the doughnut shop at Celedon Place, the arcade, the Gas 'n Go Mart. Sandi would remain at the house in the event Chris showed up or called. She would occupy herself by going back through the team roster to call all of the families again to make them aware of the crisis and to ask for assistance in the search. Before he left, Sandi pulled Kip close to her and said, "Find my son, Kip."

Dense clouds spread low and dark throughout the island. From inside his truck, Kip found it difficult to spot anything, even though the rain was less fierce than earlier in the day. Tree branches of all sizes crunched under the tires in the narrow, flooded streets. Flooded lawns from both sides met in the middle of Spanish Point Road, the rains too much for the city's unimproved, eighty-year-old drainage system. In some spots, the standing water covered the truck's running boards and forced Kip to trudge on foot through the rain-swollen runoff. At every stop, he called Chris's name in case Chris planned to ride out the storm, to wait for someone to find him and take him home.

This was already the longest day in Kip's life. Behind his eyes, daggers carved out painful memories reinforced by the sand-covered shirt and stained shorts he still wore. His head throbbed. With every lightning flash, he saw the blood-splashed canvas cover on the boat at the dock.

He drove around the McTeer Memorial Bridge and the marina, then around the Naval Hospital and Fort Frederick, where Chris often went to look for the treasure. He drove around Port Royal and down to the water's edge near the marsh to find any sign that Chris had been there. Chris was a good swimmer, but the incident with the snake the week before haunted him. It was dark now, and the rains had long filled any snake holes; they could be out and active once again.

Kip pulled into the Stop-N-Go adjacent to the marina, found a working pay phone, and called home.

"No, nobody has seen him," Sandi whimpered. "I have called everybody on the team. Nobody else is missing. Several saw Chris after the game, but they admitted they were quick to load up and run to beat the worst of the rain."

Conditions had not improved. Power was out south of the hospital. A handful of lights blemished a blackness which rivaled deep space. The only vehicles Kip saw were the emergency power crews out at work on a few transformers that had been plucked from their poles like cherries. The rain had diminished, but the wind had begun to pick up — a signal for another bout of rain.

The thunder rolled in through his left ear and rumbled out his right. He braced himself against the winds, and yelled into the phone, "Maybe Chris never got a ride from the field. Maybe he is still over on Lady's Island. I'll head over to the field and work from there. Maybe I can find something. I'll stay out here to look. You get some sleep."

"Damn it, Kip, I can't sleep. My son is lost in a storm that has yanked trees out by their roots and flipped rooftops. I've had my head next to the phone for three hours. I am not about to sleep! When you called, I about fell off the couch to answer it. I am scared." She paused. "This is not like Chris. Someone must have him." She began to cry.

"I'll call you when I find him if I can find a phone that works. Try to rest. I'll—" The receiver went dead. Even the normal squelch static in the phone line was gone. The phones were out. All lights at the convenience store property went black, as if they had been swallowed by a whale. Within seconds, Kip heard a generator cough on the far side of the property, which brought the lights back up, one by one. He slammed the truck into gear, headed over the bridge to Lady's Island, and down Highway 802 to the Beaufort Academy field.

A gust of wind lifted one of the yard marker signs and blew it into Kip's leg as he waded across the football field. Litter from the stands and equipment from the utility shed cluttered the entire area.   He found a monogrammed canvas bag wrapped around the metal supports under the rusted bleachers, but no signs of Chris. Kip knew he had to drive the roads if he had any chance of seeing the boy in this storm. Most of Lady's Island remained undeveloped despite the coastal real estate boom. Kip knew Chris would be totally lost if he tried to thrash his way through acres of scrub oak and prickly wait-a-minute vines; Chris had to be near a road.

The moan of the wind had numbed Kip's senses until a fireball of white light rocked his truck like artillery. Seconds later, a transformer the size of a fifty-five-gallon barrel crashed in front of him. He panicked, slammed on the brakes, and swerved in the sand. Smoke and steam from the block of wire and metal fogged his view as the transformer smoldered and hissed, inches from his bumper. He used his entire body to open the truck door against the wind. About the time his hip cleared the door, a gust jerked it from his grip, slammed it hard enough to break the side mirror, and hammered him into the drainage ditch. The rain was now a screaming demon that bruised his face and deafened his ears. With a cloud of steam around the charred transformer, he knew it was too hot to move. He wrestled with a nest of vines for fifteen minutes to clear a path for the truck, and he spent another ten minutes to stop the bleeding from a gash the vines had left in his forearm. With a water-soaked rag around his wound, he rocked his truck through the opening and continued on.

Down every road, the same scene repeated itself. Debris blocked every turn. The downpour swallowed his high beams ten feet out. The roads were all rain-warped and rutted, like a sandy washboard. On a sunny day, the search would have been a piece of cake, but the gale ripped limbs from the trees and lifted lawn furniture that came at him like a game of space invaders.

He worked his way to Surf Road on the marsh side of the island, where the top of a large oak tree blocked his passage. Like bugs in a spider's web, just about everything clung to the brush. Newspapers, trash can lids, a downspout. A pink bike with training wheels, a twisted aluminum lawn chair, and beneath that, a ball of some cloth or someone's laundry. He wrapped a chain with a small anchor around the pile of brush. As he headed back to the truck to pull the heap off of the road, he noticed that what had appeared to be a bundle of laundry was actually a small set of football shoulder pads with the soaked, ripped Buccaneers jersey with the number 27 on it. Chris's pads.

His stomach filled with butterflies. He yelled, "Chris!" The whoosh of wind through the trees swallowed his cries. "Chris!" No response. He turned the opposite direction; rain blasted his face. "Chris, can you hear me? It's Dad." The wind howled, and made it impossible to hear any reply, only the angered torment of the storm. He pulled the pads from the mesh of tree and moss and tossed them onto the floor in the cab. He checked the chain once more, then revved the truck and yanked the treetop out of the way. Sparked by new hope and anxious desperation, he released the chain, tossed it into the bed of the truck, and moved cautiously down the road, which ran two hundred yards. In daylight, he could easily see the other end; at night, with high beams, he could see half as far. In the storm, he could not see anything. He was wide awake now, pumped by adrenaline. He glanced from side to side on the road, then eyed the pads and torn jersey on the floor next to him. He has to be here. At the end of the road, he climbed out of the cab and back into the jaws of the storm. He staggered around to find another sign that Chris was near.

Kip began to hallucinate. He thought he saw Chris, but he didn't. He worried he would not make it to sunrise or he would not find a station with power to pump gas. He backtracked down Surf Road, and then his intuition told him to continue back toward where he had started.

Although the gusts continued to wreak havoc, they were now less frequent, and the rain had tapered to a mere drizzle. Kip pulled back onto Little Capers Road, turned right, and headed north. At the fork in the road, he headed east down Holly Hall Road; then, for whatever reason, after all he had been through, the Reader's cards started to reappear in his head again. Two cards: the Hanged Man and the Skeleton of Death. He saw the Reader's face, her hands, and her stooped movement from the washstand with the box. He shook himself from his stupor, and with a sudden change of plan, he pushed hard on the gas pedal. His tired truck coughed; then gravel, branches, and rocks hit the undercarriage; it sounded as if something was ripping the metal off the frame.

His haste to get to Morgan River Drive nearly cost him his truck. When he rounded the turn on the washed-out sandy road, his truck bottomed out, which left his rear wheels suspended in a swollen drainage culvert, the belly of the truck pressed firmly into the wet sand. He fumbled for his flashlight and grabbed a D-handled shovel from the saddle tool box in the bed of the truck. On his belly, he scraped the sand from under the truck.

He had rarely used the four-wheel drive; he wasn't even sure it worked. But he climbed back into the driver's seat, and when he engaged all four wheels, only the rear wheels sprayed sand out of the culvert.

Kip turned off the truck to save gas. He jumped out and frantically shoveled wet sand into the bed of the truck. After ten minutes, he turned the key; the truck coughed, but it would not start. "Shit," he said, as he slammed the steering wheel with his fist. He knew he was low on gas. He wrenched the key harder and cranked the truck—with the same result. He leaned his forehead on the worn steering wheel cover and exhaled a deep sigh. He then sprang from the cab and jumped into the bed of the truck. There, on the bottom of his storage box, was the orange gasoline can. He remembered he had picked up gasoline two weeks earlier for some tree trimming. Not much, maybe a gallon, but enough, he thought. He poured what he could into the tank, using his smashed funnel. The truck cranked and heaved, but it would not start. He tried again. The truck cranked and coughed, but it would not turn over. Again and again. The sound of the starter motor slowed with each crank, until, finally, it turned over. The engine whirred and knocked as he pumped the pedal. Kip jerked the gearshift into drive. The truck lurched forward, but it would not come out of the rut. He slammed it into reverse, and then back into drive. The truck climbed out of the ditch and shimmied down the sandy connector trail to Morgan River Road.

Kip continued to scan each of the yards—left, then right. Then he saw it, the Buccaneer logo on a ripped canvas bag snagged by the long needles of a young loblolly pine. He was two miles from the field where the team had played. In the storm, it was possible the wind had carried it there, but the site was north of the field. The wind was gale force, out of the northeast. He mashed the brake. The truck slid to a stop. He was yelling before he opened the door. "Chris! Chris!" No response. He ran to grab the bag from the tree. Inside it, he found the ziplock plastic bag with orange slices and a blue mouth guard. "Chris, can you hear me?" he screamed, eager for a response. A moment later, he heard the faint words he had longed to hear all night.

"I'm in here," Chris said, his voice coming from inside a small wooden shed under nearby brush.

Kip vaulted over a toppled palmetto tree and shoved himself through the splintered door that blocked access to the shed. He entered about the time Chris sat up, still covered by the blue plastic tarp he had used for warmth. Their simultaneous surprise and relief froze them, instantly, briefly. They embraced. Chris was safe and in Kip's arms.

In the truck, there were no questions of where Chris had been. Kip gripped the steering wheel to keep his exhausted body upright as he drove. Chris dozed in and out, with his knees pulled to his chest and his body scrunched against the door.

"Are you hungry?"

"Where's Mom?"

"Are you cold?"

"Where's Mom?"

They coasted on fumes past several gas stations before they found one open on Highway 21. Kip bought some chips, soft drinks, and a bag of Oreo cookies, their Sunday breakfast.

When the truck pulled into the drive, Sandi raced to look out the side door. As soon as she saw Chris in the passenger seat, she bolted through the door, arms outstretched to greet him. Chris waived all the normal twelve-year-old-boy reservations and held his mother in a bear hug; he fought back tears, Sandi allowed them to flow. Still without electricity, yet thankful the house was equipped with a gas water heater and stove, Sandi tucked a flashlight in his hand and sent him off for a warm shower while, under candlelight, she fixed his favorites: grits and fried eggs, sunny-side up, with lots of burnt-to-a-crisp bacon. Still dehydrated and drained, while seated at the table, she did not pursue the questions of why or where; she just talked with her son, and in the back of her head, she thanked God for delivering Chris home safely.

Though seated at the table with Sandi and Chris, Kip did not join in the conversation—and he never noticed them head upstairs.

Kip, too, was glad Chris was safe, but he thought more about Sparta. He wrestled with the motive, and he always ended with a blood-stained puddle and the five black spots on the deck. Were they threats from an angered trio at Taggett & Vystroon? Or were they a hex only the Reader seemed to understand? The events of the day left him too tired to think, too tired to climb the stairs. He put his head on the table and passed out.

CHAPTER 18

In the far corner of the church parking lot, a latecomer, a scrawny black man, stuffed his oversized car into a corner slot by the woody ligustrum plants that scuffed the passenger side of the yellow, rust covered Buick LeSabre. The hinge of the heavy car door creaked as he slammed the door closed. He hustled through the parking lot. The drone from within the church echoed louder as the latecomer gripped the handrail, climbed the three outer steps, and looked into the open-beamed, white-and-gold-gilded church. The latecomer remained in the narthex and listened to the buzz. The words the congregation slurred together were the Lord's Prayer, and nobody heard a word that was said.

"Our Father, who art in Heaven, hallowed be Thy name."

The storm that juked, jabbed, and knocked Beaufort to its knees the night before left scars in yards, marshes, highways, and byways. Even though the debris covered roads, downed power lines, and swamped intersections, the congregation of Saint Peter's Catholic Church came together for worship and thanksgiving, as they did every Sunday at eight o'clock. Their special intentions for the week included communal thanks to the Lord God, who had spared them from storm-related loss of life. Like so many others, Father Anthony Messimi had spent most of the night in the dark. Unlike the others, the five-foot-six inch padre from the South Side of Chicago had knelt in the sanctuary of the church, praying the rosary for the safety of his congregation, with petitions to Saint Medard and Saint Clare, the patron saints for bad weather and good weather, respectively.

"Thy kingdom come. Thy will be done on earth as it is in heaven."

In the shadow of the priest, stood the blurry-eyed deacon, Jody Snow. Sleepless for over twenty-four hours and exhausted from his efforts behind a chainsaw through the thick of the storm, the daily bartender turned Sunday deacon showed the scourge of the night: deep black circles under his eyes, stubble on his face, and matted sandy-brown hair on his head. He stood a foot taller than his pastor. Dressed in green vestments common to the ordinary time of the liturgical year, Jody looked like a tired, shaggy tree behind the altar.

With the usual variety of attendees, the Father Tony did not waver from what some Catholics consider the Eleventh Commandment—the obligatory "one-hour-service" rule: get them in and let them out in under an hour. Older spouseless singles, beads in hand, prayed the rosary with fervor and paid almost no attention to the priest. A preteen played peekaboo with the baby shouldered by a young mother one pew up. Young families with preschoolers, who sat on the kneelers, each with a mouth full of cereal and running die-cast toy cars or dolls through an imaginary world, were oblivious to the solemnity of the miracle of the bread and wine at the altar. Teenagers separated into groups inside the building to rid themselves of the stigma of Mom and Dad, many of whom were seated, uninvolved, on folding chairs in the social hall, where they were half in and half out of church, but still punched their ticket for sinless weekly attendance.

"Give us this day our daily bread . . . "

While the parents inside the church joined hands for a congregational human chain to recite the mantra of prayer, heads of churchgoing children popped up like groundhogs from behind the pews. Hands draped over the back rests, with noses and eyeballs just above them, the church looked like the backdrop for a Kilroy poster.

With arms outstretched like a crucified Christ, Father Messimi rotated his torso to make eye contact with his flock.

" . . . and forgive us our trespasses as we forgive those who trespass against us."

Ushers prayed along with the congregation as they moved to open the front doors to the church. Clouds of the previous night continued to blot the sun, while the cool morning breeze off the marsh gave the morning the welcome freshness and calm after a big storm.

"May the peace of the Lord be with you always," Father Messimi said, as he opened his arms wide, then closed them with his hands folded in prayer.

In harmony, the participants replied, "And also with you."

"Let us offer each other a sign of peace."

Immediately, the church bubbled with many tongues. Families turned to hug and kiss each other. A few souls ventured a step or two down the pew to shake hands or exchange cordial greetings of "peace" with the neighbors behind and in front of them. For them, it was an ecumenical way of saying "Hey" or "Hi" or "Have a nice day," with not much "peace" intended, seldom even a smile. The round robin of "peace" provided a noisy distraction for the latecomer to slip into the nave. He eyed the crowd and looked around the church for a certain someone that he never found. As the crowd slowly settled back into their state of semiconsciousness, he began his stroll up the center aisle.

Dressed in a shiny light neon blue satin suit with a brilliant white shirt made of Sea Island cotton, stained slightly by the pocket, and a tie with flowers of metallic blue and yellow-gold, he was a familiar face, yet still a stranger to just about all who attended St. Peter's. People did not notice the slight bulge under his coat or his white cap-toed, lace-up Oxford shoes as he breezed up the middle aisle with giant strides. His left arm dangled loosely in an exaggerated swing; his other arm remained board-stiff, something clutched in his right hand. When he reached the front pew, he stopped.

After his walkabout to shake hands and pat the elderly ladies, Father Messimi returned with his back to the congregation. Jody Snow was the first to notice the latecomer, who now stood at the front of the altar. Jody motioned to the priest. The priest turned around and saw the scrawny black man as he climbed the steps toward the altar. The murmur in the church hushed to a whisper when the visitor began to speak.

"Peace," he said, with a gesture to the celebrant bedecked in church vestments. Then he turned to face the congregation. He cranked up the volume of his greeting, "Peace." The second greeting caught their attention; the parishioners looked toward the altar and the visitor. Unexpected, to say the least. Unannounced, for sure. Not a clergyman.

He turned his head over his right shoulder and said with a nod, in a soft tone, "Peace to you, Reverend."

And peace to all of you," he added, as he spun back toward the pews.

From the congregation, a handful of inattentive people responded with "Peace," the usual reaction to hearing those words from the altar. Obviously, they had not bothered to look, or they could not see that the words were not those of their pastor.

Father Messimi dipped his brow in amazement. He showed no visible signs of concern, but he reflected the astonished looks of all the people in the pews. The pew dwellers assumed the latecomer was some sort of guest lecturer, but they wondered why, at this point in the

Mass, he would rock the traditional order of the Vatican-approved liturgical service.

"I have come to you today as a disciple, a prophet, a messenger." His voice, though not projected through a microphone, carried the length of the church. His diction and pronunciation were crystal clear. "Our Lord and Savior, Jesus Christ," he said, with a heavy downbeat on both names, "has sent me to you. He has spoken to me. He has commanded me to share his message with all of you who come together to worship him in this house."

The startled crowd began to settle a bit. Something was not right. They were quick to determine this was not a part of the planned liturgy. The ushers huddled in the vestibule to dream up what they should do.

"My brothers and sisters," he started; then he allowed his voice to trail off a bit.

"And you are my brothers and my sisters," he added, as he began to pace along the top step. "The great and glorious God we call Abba, our Father, to whom you have just prayed . . ." His inflection and meter were staccato and poignant. "He does not believe you." He paused. "In fact, God knows you do not even believe yourselves. He hears no sincerity in your words. He sees no sincerity in your ways. He feels no sincerity in your deeds. And among you are sinners, one grave sinner, and the Lord says the sinner must repent."

The congregation remained on their feet. Nobody sat; for once, everybody listened. Nobody talked, not even the children—all in sharp contrast to moments earlier, when they were entranced, speaking in tongues, words flowing with no meaning, no heart, no listening. Their ears now recorded every syllable; their eyes noticed every movement. Even the teenagers on the folding chairs in the social hall looked through the glass wall, amazed, but none talked or made any attempt to leave.

Ida Mae Smorado, the hunchbacked, white-haired widow who was too short to see much with everyone standing around her, leaned into her tall grandson and asked, "Who is that up there talking. It's not the priest is it?"

Her grandson turned toward her, bent down, and whispered in her eighty-nine-year-old ear, "It's Obadiah Whyteson, Nana."

Ida Mae wrinkled her nose and crinkled her brow, and replied, "Who?"

Her hearing, like most people her age, was not what it used to be. For a second time, now louder, and loud enough for others around to hear, he said, "Obadiah Whyteson is up there talking."

She rolled her eyes. "What in the Sam Hill is he doin' up there?"

Arms outstretched, Obadiah formed a human cross, his Bible visible in his left hand. "Look around you. Don't be shy. Go on."

He thumped his Bible with the palm of his empty hand and raised his voice. "Look around you. Find all my people here."

And like sheep for their shepherd, heads turned, necks craned, bodies swayed, but the silence reigned.

"That's right. There be none here."

He was the only black person in the church. His emphasis on the color of the congregation, or rather the lack of color, fueled his rage.

"Race is the sin that stains our country."

He continued to pace like a man locked in a cell for years. Sweat now poured from his brow. He looked into the crowd to identify one particular member. He fidgeted with his belt buckle, cleared his throat, and continued. "My people are praying out on Coosaw Island and St. Helena Island and in town at the AME. They are in there praying for 'peace' — real peace — for you, their brothers and sisters. Real peace between blacks and whites. Real peace between the poor and the rich. They are praying because they know; ah, they know, like the Lord J-EEEEE-SUS told us; they know; the only way it will happen is through prayer."

Obadiah railed against the whiteness of the crowd in a blustery sermon. From the narthex, the ushers planned to move along the outer aisles, masked from the speaker's view. Deacon Snow stepped forward and whispered into Father Messimi's ear as the ushers approached. Obadiah, again with arms opened wide, turned his head toward the movement on his left, then on his right. Nervous for the first time, he dropped his arms, opened his Bible, and fumbled for a marker he had placed inside. He wiped his brow with a white handkerchief, then stuffed it back in his chest pocket.

"Your readings today, they spoke about the vineyard workers," he read, firing the verses at the congregation in a staccato monotone: "'Take your earnings and go. I choose to pay the last-comer as much as I pay you.' 'Why be envious because I am generous?' 'Thus the last will be first and the first, last.'"

He closed the Bible and raised the good book above his head. "This is the word of the Lord," he said emphatically.

"For most of you who were asleep during the readings today, this is what the Lord has commanded," he said, striking an evangelical tone. He opened his Bible again.

"From first John, chapter three, verses sixteen through eighteen." He continued reading with fiery zeal. "'Hereby perceive we love of God, because he laid down his life for us: and we ought to lay down our lives for the brethren. But whoso hath this world's good, and seeth his brother have need, and shutteth up his bowels of compassion from him, how dwelleth the love of God in him? My little children, let us not love in word, neither in tongue; but in deed and in truth.'"

The ushers saw Obadiah had his eyes on the book, no longer watching them; he was preoccupied in prayer. Four ushers, two on each side aisle, and a fifth usher still in the back of the church, simultaneously looked at Father Messimi, who said nothing, but raised his hand in a motion that passively said, "Stop. Let him continue."

The ushers backed off. They remained in place with their arms crossed. Scowls painted their faces as they watched and waited, eyes and ears on Obadiah.

Speechless still, people began to fidget on their feet. Outside, the natural breeze became still while the fire and brimstone served up inside the church grew more agitated. People, mainly the older women, used the weekly bulletin to fan themselves. Others waved their hand in front of their face. Most just bobbed left and right to catch a better look at the speaker.

"I . . . I . . . I," he stuttered in frustration. "I witnessed what you said. You . . . you said, 'We believe,' you said. 'We believe in one God, the Father Almighty.' The Almighty."

He walked to the other side of the altar. "He is the Lord God Almighty," he repeated. "'The Creator of Heaven, and . . . and Earth.' And you said you believe that? All of you. Each and every one of you stood there and said, 'We believe.' But do you? Do any of you even know what you said? Did any of you listen to what you said?" He paused, and challenged the stares of the people in the front pew.

For the congregation, it was like watching a tennis match. Eyes followed him back and forth across the steps of the altar. This way, then that. He would not stand still. As he walked, he thumbed the worn pages of a tattered Bible. He paused only long enough to take a deep breath; then, he recited, with only a glimpse at the page. "First John, chapter two, verses fifteen through seventeen: 'Love not the world, neither the things that are in the world. If any man love the world, the love of the Father is not in him. For all that is in the world, the lust of the flesh, and the lust of the eyes, and the pride of life, is not of the Father, but is of the world. And the world passeth away, and the lust thereof: but he that doeth the will of

God abideth for ever.' And forget not what James said in chapter four, verse seventeen." He froze. He stopped walking.

His last words took away his pleasant demeanor. He frowned deep, and his face, the gaunt reflection of a hard life, sunk deeper. Wide eyes turned to slits. With his hands at his side, an ageless scorn erupted. "'Therefore to him that knoweth to do good, and doeth it not, to him it is sin.'"

Once again he became animated. Sometimes, he waved his arms as if he were tossing confetti into the air. Other times, he pounded his finger into his chest.

"God is not small, and he commands us to follow his light—in his life, not in his shadow. The Lord Jesus says, 'Listen TO me.' He says, 'LIS-TEN to me. Listen to ME.'"

Three times he spoke, and each time with emphasis on a different word.

"ONE among you has sinned against my sisters and brothers."

Feet planted, he flexed his knees and bobbed in place.

"ONE among you plans to end the lives of thirty-seven of my sisters and brothers," he bellowed. He . . . is . . . wrong. He . . . is . . . a . . . killer!"

His hand pointed like a pistol to targeted listeners, from left to right. "A killer in your midst."

Again, he looked beyond the front pews and around the congregation to find the one person.

Though his voice had been high-pitched, he allowed it to slip deeper, turn guttural. His accusation turned into a prediction. "He is wrong, and he must . . . suffer! And suffer he will!"

He had their attention. With his Bible closed in one hand, he raised both arms and pointed to the heavens beyond the ceiling. He looked skyward, then lowered the book to his chest.   The other hand dropped and pointed, and his shouts now diminished to the low, possessed tones of a forceful whisper, he began to prosecute his witnesses as if they were the accused. "One . . . among you has stolen and cheated my Gullah people out of several livelihoods."

Then, with a louder inflection, he spoke, "One among you is the evil one."

He shifted his attention from one unsuspecting soul to another in search of the accused, looking through the crowd for one particular face—the face of Kip Drummond. "Behind a false smile and meaningless handshake, one among you is living a lie that will soon be revealed."

From the loudmouthed car dealer Thad Dawkins, gold chains around his neck and a Rolex watch on his fat wrist, all the way around to Miss Josie Hibbard, who had fired more cleaning ladies for "stealing" things that had never been stolen, every white-skinned churchgoer commenced their introspective soul searching. *What did Obadiah know about me? What does he mean by "suffer"?*

Then, as if possessed, Obadiah began to shake. Violent tics twisted and turned him. He wrapped his arms around his chest and shivered with cold chills, though sweat streamed down his face. He held himself, eyes closed, his head shaking out of control. He covered his ears to cradle his head to stop the rapid movement from side to side: left, then right. He let out a yell like a wounded animal and stumbled to his knees.

From back of the altar, Father Messimi began to move forward.

Obadiah staggered down the steps to the floor. All eyes were on the man they knew as Obadiah Whyteson, the man they also knew as Rootie Kazootie, the free-spirited, but daft, scrawny black man who directed traffic on nearly empty streets. On any given day, he could not carry on an intelligent conversation, but on this day, in ten minutes, he had shamed the entire church into guilt. His unintelligible Gullah dialect been transformed into to the perfect English of a Vermont country schoolmarm, albeit with an expected Southern drawl. The churchgoers and Jody Snow and Father Messimi all watched, prepared for more wailing.

Rising from the floor like a seedling to the sunlight, Obadiah leaned, his knees unsure. He reached for the bulge inside his suit coat, put his right hand on his heart, and stood there, dazed, his eyes rolled back. When he pulled out his hand, it was no longer empty. Firm in his palm was revealed a shiny tip which he turned to aim back at the altar and Father Messimi. As he turned, the people in the front pews saw the round chrome finish that protruded from his hand. Two ladies closest to him screamed. Jed Pope, the head usher shouted, "He's got a gun." The ushers froze. Deacon Snow dropped to his knees. People throughout the church who had stretched and strained to see dropped to the floor behind the cover of the pews.

Obadiah turned to face the altar, his balance unsteady. Then he lifted his hand higher and higher to reveal a tubular crucifix.

"Abba, Abba, I put my life in your hands," he shouted. Father Messimi responded with lightning quickness. His voice quivered. "Go now in peace, my son."

Obadiah turned toward the people. One by one they popped up from where they had hidden, quick to see who was the first to leave the safety of the pews. Obadiah's gaze was hypnotic, drawn toward the enormous open doors and the late morning sun outside. Chin up, his Bible in his left hand clutched over his heart, he raised his right hand with the crucifix. He walked tall down the center aisle with a confident strut. People watched and stared, but nobody moved. Even the children now stood on pews to jockey around belt buckles to peek at the man in the aisle. The ushers held their ground, and like the others, they stared dumbfounded by what they had just witnessed.

Obadiah left the church, untouched, unhindered, and walked slowly to his car. Nobody followed him, and with his Bible now in his other hand, nobody noticed the other bulge under his jacket, one that looked like something tucked in his belt. It would wait for another place, another time. He placed his Bible on the seat, then drove off.

CHAPTER 19

One Liberty Place, Philadelphia, Pennsylvania

Has that son of a bitch ever been on time?" Alex Stringham shouted. "I mean EVER? Page him!" He yanked down the knot on his tie and unbuttoned his collar.

"Assurdo! Faccialo voi stessi si grande, jackass." Manny Ventresca flicked his middle finger from under his chin and turned away from his American contemporary.

"Hey Pizano, in Rome, do as the Romans do. In America, speak fucking English, ya rube," the athletic Stringham replied, his manhood challenged by the walrus-sized figure at the opposite end of the table.

"Look, I already tried, buco," Ventresca said, facing Stringham again. "He's not answering the fucking page, all right?" Ventresca, the Italian member of the consortium, leaned back in the black leather chair. He began to file his nails with an emery board.

"Is he in town?" Stringham asked.

"He was scheduled on the "red eye" from LAX," Ventresca replied.

"Weather some sort of problem on the left coast?"

"I don't think so."

"What about our village idiot friend?" Stringham asked, referring to Kip Drummond. "Is he in town?"

"I asked Barb to check when I came in. She had confirmation from the Crowne Plaza that Drummond and his redneck Sancho Panza attorney buddy, 'Mistah' Tripp Stansel, both arrived last evening, late." Ventresca, slouched with his legs crossed and suit jacket unbuttoned, did not bother to look up; he continued to file his nails. "She left the envelope with the read-ahead documents and agenda for today's meeting with the front desk at the hotel. They should be quite aware of the start time for today. They should be here."   And they were.

When the elevator doors slid open, they revealed to Kip and his attorney a smoked, opaque glass foyer. Etched in the glass was an elaborate crest of bodies, branches, and a mound of coins. The figures and the foliage, carved by a masterful artist, appeared lifelike in the thick wall of glass tinted soft as a gray cloud. The crest showed three-dimensional representations of the Michelangelo Buonarroti frescos in the Sistine Chapel. There were buxom women, full-bodied and muscled. Colossal masculine characters stood beneath a large tree. Six in all and each of them nude, they groped and pawed tastefully—not at the women, whose skin pushed hard against theirs, but at a pile of gold coins between the six.

The unique feature of the entrance art was the brilliance and the lure of the gold. The coins were real: twenty-eight Saint-Gaudens Double Eagles coins, twenty-dollar pieces lumped together by metallurgical magic and all dated 1928, the year the firm was founded. The coins, with a total face value of under forty thousand dollars, had a collectors value of over a million. Through the Great Depression, recessions, wars, and post-war growth, Taggett & Vystroon had built themselves into an international conglomerate and flaunted the fact garishly.

Beyond the screen of glass and gold were myriad opulent offices. Walnut-paneled walls were adorned with original small and large works of the Great Masters—Rembrandt, Turner, Van Gogh, Lautrec— presented in ornate, gilded frames with museum lighting: simple statements of beauty and creative genius. Antique tables with the usual bric-a-brac of the trade artfully mingled with traditional items and classic works of art. On one table was a pure-silver recasting of Remington's The Outlaw, and beneath it, displayed in a small, unassuming cube of hardened silicon, was a microcopy of a prospectus which offered fifty million shares of PFG, Inc., at a price of thirty-five dollars per share. It was one offer—one deal equal to one and three-quarters of a billion dollars. Other tables were similarly unique.

Four separate seating circles spaced far apart throughout the room allowed conversation outside the normal hearing range. The receptionists, positioned in the middle of the open area, greeted guests from behind their circular island of walnut-and-gold filigree, which bore the same company logo that had been carved into the thick walnut base of the welcome area, again with a pile of gold coins.

Cute, curt attendants with headphones managed a bank of phone lines and transferred business calls to available partners throughout the firm.   Totally segregated, the group was all female, all smiles, all foxy, and each clothed in a wardrobe inspired by the boutiques and haute couture of Rodeo Drive.

"Gentlemen, welcome to Taggett and Vystroon," said Barbara Campbell, the bright, elegant, all-business practice manager for the Corporate Office. "Please follow me."

Fronds of the potted palms bobbed as the tall, natural blond with piercing, azure-blue eyes and luminescent skin hurried down the long connector hall toward the meeting room. "Quite a view wouldn't you say?" she said, and she dipped her head to point out the Philadelphia skyline as they walked along the glass perimeter of the suite. The streets below were littered with dots and dashes of people, cars, and buses mixed in lines of crisscrossed Morse code.

Once the three of them had made their way through a set of gargantuan doors marked only with brass pulls, the lavish décor of the grand foyer transformed into a high-tech sweat shop. Cubicles in quadrangular arrays of sea-foam green and tumbleweed-brown reinforced the corporation's support from the dapper legions of employees quarantined under dim lights and hypnotized by the constant flicker of monitors. Men in suits of grays and browns, blues and blacks. White shirts. Ties of only a few colors and shapes — no cartoon characters or sports images, but only classic reds and blues with boxes or stripes. Ladies in pantsuits and skirts, stylish and long; all with jackets. Jewelry was modest in style, but plentiful for all. Gold and silver necklaces. Rings and bracelets. Stones of deep, deep green and blue.

At the end of the corridor, Kip and his lawyer met their hosts.

Without greeting, Kip entered the Board Room, dropped his briefcase at a spot midway down the table, unbuttoned his blazer, and tossed it on one of the chairs along the wall.

"Let me get this meeting started, gents," he said as he walked to the sideboard to pour a cup of coffee, without any suggestion of the customary handshake. His sweaty palms belied his cockiness.

"Oh, pardon my manners, Mr. Drummond and Mr. Stansel. Would you like some coffee?" Manny Ventresca asked, showing his disdain for the good ole boys from South Carolina.

Kip looked back over his shoulder to acknowledge his sarcasm. "You guys dragged me . . . " — correcting himself as he nodded toward his attorney, Tripp Stansel — "us up here. We've been through these numbers before. What has changed? This trip better be worth my while."

According to the prearranged script he had made with Kip the night before, Tripp reached into his buckled brown leather briefcase and pulled out the read-ahead packets and then another set of folders, each marked with the Indian head logo of the Lady's Island Oyster Factory. Tripp leaned over the table, his shirt untucked in the back. He slid the folders to the three savvy businessmen—past a crystal carafe of water and a stainless steel ice bucket, which formed a line of demarcation down the middle of the long table. While Tripp distributed the discussion materials, Kip reached into his satchel for a folder and his packet blanketed with notes, talking points, and highlights; then he stood and locked his knees.

The threesome from Taggett & Vystroon rummaged through their packets, eagerly seeking one specific document bearing Kip Drummond's signature.

"If you look at the contents of the files Mr. Stansel passed out, you can plainly see how sound our business is," Kip said. "The debt, though it might seem significant to some, doesn't hamper our daily operations. I trust you can read those articles from the various newspapers in the file. The Savannah Morning News rated my business as 'The Best Place to Work in the Low Country.' The Savannah Tribune, as well as the Charleston Post and Courier, rated the business as 'The Best Entrepreneurial Turnaround.' The Charleston Daily featured the business, and me as the owner, as 'The Best Overall Opportunity.' "

The team from Taggett & Vystroon continued to thumb through the files like skunk bears over a dead mule. They cocked their ears, with only an occasional peek at Kip, who hid his nervousness as he turned his back on the table and walked to the sideboard to top off his cup of coffee. Kip used the silence to ready his next point.

Stringham looked up from the table and pushed his glasses back up the bridge of his nose. "Mr. Drummond, we can see—"

"Ask anyone," Kip interrupted. "My business is a true success story in the eyes of the community. We receive more positive press than any single business in the coastal region, including Hilton Head. Our appeal is widespread and far-reaching."

Ventresca and Khouri were locked heads down in a side conversation, not the least bit entertained by Kip's awkward and unorthodox representation of the business. Their eyes flicked from side to side—across forms, reports, articles, and financial records. As an item of interest in the newspaper articles caught their eye, they would mark it quickly, then doodle a bit with notes in margins. They realized the agenda was hopelessly lost on this guy, at least for the moment, knowing there were other details to discuss. They waited for Stringham to reel this fish in and get down to the real business matters for the day.

"In addition to these ratings for my business, if you refer to the yellow tab marked with a capital G, you will find the records for the past four years. You can see where the assessment of the business, based on performance, shows we have been solid as a rock, tracking nicely against a plan, year after year, to develop the business." Kip finished his coffee, placed the cup and saucer back on the sideboard, then proceeded to detail the financial reports from the previous years. He used a rehearsed spiel his accountant had put together to ram down Stringham's, Ventresca's, and Khouri's Ivy League throats.

The longer Kip rambled, the thicker grew his mask of perspiration—from fatigue, the aftereffects of fitful sleep; from the heat of the closed chamber; and from adrenaline, pure and simple. To break the cadence of his delivery, he would turn away from the listeners, take a sip of ice water, then slide his chilled wet hand across his brow and dab it dry with the monogrammed linen napkins.

"Mr. Drummond, we want to thank you and Mr. Stansel for accepting our invitation to visit with us at Taggett and Vystroon," Stringham said, acknowledging the Beaufort contingent with simple nods to each of them.

Tripp Stansel returned the nod as Stringam continued, "We are grateful that you agreed to take time away from your business to meet with us here. We trust your trip will be a significant one and not time wasted."

Kip leaned back against the wall and twirled his pen with his fingers like a miniature baton.

"As you well know, your business remains an interest of ours," Stringham said. "We believe we can create an opportunity for both of us to do rather nicely." He took a few gulps of water, then brought the discussion in line with the agenda. Khouri motioned to Ventresca.

"Allow me to cut right to the quick of the matter, Mr. Drummond," Ventresca said. "We realize you are a very busy fellow, and despite your presentation here this morning, we realize you do not have resources within your business to capture your true value. I am not quite sure who prepared those sheets you handed us."

"I worked them through with my accountant," Kip said.

Stringham eyed him with a smirk and a look of pity. "Over the months, our staff has done an incredible amount of work analyzing your business. They found it most interesting, at times fascinating, what you have done with that business right from the very beginning. We wanted to share some analysis."

He walked to the credenza where he picked up a laser pointer and a remote control.   As the lights dimmed, a hidden projector appeared; its lamp cast a fuzzy image on a screen that materialized from an inconspicuous slot in the ceiling at the far end of the room. As the lamp warmed, the image of the financial charts on the screen sharpened.

"What we have here is a summary of your Lady's Island Oyster Factory business," Stringham said. "It reflects your operation during the period of your ownership."

Kip sat motionless in his chair to contain a fury that continued to grow with every sentence. What appeared on the screen was extremely detailed — far more so than what his accountant had prepared: graphs and charts; projections matched by actual figures — details that even Kip did not have. He failed to understand.

Tripp Stansel leaned to his left and whispered something in his client's ear. Kip's eyes remained glued to the screen; he shook his head in a negative response. A moment later, he slapped his folder down on the table in front of him.

"Your crackerjack staff missed the mark on this one, guys," he said with a snort, his tone hateful. He aimed a two-second stare at each of the presuming faces across from him. "Are you guys deaf or just not paying attention to what I just went through? I just showed you proof that what we have going with the business has the eyes and ears and approval of just about everybody watching down in our neck of the woods."

With the outburst out of the way, Alex Stringham hammered the first nail in the coffin. "All in all, Mr. Drummond, that business of yours does not appear to be running quite as well as you let on these days."

Kip scowled and leaned forward in his seat, interested to hear the rationale. Stringham returned to his seat and sat with his legs crossed.

"Again, we appreciate your presentation and the articles you shared, but they are a bit dated. They represented your first year in the business."

Kip clenched his fists. He knew the Taggett & Vystroon analysis was stronger than anything possible back home, but he remained reluctant to acknowledge their facts. He knew Grant Lesieur, his accountant, was a small-town, home-grown personal finance accountant who made a killing preparing taxes for the older, wealthy residents of Beaufort. His knowledge of business accounting was limited to a successful, but small, bookstore and a family-run chocolatier. The more Kip had listened to the threesome and had digested what appeared on the screen, the more his stomach had churned.

"Since that time, Mr. Drummond, it seems there is a completely different story we need to discuss. Our analysts project your cash flow picture, near term, looks more like this." Stringham changed the slide and scrolled the laser pointer to a column on the screen. "These loans are based on your business, your available lines of credit, and your personal holdings. The numbers on the left represent the real world as it is today. Note they die out after eighteen months. The panel on the right has a slightly different look."

Kip tapped his pencil on the table. With loans, the numbers gave him an extra year before all the black numbers turned blood red. The screen looked like a numerical murder scene of red ink. He did not breathe. His eyes scanned as fast as he could focus. Before he finished his scan, Stringham presented a second slide.

"How in the hell did you get this information?" Kip erupted, his chair careening off the back wall. He stood, then bent over with his hands on the table, his eyes pinched by angry wrinkles of anger. "This is my personal information. Where the hell did you get it?"

Kip looked at Tripp Stansel, who shook his head to deny any collusion. The lawyer, who had been calm throughout the proceedings, now fidgeted like a whore in church; then he reached for the small pocket tape recorder he was using to tape the session. He whispered something into it at close range, something the others could not hear.

Kip rushed to the screen. The projection of the slide was now as much on him as it was on the reflective surface of the screen.

"Where did you get that?" He slapped the screen and blasted Stringham, who was still holding the laser pointer. "You have your hands in my bank's pockets?" Kip lanced all three with stares, his face crimson with anger. "No doubt there is somebody down there willing to do my ass in to make a little money off of me, someone who could get their hands on my records."

He walked back toward his chair, blinded by the projector lamp. He squinted, then poured himself a glass of iced water, hoping the ice would cool his temper while his eyes readjusted. His emotions charged through his body like racing freight trains.

"Mr. Drummond, I can assure you, we would never do such a thing," Stringham said. "We are a worldwide operation. Our analysts are able to collect information on most any topic, even business data on a privately held business. Our methods are forthright and honorable. We would not dare compromise our integrity."

Ventresca clicked his ballpoint pen, continuously faster, as he listened to the exchange, his short fuse lit.

"Right!" Kip shouted. "And my personal data? How do you explain that? My personal finances are private. I share that with very few people, trusted people, the details of which remain confidential."

"Well, Mr. Drummond," Ventresca said, his Italian blood boiled to a point where he was unable to sit and listen to this Lowcountry bumpkin go on.

"Some people can be careless with how they dispose of their personal information. Now, mind you, I am not suggesting that you have mishandled your personal matters, Mr. Drummond, but—"

"Then, what are you suggesting?" Kip asked before Ventresca could finish.

"We understand times are very difficult for you lately, Mr. Drummond. That you might be under a great deal of stress. As the charts reflected, the recent price increases to your suppliers and their willingness to sell their goods elsewhere—"

"And the tragic loss of your dog," Khouri interrupted, to break his silence and enter the conversation . "Oh, and the way he was butchered!"

Kip's attention snatched the words like a magnet over a box of tacks. "How do you know about that?" he asked, curious to make a connection. "Better yet, what do you know about my dog?"

"As I mentioned, Mr. Drummond, we have ways to amass information on clients," Stringham said; his words matched a sense of no good in his eyes.

"And did I also hear your son disappeared?" Khouri asked. "What a terrible scare! It was fortunate that you found him when you did. I mean, who knows what might have happened to the boy? Life is full of those unexpected events. They seem to happen more frequently for some than others." Khouri's expression suggested the possibility that another disappearance might not have the same fortunate end.

Tripp Stansel slid forward in his chair. "I certainly hope your comments were not intended to threaten or intimidate my client, Mr. Khouri," Stansel said; his jowls bounced, but his thin lips barely moved as he peered over glasses low on the bridge of his nose.

"No, Mr. Stansel, just observations," Khouri said. "Seems Mr. Drummond's luck has been less than good lately. How can we imagine his fortunes in business would be any better? I mean, Mr. Drummond has never run a business. Has never been trained to run a business. And, academically, well, Mr. Drummond had similar misfortunes." Khouri spoke in a dismissive tone, certain that any debate on these points would be short-lived.

"Mr. Drummond's business is unstable and will be for the next four quarters," Stringham said, with insolence meant to suck the wind out of further argument. "The cash flow could never cover the people expenses. Improvements he needs to make to the physical plant in order to pass safety codes are beyond reach. I am sure I don't need to remind your client that those improvements are due by the end of the year. That's less than ninety days."

Kip tuned out the cockfighting in the room and mentally lapsed into the events of the previous weeks: Sandi's constant bickering, Chris's indifference, Sparta's blood on the boat, the words the Reader shared over the cards. The pieces of the puzzle did not fit together. He grew restless; his legs twitched. Again, his palms began to sweat.

When Tripp Stansel cleared his throat, Kip popped out of his trance. "Where are the numbers? Let me see the numbers. Give me the details behind your slides. I want to see every bit of the background for this stuff. All of it, including my personal stuff. And I want to know where you got it."

Stringham folded his hands on top of the sheets in front of him. With that cue, Ventresca pulled two thick folders from a briefcase under the table. He gave each of the guests a folder.

"Gentlemen, I believe you will find these numbers slightly different from those you presented earlier. There are conditions with these numbers, as you will see when you read through your packets."

"I believe Mr. Drummond and I will need some time for this," Stansel said, while he paged through the packet; it was obvious to all that it would be a lengthy conference. The trio on the opposite side of the table granted the request.

"When you are ready to move forward with the discussions, please ask Ms. Campbell to page us," Stringham said after his two companions left the room; then he closed with an air of confidence, "We will reconvene to finish the arrangements."

For three hours, Kip bounced questions off Tripp Stansel. They reviewed, discussed, and argued the stats from the slides, the numbers in the files, and the terms of the offer on the table. For Kip, this was not a done deal. He had multiple reasons to walk away from it. He wanted to intimidate the trio further, to wrest their overconfident resolve, and to derail whatever scheme they had. He swallowed hard the insults of Mazan Khouri. Degree or no degree, experience or no experience, that business was his, and he was the owner—the ownership his lifelong dream and aspiration. As they talked, a cavalcade of faces with feelings trooped through his head: Gunny and his Gullah people; Sandi and her fatherless son; the hobbled Reader with her cards spread on the table. Tripp Stansel maintained the level head; he was not far removed from the outcome. He knew there would be much talk about Kip's decision. People would link Stansel to the deal.

Two hours into their deliberations, they paged Ms. Campbell. Before she responded, she alerted the principals. Stringham, Ventresca, and Khouri were poised to march back into the conference room until Campbell informed them that she had been paged to refill the carafe of water and to bring more ice.

At 3:17 p.m., Kip Drummond buzzed Ms. Campbell. Within a minute, she slipped unnoticed through the door while the two continued to confer. It was her perfume that announced her presence and pulled Stansel from his concentration. He looked up, then nudged his client.

"We need to see Stringham and his cronies," Kip mumbled, as he looked down toward the spread of papers on the table, constantly tapping his pencil on it.

"My pleasure, Mr. Drummond. I will page Mr. Stringham and his associates and tell them you are ready to continue."

Stringham, Ventresca, and Khouri returned to the room, confident and quiet. "So Mr. Drummond," Stringham said, "I trust you now agree the details we presented earlier provide a clearer look at the projected future for your business. That said, the final offer we have placed on the table is extremely generous." He expected an immediate concurrence and stood behind his chair on the far side of the table.

Stansel responded soberly. "Gentlemen, my client and I agree that the offer is most generous, but at this time, he is not predisposed to accept your offer."

Kip fumbled with papers, not immediately inclined to flaunt his victory.

"You've got to be kidding? He's not accepting the deal?" Khouri said to Stringham. He pushed back from the table. "I knew you were a dumb shit, Drummond. You must be out of your ever-loving mind."

Kip looked up, but refrained from commenting.

"My client believes in his business," Stansel said. "He believes in the people who make the business. He believes that, although generous, your offer does not provide for the value of the business or of the property on which the business rests."

Stansel droned on and on with more legalese while the three stunned dealmakers listened half-heartedly and scribbled notes between themselves. Ventresca reached into his briefcase and pulled out another bundle of documents held together with a large rubber band. He rifled through the papers and pulled one frayed folder from the mix. He handed it to Stringham and, in an aside, pointed out some specifics of the contents.

Kip rolled his tongue across his teeth, his mouth dried by the tension. He sensed a rebuttal or, possibly, a change to the offer — something.

"So you see, for Mr. Drummond to agree —"

With his right hand in a loose fist, Stringham knocked on the table, two hard knocks with his knuckles, then stood straight and tall. "Mr. Stansel, pardon the interruption. We do appreciate your words. Your explanation is duly noted. We understand the reluctance on the part of your client to divest his interest in the business, a business that he has coddled for years."

Stringham inched down the long conference table toward the projection screen at the end of the room. He pushed the remote button, and the screen retracted back into the ceiling.

"We all know we've been through these numbers over and over again. We thought presenting some of our research this morning would have shed greater light on the numbers and highlight the willingness of Taggett & Vystroon to provide a suitable upside to your client's investment and business overall. You know, it pains us greatly to hear that our research efforts failed to convince you and Mr. Drummond."

Stringham turned away from the table, but continued to talk. "We pride ourselves in our research. As you have seen, our analysts are able to assemble facts and details that may escape others. Their efforts maximize the outcome for businesses like yours."

He turned back toward the table and looked directly at Kip, who had followed Stringham's movements like a mongoose tracking a cobra.

"Our team has done exceptional work for you, Mr. Drummond. They prepared the analysis we shared this morning. That was no small effort, you would agree? Certainly not a capability you have at the Lady's Island Oyster Factory or in Beaufort or Hilton Head or even Charleston. Mr. Ventresca just brought a few things to my attention. I feel we should share these with you as well. These were items we overlooked earlier, but they might be germane to our discussion here."

Stringham pulled out a swivel chair at the far end of the table. He did not sit down; he stood behind the chair and began to spin it like a roulette wheel. He gave the chair a gentle push, then stood and watched it spin.

"How did you end up in Beaufort in the first place, Mr. Drummond?" Stringham asked as he selected a sheet from the battered file Ventresca handed him. "Says here you were a commercial real estate broker in Charleston. Spent time in the Army. Went into real estate. Made it big, I guess, on the commercial side of that business? Or did you? Big enough to buy a business for over two million in cash? Why would any good real estate broker pay cash for a business in Beaufort, South Carolina?"

Stringham chuckled as he looked down the table toward his colleagues, then toward Kip.

After three hours of point and counterpoint with Stansel, Kip leaned back in his seat with his arms crossed, bewildered and confused by Stringham's mind game.

Stringham nodded to Ventresca, who with a simple backhanded flick of his wrist, sent a thin folder across the table to Kip. When he opened it, he found two sheets of paper. One was a newspaper clipping from a copy of the Philadelphia Inquirer dated November 27, 1986, Thanksgiving Day. The article headline read: "Largest Super 7 Jackpot," and the article reported that a single ticket sold by a 7-Eleven in South Philly had the winning number for a jackpot of six million dollars, the largest single winner in the history of the lottery in Pennsylvania. The article touted the lottery for its contributions to the Commonwealth's older residents for the previous fifteen years, but it never listed the name of the winner. Although the prize had been claimed, the winner had expressed a desire to remain anonymous.

The second sheet was a tax form bearing the name of Thomas K. Drummond and listing his residence in South Carolina.

It did not take long for Kip to piece the forms together. In themselves, they revealed some history into the beginning of Kip's career as a business owner, all in all very little of that history, but they revealed an undisclosed look at his past. Kip closed the file. He did not speak. Tripp Stansel motioned for the file, but Kip would not release it. His gaze drifted above, beyond, and through his business hosts toward the artwork on the walls, on the sideboard, and in the corners, his focus deeper in his head.

"I believe Mr. Stansel and I should discuss this," Kip said. "If you will excuse us."

"As you prefer," Stringham said. He led Ventresca and Khouri out of the room.

Kip spent the next ninety minutes with Tripp Stansel, then fifteen minutes with Stringham in a private session, then another twenty minutes with his counsel, when he highlighted a few key points.

Despite his tousled appearance, Stansel was a tenacious negotiator, far better than Kip and the main reason he left the seersucker-clad attorney from Beaufort in the room with the dogs from Taggett & Vystroon.

Kip rode the elevator solo to the lobby, walked past the concierge desk, and hailed the lead cab in the short queue.

From a bank of pay phones at Hartsfield International, Kip called Stansel in Philadelphia, who was still at Taggett & Vystroon and still negotiating. Over the phone, the two fired short questions and answers back and forth. When they were finished, Kip agreed to the terms and arranged to meet Stansel back in his law office on Port Royal Street the next morning to finalize the paperwork. With a sigh, Kip hung up the phone and boarded the puddle jumper connector from Atlanta to Savannah. Once on the ground, he grew anxious for the one stop that remained before he could head home.

Chapter 20

The flight out of Atlanta was delayed. Over the intercom, in a voice that sounded like someone with their hands over their mouth, the pilot announced, "Well, folks, from the flight deck, it appears we have a mechanical problem, nothing serious." Most problems are never serious on the ground. It took the mechanic an hour and a half to replace a faulty switch before the plane could make the thirty-seven minute hop, wheels up to wheels down, from Atlanta to Savannah. Kip knew he would be late for his appointment.

Like a blind sprinter, Kip bounced off travelers as he dashed for the door, his nose in his canvas briefcase as he rummaged for the parking receipt. He pulled out pens, paperclips, a boarding pass for the flight to Philadelphia, and a tag with a red-nosed Rudolph on it. It read, "Merry Christmas to our favorite businessman." It was signed, "With love and joy, Sandi and Chris." He recalled the Christmas day when they gave him the briefcase, five years earlier.

He headed north on the interstate, a familiar route he drove hundreds of times before, often too intoxicated to recognize the signs alongside the road, but tonight, it was his speed and the banks of coastal fog that caused him to miss his turn. He cut through the emergency crossover in the median, reversed his direction, and went back to the Hardeeville Exit, where he picked up a backwoods, two-lane road toward Beaufort. He jockeyed the truck around the weekend golf-and-cocktail-partier traffic. Behind the wheel, pressed for time, his angst gnawed at him like a bear on a bone. He was uncomfortable that the bastards had him over a barrel, or so they thought. The documents in their folder meant someone had deceived him, had left him exposed.

His instructions to Tripp Stansel had been very specific. He needed Stansel to handle details. The thought that they could meet the following day to dot the i's and cross the t's and make it all a done deal did not settle well with him. He could not bring himself to think about it—at least not until he finished his appointment at the shack on St. Helena's Island. He was already late for his meeting with the Reader.

His head slammed the cab top as he raced through the hidden turns and bounced down the rutted lane to the house familiar to him now. The headlights sprayed the porch with a blurred, yellow beam. As he switched off his lights and opened his door, the porch light flashed, then exploded with a pop, like a cork gun. With only the dome light, he spotted a push lawn mower in the tall grass, but he failed to notice the tire tracks to the tailfins on the corroded, yellow Buick tucked behind a dilapidated shed, smothered by a plague of kudzu. When he closed the truck door, the pitch of night stole his vision for an instant. As he walked, he stumbled over a rusted bucket. Quickly, a blast of early-autumn night wriggled through his clothes, chilled his nervous sweat, and generated a rash of unmanly goose bumps. He recalled his last visit and the prophetic final words he had heard from the wooden stoops. "You will see your friend on the boat." He remembered Sparta, the racked, grotesque body on the Carpe Diem a week earlier. As he approached, more and more light oozed from between the cracks around the windows. The door opened, and the candlelight from inside lit the sandy path to the doorway, where he spotted the stooped figure of the Reader. She clenched a hand-carved wooden cane and the doorknob. Tie loosened and suit jacket in the truck, he moved toward the woman with his head down. His eyes glanced up only occasionally to see the intimidating watch of the Reader.

He climbed the steps to the porch, while the Reader leaned heavily on the cane in an unsteady shuffle toward the room with the table, where he had sat for his first reading; the candelabra in the shrine at the end of the short hall lit the way. Sconces flickered like stalagmite flares of layered opaque wax and cast an eerie glow on the walls, on the curtains that covered the narrow window, on the washbasin stand, on the four wooden chairs, and on the distressed table in the center of the room. When he entered the room, memories rewound to his last visit; then, something unexpected happened.

The old woman did not take the seat; instead, she hobbled to a place out of sight. He worked his way around the table as another figure entered the room.

"Where did the old lady go?" he asked without hesitation. "I came to see her. I have questions for her. Get her back in here!"

"Mr. Drummond, we have met. I am Bheki Uwtando. I have been with Madam Ayanda for thirteen years. She has shared her spirit with me. Her thoughts are my thoughts. Her feelings are my feelings. Her eyes are my eyes. We share everything but the path through life which she has traveled well ahead of me. During your first visit, she doubted you and your belief in the cards."

She looked away, back toward the curtain where she had entered. "She sent me to warn you, Mr. Drummond. The five of spades. You came to see her to ask about the five of spades." Kip leaned forward.

"Madam Ayanda tried to warn you of the hex. Your friend. Your dog . . . on the river. Now your family."

"What do you mean my 'family'?" Kip asked.

"Madame Ayanda says the cards tell her you are different now. The cards say you have different feelings. You are here because you believe. Madam Ayanda says I should assist you."

Kip placed his elbows on the table and rubbed the stubble on his cheeks with the palms of his hands. "OK, look. The last time I was here, I'll admit I was just curious. People mentioned tarot to me. I had my doubts."

The thick black lips of the psychic pursed tight. The edges of her mouth drooped. Her brow wrinkled. Kip stopped. The young black girl closed her eyes, clasped her hands, and turned her head away from Kip toward the curtain in the corner of the small room. When she turned her head back and opened her eyes, Kip continued.

"That was last time. Since then, a lot has happened in my life, and just about all of it were things Madam Ayanda had mentioned. The cards explained, predicted, or suggested these things would happen. What little I understood from that first meeting, I doubted, and most of what she said, I didn't understand at all."

He leaned forward. "Now I understand. Now I believe." His hands shook with a nervous tremble.

"Don't be scared, Mr. Drummond," Bheki Uwtando said.

"I have another question to ask." He cleared his throat.

Bheki Uwtando pushed back, walked two steps to the washbasin side table, and returned with the small box of tarot cards. "Mr. Drummond, I will spread the cards for you again. Beware the cards you see. They reflect the deepest level of your memories, the voice of your inner self, your awareness. They are the voices you hear whispering to you, the voices you strain to ignore."

She closed her eyes, lowered her voice, and spoke in Gullah, "Oonuh mus b'leebe."

Tense as a wound watch spring, Kip snapped back, "Goddamn it, I told you I believe." No sooner had the words left his mouth than he raised his palm, gesturing his apology for losing it. "Sorry. Sorry." His head and eyes drifted down toward the table and back up, then locked on her. He stared at her dimly lit silhouette; her eyes, glowing like hot coals, burned through his gaze; neither of them conceded a blink. Raindrops plunked slowly on the tin roof. Dunk-a. Dunk-a.

She pursed her lips and exhaled a breathy sigh. As she reached for the wooden box in the middle of the table, Kip pulled his elbows back. With her willowy black fingers wrapped around the box like a net, she slid it toward her. Rain began to roll off the house like a waterfall and formed a moat around cinderblock footings. Lightning zigzagged across the sky in the distance, followed by gusts of humid air that blasted through the screen door; every candle flame bent to follow the wind. Then, the moment presented itself; the Reader's assistant invoked the spirits who had drifted in with the storm.

"With the opening of this deck, may I reach inside your soul, your mind, your heart and tell the tale they long to reveal. Tell me, what is your question?"

For some reason, the words of Bheki Uwtando left Kip awash in a pool of flashbacks. Unexplained, senseless emotion bolted like lightning, brilliantly illuminated in his mind. First, microsecond, Technicolor memories, then blackness. The imaginary world his real father once created for him, his own private world, capped by boyhood visions of the funeral in Arlington National Cemetery when he said his final goodbye. Dancing and making love to Sandi years before, the recent spat and the chasm that had emerged between them. The day he bought the oyster factory. The memory of finding Gunny's wallet, then meeting him for the first time. The first reading. His dog on the boat. Like a whirlpool, the memories sucked him in, down, and away. Focus. He did not know what to say or how to say it; his brain was numb. From the moment he left the conference room in Philly, six hours earlier until just minutes ago, he had rehearsed his question; now it was gone. Although he had asked the question of himself thousands of times, he could not remember it.

Sweat streamed down his face and dripped onto the table. He wiped his forehead with his sleeve, closed his eyes, swallowed, and said in a monotone, "What should I do with my business?"

"Take the deck. Hold the cards in your hands. Think about your question." With the box containing the cards unopened in front of her, she gingerly removed the timeworn deck of cards from the box and unfolded the colorful cloth around them, in the same manner as Madam Ayanda. She buried the top and bottom cards in the middle of the deck.

"Concentrate," she insisted. "Concentrate, then shuffle the cards until you feel you have moved your spirit into them. Allow the cards to draw from you your feelings, your beliefs, your fears, your joys, your past, present, and future. Let out your emotions. Let the cards speak for them."

She pushed the deck across the rough surface of the table, then leaned back in her chair, hands in her lap, head down, chin in her chest, shoulders drooped forward, totally limp. As he touched the cards, he felt a strange awareness of the many hands before his that had shuffled them, softened the edges, worn away the colors. A communal warmth seeped into his hand along with the concentration of all the others before him who had sought answers to their questions in these cards.

He shuffled the cards loose in his hands. He allowed the frayed edges to slide and mix. As he did, slowly, his eyes closed tightly, his face taut, strained. He repeated his question, in a whisper, as his hands juggled memories, deep memories, with each card that slipped from hand to hand. When he stopped shuffling, he trembled. The rains were softer now. Glassy-eyed, he handed the cards back to the assistant.

She divided the deck into three separate piles. From the middle one, she pulled the top card, then the next, and the next. She explained each, one by one.

"The Tower. It represents great, sudden change. A revelation, possibly."

Kip found it strange that it was the same card that had been in the center in his first reading. She pulled the next card and placed it on top of, but perpendicular to, the first card.

"The Ten of Wands: oppression. Something has boxed you in. You are trapped. Pressures, excessive pressures, are at work against you, though the problems could soon be overcome."

Kip struggled to understand the two cards together, but remained hung up on the Tower. He wondered what it meant to have the same card in the same position and that it symbolized "great, sudden change." He stared at the mystical images in surreal colors on the card. The groan of distant thunder framed his thoughts. He began to wonder if the weather itself was an omen. He sensed something strange and different about the room.

As she leaned over the table and placed the next card close to him, below the first two cards, Kip slid his chair back.

"The Seven of Wands represents Valor. You stand up for something you believe in, you are assertive, and you would take a great leap to do something good. You direct your efforts to overcome odds that could overwhelm most."

The rain had slowed to a steady drizzle as she placed the fourth card to the left of the first. Kip looked on, unable, still, to weave together any meaning; the Tower was still his focus.

"The fourth position represents past experiences and fading concerns, which have been taken care of." As she turned the card, Kip recognized the Hanged Man. It, like the Tower, was a card he had seen in the same place in his first reading.

"Wait a minute," Kip said, as his hands slapped down hard on the table. "I'm not feeling any of this."

"The cards tell your story. If your energy calls for those cards, they present themselves," Uwtando said.

"Look. I just want my question answered, OK? This isn't getting any closer here."

"Oonuh b'leebe? Ent de cyaa'd reveal trute ta oonu duh fus' time?"

Kip turned to catch movement from the shadow behind the curtain under the wall sconce. He recognized the gravelly voice, but he did not understand what she said. With two hands on her cane, Madam Ayanda crept her way toward the table.

"Yo h'aa't iz burdened wid a secret. Oonuh hab bil' yo bidness 'pun 'um. 'E is fixed fashi'n a spike in yo recishun."

Kip turned to the Bheki Uwtando, his hands raised with palms up. "I don't understand a word she is saying."

"She said your heart is burdened with a secret. You have built your business on it. It is fixed like a spike in your decision."

Standing next to him, his sense of sight now deferred to his sense of smell. As the stooped black woman approached, he sensed the unforgettable smell of the fields and the factory. The smell of sweat, of dirt, of oysters, of salt water. Not repulsive. It was the Lowcountry; it was the perfume of the Gullah. Her strained voice continued.

"Bus' out dat spike. Free yo h'aa't an dem h'aa'ts ub all dem oonuh hab suppressed all dese yeah. Oonuh are the only one kin do dis', and oonuh know dat."

"She said you need to get rid of the spike, to free your heart of all that you are holding inside. You are the only one who can do this, and you know it."

Kip looked away, then back at his translator. His body shook, visibly. He looked down at the cards on the table. He ran his hands through his hair, then motioned for her to continue.

Madam Ayanda placed one hand on the back of the young girl's chair and watched as she placed the last six cards in rapid succession. Her words cut to the quick. Failure. Cruelty. Strength. Ruin. Judgment. She ended with the Ace of Coins, another card Kip saw in his first reading. He did not challenge that card or any of the final cards; he just listened, his senses too fixed to measure energy fields or translate images. Echoes of the storm rumbled across the island; remnants dripped from the trees. Inside the tiny house, the spread and the explanation were complete. Kip massaged his brow with his right hand while the fingers on his left hand traced scars on the table in a bewildered search for some meaning to what he had heard.

Finally, he extended his arms up over his head. "I give up!" he said, with a sigh of frustration. "This thing, this hidden thing, a 'secret,' zaps my energy and continues to push me in the wrong direction."

He lowered his arms and looked dead in the eyes of Madam Ayanda. "And if I change, all will work out just fine. Great! And what about the company? My question was, 'What should I do with my business?'"

With fire in her eyes, Bheki Uwtando jumped to her feet. "What is your business? Is it not people? You work your people too hard. They've been there all their lives."

"T'ink. B'leebe duh ca'ads. B'leebe yoself."

Kip slumped in his chair. Uwtando sat back down and remained silent.

Kip waited for more. When nothing was said, he began to stand, but he slowed his departure as he heard the two women talking Gullah gibberish on the other side of the table.

"Madam Ayanda says she gave you advice. You do not listen. No matter what you do, the hex is on you, and it will hurt you again unless you accept the will of God, who puts energy in you. Once you accept what God says, you will live your answer. Life has no rewind. Every day is another X in a block on a calendar."

Kip slammed his chair aside and stepped toward the door. "If you will pardon me, I have a business to deal with. I need some sleep, and listening to you two doesn't make sleep come any easier. Good night."

The fragile old lady tested her balance as she pulled one hand from her cane and jabbed at the middle card as if she were nailing it to the table. Her assistant spoke for her, "You see that Tower exploding. That's you. You will see that again and again. Beyond it, you will reveal a bountiful new world. Always remember, silence is a deadly disease."

He heard the warning as he walked through the door and out of the shabby little house. On the drive in, he had been so confident that the reading would provide a simple "yes or no" and confirm the instructions he had left with Tripp Stansel in Philadelphia, but driving home, he was more confused and more tired than before. He drove slowly passed the Chapel of Ease, where a few eventful weeks earlier, dust, nails, and dirt in a bottle had become a hex that turned his world upside down.

Pockets of fog left by the earlier storm slowed his return home. He crawled through the dense haze by the Penn Center. The headlights of the Buick LeSabre that had followed him from the Reader's shack turned off there and parked in the mist beneath the muted glow of the outdoor lamps.

For Kip, the drive home took him in and out of variable fog. Clouds brushed aside by cool air unveiled the waxing moon and the low tide marsh. He did not want to wake Sandi, who would grill him on the results of his meetings with the shysters from Taggett & Vystroon. At this point, he just wanted to curl up somewhere and sleep.

When he turned off Spanish Point Drive, he dimmed his headlights. The fog was thicker, here, closer to the marsh, but he knew the bends of his driveway well enough to pull in without splashing the house with the car lights. At a snail's pace, he pulled about halfway down the drive, stopped, and parked. He would walk a bit further than usual to avoid waking the household. As he walked, he realized how much easier it was to sneak around the property without the watchful eyes and ears of Sparta. A lump formed in his throat as he imagined Sparta darting down the drive, barking wildly, to greet him. He knew it would not happen tonight; it would never happen again.

Streams of moonlight slipped through the moss on the oaks. Even with the fog, he managed to make it to the side door nearest the carport without the aid of any lights. Normally, the front porch light would be lit. Either Sandi had forgotten to turn it on, or the bulb had burned out, again. He was always putting in a new bulb out front, he thought.

No smells were left over from cooking supper. Strange. They must have gone out. Sandi and Chris enjoyed their dining-out opportunities. Tonight had to be a good one. Although he was hungry, Kip was too tired to eat; he just wanted to crash. He made his way down the hall; the century-old floorboards creaked with every step. He went into the family room, pushed the newspapers off the couch, and lay down, using the seat cushion from the rocking chair as a pillow. The sounds of the night made it impossible for him to think or sleep. Exhausted, he lay there, tormented by the events of the day in Philadelphia and during his evening on St. Helena Island. The orange power light at the foot of the freezer, its bulb blinking and flickering, caught his eye as he nodded off.

CHAPTER 21

He rose before the sun, opted out of a shower for fear he would wake Sandi or Chris, grabbed a cup of yogurt and a small carton of OJ from the fridge, and walked quietly out the door he came in the night before.

A thick cloak of fog still lingered over the blackness of the morning lawn. Kip bought a cup of coffee at the Stop-N-Go just before the bridge. In the distance, he saw the street lights from the sleepy city. It was a Friday morning, in the fall. Nobody else had braved the day. He shared the roads with an eerie fog, but no traffic. It was not his normal routine to drive to the office this early; this was always Gunny's time to get the place cranked up.

On a single sheet of lined paper, he scratched out his confession. Thirty minutes later, he heard the tap on his door. It opened.

" 'scuse me, Mr. Drummond. How was de trip to Philadelphia?" Gunny asked.

Kip looked up from his writing. "Things went fine, Gunny, just fine. Say, once you get the line up and running downstairs, can I see you for a few minutes?"

"Sure. Yes sir," Gunny said. "I'll get dem loads off de dock and into de works. Dat will takes me a little time, but I should be able to get all dat done by 9:30."

"Good. See you then."

After Gunny left, Kip continued to stare at the empty doorway.

The factory looked almost exactly the same as it did in 1939, hardly a reflection of the growth in Beaufort. It was the pride of Lady's Island, a landmark in its own right. For Kip, there was no debating that without Gunny, he would have lost the business years ago, along with his investment.

The morning sun had arched high in the cloudless blue sky. On the floor below Kip's mezzanine office, the threadbare conveyor belt, laden with the muddy clusters of shells, squeaked a telling discord to the history it had known. Outside, in the lot, the unmuffled Buick LeSabre came to a stop, the car door opened and closed with a groan, and Obadiah Whyteson worked his way around the factory to the dock.

"Weh is Mr. Gunny?" Obadiah asked, a disturbed, worried look on his face. "Uh needs to see um."

"He be headed up to talk to Mr. Drummond," Micah said, and pointed toward the middle of the factory floor. Obadiah limped as fast as he could to catch Gunny.

"Mr. Gunny, uh haffuh talk'um wid oonuh," Obadiah said. "I hab dese papuhs yuh dat oonuh needs to see."

"Look, I have a meeting with Mr. Drummond right now. Stick around. I'll look at dem later."

"Please, Mr. Gunny, look at dese yuh papuhs b'fo' oonuh go up. Dem is 'portun'." He held the file of papers at his side.

"I'll be finished in a few minutes and look at dem, Obadiah."

Before Gunny turned and headed up the stairs, Obadiah extended the folder toward him. The tab on the folder read "TV."

"Deseyuh papuhs uh t'ief from Mr. Drummond's desk," Obadiah said, but not loud enough for Gunny to hear above the ever-present spirituals of the Gullah workers. Then Gunny hurried up the metal stairwell, two steps at a time.

At the open doorway, promptly at 9:30, Gunny cleared his throat to get Kip's attention. "OK to come in now, Mr. Drummond?"

"Sure, Gunny," Kip said. "Come on in. Push the door closed."

Gunny nudged the door closed, but it stopped short of the frame. Obadiah hesitated for a minute, looked around, then, with folder in hand, he dragged his bad leg up the staircase, one step at a time. He stopped short of the door. He did not bother to knock or announce his presence. He figured he could talk to Kip with Gunny present, but first, he just listened through the door left ajar.

Kip had waved Gunny in. "Lookin' tired there, Gunny," Kip said, trying to ease into the conversation. "Been a tough day down on the floor?"

"Same as most days," Gunny said. He leaned against the back of the stained couch that had not changed since the business opened its doors.

"Gunny, ya know, I . . . " Kip started. "Gunny, I don't really know how to say this." Kip crumpled the scribbled notes in his hand.

"I'm selling the factory, Gunny. I've been made an offer I cannot refuse. I want you to pull all the people together tonight for an announcement here at 7 p.m. I'm sorry, but it's the best thing for all of us."

Gunny's eyes drifted toward the floor. Even though Kip was a few years younger and over thirty pounds heavier, Gunny's first impulse was to coldcock Kip right then and there.

Obadiah's reaction from just outside the door was more immediate. He slipped on the wet stairs in a hurried descent and headed for the dock. As he passed by Micah, he mumbled, "'E be sellin' duh factory!" then limped to his car, pounding his chest and mumbling to himself. The Buick cranked and stalled. On the second try, he rammed the gas pedal to the floor, which shot a rooster tail of sand thirty feet back. His first stop in town was the Piggly Wiggly, the hub from which all rumors evolved.

"Six years ago, I found a lottery ticket in a wallet I picked up in the alley by the John Bull Tavern," Kip continued, his stomach churning. "It was your wallet, Gunny. The only contents were three one-dollar bills, your driver's license, a Super 7 Lotto ticket purchased in a 7-Eleven somewhere in South Philly, a membership card of the Marine Corps Association, and a picture of you in your dress blue uniform with Joetta on your arm. The banner above the two of you read, 'Marine Corps Birthday Ball, 1775–1975.' I can see those things in my head as if they were on my desk right now."

"I noticed the lottery ticket, but at first, I didn't do anything with it. At some point, I called a local Realtor in the Philadelphia area to ask some bogus question about their market. Then, I slipped in some random question about the lottery, and the guy told me somebody had won six million dollars on the Wednesday before Thanksgiving."

Gunny remained behind the couch as Kip began to walk around the room. The more he revealed, the more relieved he felt, and the more his confession flowed.

"So then I called the Pennsylvania lottery office and said I wanted to come in with a winning ticket, but I wanted no publicity, none. They agreed. I took the cash in a lump sum, a little over three million. I concocted the inheritance story, and despite all the talk around town, nobody ever challenged it. Beaufort was the perfect place for me to buy a business and not have to worry about high society hounding me for money."

Kip moved back when Gunny stepped around the end of the couch without a word. Kip reversed his direction and worked his way back toward the safety of the desk to put more distance between the two of them. He wiped the sweat from his face.

"When I bought the business, it bothered me that you worked here. For some reason, I thought the best thing for me to do was to take care of you as much as I could. That's why I asked Lucas Rogers to retire early: so I could move you into a better position where I could do things for you and give you a chance to shine in the community. In the end, the decision was a good one for other reasons, but it also helped me live with the guilt. And I have lived with it. I have felt the guilt day in and day out for six years. Every time I walk out of my house in Port Royal and into this factory, I think of your wallet. I see it lying there in the alley, and I ask myself why I didn't give it back to you. Why did I keep it? And I can't answer that. I don't know."

Kip was drained. His lengthy apology left him with a dry throat, sweaty palms, and a head that echoed like the inside of a kettle drum. He reached for the carton of juice he had brought from the house. The few drops that trickled out offered little to quench his thirst.

"I had what I wanted, Gunny. I had the business and the success that were the goals in my life, but it cost me my honor, my honesty, and my integrity. Although things seemed perfect for the Drummond family, inside I've carried a heavy load of guilt which affected everything I did. When this land deal first started, I didn't think much of it. I owned the factory, and there was nothing they could do to take it from me, or from you, or from all your people. Then, I saw a chance to make things right. I didn't cave in. I battled them for a better deal. At the meeting yesterday, they upped their ante on the price. I told them to draw up the papers for the sale."

It was late in the morning by now, and the sun on the tin roof above offered little comfort in a plant that had never meant to be air conditioned. The window unit in the office was too small and too loud. Kip rarely turned it on. Today was no exception, although, at this point, he wished he had turned it on. Both windows were open a crack at the top to allow the building heat to extract itself, but no cool air came into the closed room. Working in a tin can was hot, even in October. And his workers did it every day.

Kip wiped his brow and ran his hand up over his forehead, onto his scalp, and down the back of his neck. He raised his eyebrows, took a deep breath, and said, "Gunny, I am going to pay you back every penny, every penny you would have won with your ticket, every cent plus interest."

"What makes you t'ink I want de damn money?" Gunny punched his fist into the palm of his other hand as he came around the couch and put his nose in Kip's face.

"What makes you t'ink I wouldn't want dis business? To you, dis is a rundown old building dat stinks like dead fish, sea salt, and sulfur mud. Fallin' down rafters.

Machines dat need fixin'. But for me, for my people, dis is our life. Can't you understand dat? Maybe it's not about de money, Mr. Drummond. Did you ever t'ink 'bout dat?"

Gunny turned to look at the walls and out the small window; the sound of his fist against his palm choreographed the tension. Kip looked on in disbelief.

"Why are you so quick to sell a business dat you bought with money dat was mine, huh? Why do you t'ink you can sell it at all? Why don't you give me de business? Maybe I don't want de damn money. Maybe I want dis business instead. Did you ever t'ink 'bout dat, Mr. Drummond?"

"Gunny, that's crazy." With his eyes still on Gunny, Kip rummaged through his briefcase and pulled out the folder he had received in Philadelphia. "This business is history. Here I can show you the charts, the graphs, the receipts, all the business records. Without extra cash, you couldn't keep this place alive. That's why I thought you would want the—"

"Want de money? Is dat what you thought?" Gunny charged the desk. He slammed his hands down hard. Papers, pencils, and pens flew everywhere.

Kip rolled backward in his chair to avoid Gunny's right hand when he grabbed for Kip's throat. "What I want is to kick your ass and roll you down de steps to let dem ladies down dey finish you off. By God, dem could and dem would if dem knew what you had done and what you are plannin' to do."

Though heavier and younger, Kip did not want to tangle with Gunny. He had a past. It was hard to tell what he would turn into if given the opportunity under the circumstances. Besides, for Kip, it was a "no win" situation: he against an older black man.

"You thought I'd take de money, is dat it? Yeah, take de money and tell dem ladies downstairs to go piss off? Is dat what you thought, Mr. Drummond?"

Gunny stepped back away from the desk, but he was still close enough to dive across it and knock Kip out of the chair. "I want dem ladies to have lives, real lives. Lives in de business dey helped build for decades. Yeah, decades. Dey kept dis business alive. Not you. Not me. It was dem ladies. And dey are tired, Mr. Drummond. Dey are tired of bustin' dem butts and listenin' to rumors and puttin' up with your shit, just because you wanted to run a business. I am tired of it, too—all of it."

"Gunny, this business needs a lot more than prayers and gospel singing to stay alive."

Gunny chewed on the inside of his mouth and looked away. Moments before, Gunny could have killed Kip in a justified rage that anyone could have defended in court. "Once a Marine, always a Marine!" A hero defending his troops.

Kip was dumbfounded. He had not expected Gunny's reaction. He said what first came to his mind. "Gunny, if you want the business, you can have it! Take your pick. The money or the business. What do you want?"

Kip was stern with his message. "Think about it, but I need to know, today. What way do you want to go? You need to call Stansel's office today, because I need to talk to the people tonight and tell them what is happening."

Gunny leaned forward, straight-faced, his eyes red with hate. In a hushed voice, he asked, "When you want to talk to my people, and what you plan to say?"

"Have them together, downstairs, at seven tonight. I have to go into town to go over all of this and other paperwork. It will take me all afternoon. Call me there with your decision.   Let the people finish their work today, and order some food for dinner here. Chicken, barbecue, Frogmore Stew, hush puppies, sweet tea, whatever they want, and have someone bring it out."

"Some of dem people have other jobs and families to take care of," Gunny said.

"Look, this is going to be tough enough as is. If they need time to make arrangements for tonight, then let them take some time this afternoon. It really doesn't make any difference on production at this point, but I need everyone here at seven tonight."

"What you goin' to tell dem?"

"I'll tell them the truth," Kip said. "Either I tell them you are now the new owner, if that's what you want, or I tell them I am selling the business." His voice was spiked with irritation.

"You goin' tell dem about de ticket? About what you said you were goin' to do with de money?"

"No. Gunny, I can't. The ticket was yours, and the money was yours, and the money will be yours, but I want that to remain our secret for now. Can we agree to that?"

Gunny hesitated. He still had doubts. He wheeled around and again leaned forward, his hands on Kip's desk. Like a drill instructor, he placed his nose about three inches in front of Kip's. "I ain't so pissed off for me." Spit from his punctuated verb splashed on Kip. "It's my family dat took de hit. Joetta put up with dis shit for six years. How do you pay dat back, huh? My poor wife. And me. Hell, I probably would've stayed yuh and worked with dem people because dey ain't got nobody else to turn to. Course, de business might have been shut down back den if you hadn't bought it. Guess I could have bought it myself and run it myself to keep de doors open. And now what'll I do? What about dem people?"

"Give yourself some time, old man," Kip said, his tongue bold but sympathetic. "Call me and have all the people here at seven so I can tell them myself. I need to get into town and work on details with Mr. Stansel."

Kip hesitated. Bags under his eyes drooped; his face was ashen; his voice was choked and strained. "Will you have the people here? Can I count on it?"

Gunny doubted Kip's contrition after he had hoarded the secret for six years. It all seemed too simple. He had spent the previous day in Philadelphia; there was no telling what scheme the consortium had set in motion. Gunny scowled, then turned and walked to the door. He placed his hand on the doorknob. "I will call you. Just remember, dis deal is my decision. I hold de cards now, Mr. Drummond, not you."

He pulled the door open, stepped through, and slammed it hard enough to rattle the trophies on the wall. He walked down the stairs.

Kip remained in his chair, his head bent over the wad of scribbled notes now soggy, smeared by perspiration. The only feeling that remained in him was an urge to curl up somewhere to sleep and end the nightmare, but he knew he had to get into town. He gathered folders from his desk drawer and pulled on his salt-stained Washington Redskins baseball cap. His legs felt like jelly as he walked down the stairs.

Outside the building, Kip squinted in the midday sun. He was not sure what Gunny had said to anyone. He noticed a number of older ladies huddled around Gunny, who looked up, made strained eye contact with Kip, then continued his conversation.

Kip rode a wave of panic as he drove across the bridge and into town. What if Gunny mentioned the deal to all the others? What if he mentioned how Kip stole the lottery ticket? What if Gunny mentioned Kip was paying him millions? What if he didn't bring the people together for the meeting tonight? How would he tell them about the rest of the deal he had to finish with Stansel? What if Stansel decided not to help him? The sun was still shy of noon, but the events of the morning, on top of the ordeal of the night before, which followed his day in Philly and a restless night on the couch, left him in a sad state, physically and mentally. Ahead of him awaited an afternoon full of documents and decisions, but what he really needed was a good nap. Yet he was eager to sit down with Tripp Stansel to go over the details he had hammered out with Taggett & Vystroon prior to his flight out of Philadelphia. The drive from the factory to the law office on Port Republic Street took just over six minutes, normally. Some days, today being one of them, the bridge would open to allow tall-masted sailboats to pass in and out of the marina. While he waited in the long line of cars at the bridge, Kip mulled over a litany of "what if" scenarios, all of which seemed to lead to a miserable end, until he remembered the Reader's cards.

Parking was always available on Port Republic Street near the Piggly Wiggly, even on a Friday morning. Kip found a spot behind a rusted, yellow LeSabre. He fed the meter a fist full of quarters and headed for the law office two blocks away. When he passed the rusted, yellow car, he noticed the well-worn New Testament on the front seat.

To Kip's eye, everything appeared normal for any weekday morning in Beaufort. Maybe it was his imagination or his lack of sleep, but today the normal street-talk greetings, the "hey" and "good day, y'all," weren't there. Something was different. Kip could not put a finger on it. Was it his guilty paranoia, or had his session with Gunny already begun to fuel rumors around town?

CHAPTER 22

The business of the day had allowed no rest for Kip. Except for one call from Gunny, Kip and Tripp Stansel spent the entire afternoon secluded in uninterrupted conference at the law office.

It was nearly sunset. As Kip neared his office, the only natural light came from the evening sky, brushed a flamingo pink over the marsh visible at the end of the tunnel formed by the oaks and palmettos along Oyster Factory Road. It wasn't until he pulled into the lot that he was able to see that his was the only car there. The factory was locked and dark. The outer security lamps were not on. Once inside, he looked around for signs of others, but he found himself alone in the factory, the one he wanted so much he once stole to have it. Where were the people? He opened his office window to pull in the evening breeze off the river, then plopped into the chair behind his desk, his arms dangled limp over the armrests.

The chair cried a witchlike squeal when he leaned back. Through the slit under heavy eyelids, he scanned his desk. On the corner were two small frames. One held a photo of Sandi from their honeymoon in Jamaica; the other, a photo of the happy family—Sandi, Chris, and Kip—huddled around a larger-than-life Mickey Mouse at the Magic Kingdom of Disney World, which they visited for Chris's seventh birthday.

At the opposite corner of the desk, Kip noticed the flashing message light on his phone. He had not noticed it earlier, but it suddenly caught his attention like a lighthouse through his mental fog. Maybe it's Gunny.

"Kip, Christopher and I are leaving you." It was Sandi's voice. "We left last night. I'll have Daddy's attorney draw up the papers and get in touch with you. Don't try to find me. I don't want to talk to you. I don't want to see you. You can bet I'll do everything possible to make sure you never see Christopher again, too. Goodbye, Kip." Click.

He placed the receiver back on the phone and buried his face in the rough palms of his hands. He had the urge to rewind the message and listen a second time to make sure he heard it right, but he realized what he really needed to do was rewind his life—to take a "do over" mulligan on the past six years, maybe even longer. Images of the tarot cards haunted his mind's eye for several minutes before a car door slammed outside.

He walked to the window, where he watched a string of cars and trucks roll up in rapid succession.

Gunny must have called an earlier meeting somewhere, maybe for dinner or maybe something more.

Kip heard movement on the first floor. Stools sliding. Large plastic packing crates being tossed and positioned to seat the audience at the foot of the stairs. Not long afterward, Gunny appeared in the office doorway.

"De people are yuh." His sullen tone complemented the quizzical reservation on his face.

"What have you told them, Gunny?" Kip asked.

"I ain't told dem nothin' 'cept be yuh, but de rumors in town have dem fired up, angry to de point where anything you might say jus' might cause dem to ignite. Hard tellin' what dey do. Some of dem women brought dey family with dem, dey sons and older grandsons. Dem folks didn't come yuh to hear no sermon. Dis ain't no church meetin'. Dis is a hostile crowd."

"Dey waiting, Mr. Drummond," Gunny continued. "You best go down and talk to dem. Dey saw your truck. Dey know you are up yuh. If you don't go down, dey come up, and dat's not somethin' you want. Trust me." There was no mistaking Gunny's tone.

Kip swallowed hard and willed his stomach back in place. The phone on his desk rang, but he ignored it. He stepped through the door and out onto the metal staircase. No whispers. No movement. Stares landed like daggers in his chest as he moved halfway down and stopped. From this point, he could see them all, and they could easily see him. He thought it best to allow some distance to avoid being tackled or knocked down. There were probably fifty people there, at least a third more than the payroll. He recognized the ladies, but there were many more men than the two normally seen on the factory floor.

"Thank you all for coming. I have a few announcements to share with you," he began.

Toward the back of the group, a man stood. Wearing an oversized Charlotte Hornets jersey with the number 1 on it, he pressed his hands deep in his pockets and rested his foot on a crate. The movement startled Kip. People fidgeted; he sensed their restlessness.

"Get to de point," someone yelled. Waves of nervousness rippled through Kip's stomach.

"The offers to sell the factory continue to come in with more and more pressure. I —"

Before he could complete the sentence, one of the older ladies seated in front shouted, "So you goin' to sell us out! I been workin' yuh in dis factory since 1956, and now you goin' sell us out."

"I have taken —" Kip tried again.

"Yeah, you be taken you sweet time getting' dem words out you mout'. Come on, der Mr. damn Drummond. Duh entire city be talkin' 'bout you tuhday. Sence you come, 'yuh rollin' wid all duh money en buy dis rusty ole buildin' with dese ol' women, en you been makin' dem work like slaves. Den you turn 'round and negotiates with some group uh strangers to sell duh bidness, takes duh monies and run while all dem po ole ladies, dey be jus' be starvin' en shit. Come on, man. We sees what you done."

The voice came from a black man the size of a house in the back near the dock door. Kip recalled seeing him before. He was the great-grandson of Jeneva Ramsey, the oldest worker at the factory. She had four generations of family living in her old house, a hand-me-down renovated set of slaves quarters out on St. Helena. She was well-respected for her fifty-five years of dedicated service broken up only long enough to birth seven babies of her own. She turned toward the bold black speaker with a stern look reserved for children who are out of line and one step short of receiving a few good lashes.

"Far as we concerned, you are duh one dat be losin', mister," the huge man continued. "Once you sell out dese people, dey be down on rock bottom. Ain't nobody goin' never do nothin' for you again. You might best leave town, and I be out back waitin' for you to get started." He hurled his stool against the wall and stomped away, headed for the dock through the huge sliding door, which he closed with a seismic slam.

Kip brushed his hand through his hair and continued before anyone else could add to the huge man's anger.

"I need to give you some other details. The Northpoint subdivision next to us has fifty-four acres to develop. The group developing it from Atlanta wants the sixteen acres we have here. Yesterday I spent the day in Philadelphia with a different group that wants the land. They made an offer."

Once again, the crowd stirred, and Kip hesitated. "I told them no."

A buzz started through the crowd. "From Philadelphia, I called the Atlanta group and told them what was offered. They matched the deal and made a few changes. The group in Philly countered with an even better deal. I accepted their offer. They intend to construct custom homes. Our oyster business will go away."

The building came alive with moans and muttering. The younger ladies cried and consoled each other, all without jobs. Most all the older women remained stoic, stunned by the reality that they had never worked anywhere else. There was no place else to work in Beaufort except the two hospitals. Several of them never finished high school; they knew they were too old and could not pass the tests to work even the simplest jobs in the medical facilities. The majority did not have transportation to work as cleaning ladies, cooks, or nannies.

Kip had not finished. "OK, listen. Listen up," he continued. He used a clipboard to bang against the metal railing to get their attention. "Listen, there is something else. I am selling the business, but I am still going to pay you. I am using some of the money from the sale to set up a trust, a special bank account, for all the workers so you will be paid for years to come because you were so faithful to this business."

"You mean you is goin' pay us for not workin'?" someone in the back asked.

The place was abuzz. Everybody had something to say. Questions yelled from the back, hollered from the side. People stood on their chairs to have their voices heard and their questions answered. If they did not understand his initial explanation of the sale, they would never understand being paid for not working. And they sure as hell did not trust Kip with anything he said. Although he could finally breathe, he could tell by the doubt on their faces they did not understand.

"I am going to take the money from the sale of the factory and put it in the bank and send you a check every week," he said, and repeated his words to make sure everybody could hear him. A good feeling kindled inside him, but he knew not to smile for fear they would misinterpret his intentions or his honesty. Smiles and surprised looks mixed with the earlier tears for the majority of the people; some still flashed a puckered, far-off look of doubt.

Before Kip could answer any questions or continue his explanation, the dock door slid open and crashed against the wall. Everyone turned, startled by the noise. From the black corner of the dock area, someone came running toward the group at the foot of the steps. Kip expected to see the hulk of black muscle that, moments ago, had called him out in front of the crowd. He waited for the footsteps to breach the light, but before he could see the body, he heard the voice.

"Kip, there's a fire. It's your house, man. It's growing fast. The fire department is on their way from town and Port Royal. You gotta get over there." It was Tripp Stansel.

In a house with structural timbers that were over a hundred years old and that had been remodeled just a few short years ago with flammable plastics and other materials, Kip knew it would not take long for the flames to rip through the place. His fear of the crowd all but gone, he dashed down the steps and out the service door. His truck cranked, but it would not turn over on his first try. He pumped the gas and flooded the engine. He pounded on the steering wheel while he waited. He tried and tried again, without the choke, until the engine fired up. His was the first vehicle out of the lot, followed by Tripp Stansel's and a long line of dilapidated cars and trucks of his workers and their families. When he reached the bridge over the Beaufort River three miles down the road, he risked a look up the Intracoastal Waterway toward town. There, where the spit of land jutted out to meet the marsh at the bend in the river, he saw his house, the flames dancing a surreal tango above the roof out over the veranda. He accelerated, down the back side of the bridge. He could hear the whoop-whoop of police cars and the wailing of the emergency vehicles in the distance. A steady stream of sirens and flashing lights passed to his front as he waited in a line of cars to turn off the bridge and onto Ribaut Road.

By the time he reached his house, the entrance was a parking lot for fire trucks, emergency vehicles, and a web of yellow fire hoses. Most of the fire trucks had recently arrived, still not fully engaged with the fire. The blaze, seen mostly in the rear, had begun to work its way into the trees, the carport, and the old shed to the left of the house. Nothing short of the center of the sun could have been as bright or as hot. Flames licked the structure walls and whipped the nearby trees. Of the two hoses in service, one was directed toward the house, the other to the huge oaks to control the spread of fire to the trees, a fire which could easily jump beyond the limits of his property and leapfrog across other properties on the banks of the river into the city.

Kip stopped well short of the blaze, near the wilting magnolia tree in the middle of the yard, his lungs filled with the acrid air. Above the squawk of the radios and engine noises of the pumps and trucks, he heard someone yell his name. It was Toby Gilliard, one of the local firemen and a friend of his who would occasionally join him for weekend distance runs. Welded numb by shock, Kip did not turn to acknowledge the caller, even when he heard his name a second time.

"Kip, is anyone inside? Do you know if Sandi and Chris were in there?"

"No, I don't think they were home," he said, as he recalled the voicemail Sandi had left at the office.

"But I am not sure. Toby, someone's got to check!" He pushed Toby's shoulder around and pointed at the end of the house, which the flames had not yet reached. "We can go in that way, then work our way as far as we can get."

"Kip, those flames are over three hundred degrees, and inside those rooms, it's probably closer to twelve hundred degrees," Toby replied. "We wouldn't last a minute. Hell, we have our hands full to keep the fire from working its way into the trees and back up river to the city. With these winds coming up from Parris Island, this could be trouble."

About that time, a burst of fire followed a loud explosion which took out the front windows. Kip and Toby twisted away from the fire and crouched down with their arms wrapped over their heads to protect themselves from the missiles of glass and wood that rocketed past them.

Weighted heavily by his yellow firefighter suit and heavy protective boots, Toby started toward the house, then stepped back to Kip. "What kinda stove do you have in there — gas or electric?"

"The stove? It was gas," Kip said, anxious to get involved in some way, any way.

"Look, Kip, I gotta get back to the truck and give them a hand. Don't do anything stupid. I know you hate to sit back and watch all this go down. The best thing for you now is to answer questions and stay the hell out of the way, for your sake and mine."

The curtain of fire began to close down on the front of the house as Toby moved back to the truck, giving commands over a walkie-talkie.

Kip's gut revisited the same queasy feeling from the platform at the factory an hour earlier, but a voice of hope whispered to him. Did Sandi really take Chris and leave? If so, maybe they came back. Maybe they were caught inside the inferno. He closed his eyes to hide the hopelessness that tightened its grip minute by minute. When he opened them, he watched the silhouettes of two firemen as they carried an exhausted comrade away from the blaze and leaned him against a magnolia tree away from the waves of heat. Kip could not stand by and watch any longer. He began his move.

He was not sure why there were no flames on the south end of the house or if there ever would be flames. The hoses had soaked the wood thoroughly. Despite what Toby had said about the heat, he was still confident he could work his way through the house, at least as far as his office. Even if he could not find Sandi and Chris, there were some things inside the office, in his special box, that he absolutely had to save from the fire.

Working down through the small trees in the side yard, he stopped directly even with the side door, then bolted toward the furnace, which was his house. The door crashed when he hit it with his bad shoulder. Numbed by the pain and tripped by the door as it recoiled off the wall, Kip fell to the floor. He tried to breath slowly, but gagged. There was little air. He struggled to stand and work his way down the hall, but the acrid smoke burnt his lungs with every sip of air he inhaled. When he was back on his feet, the smoke was too thick to see anything or anyone. He sank down to the floor and continued on his belly.

"Sandi? Chris? Can you hear me?" Nothing. "Sandi. Chris. Are you in here?" The only response was the crackle of dried wood in the mouth of the flames. Objects fell around him like torches inside the fire. The ceiling fan. The sculptured bronze fountain near the foyer. Once he stood up long enough to see the faint outline of the banister leading upstairs. He crawled to the backside of the house and looked into his office.

Blue and orange flames feasted on his antique desk and bookshelves. Molten wax dribbled from his stacks of prized LPs into the puddle of water on the floor. Album covers for Iron Butterfly, Led Zeppelin, and The Beatles sagged, limp. The unpredictable fire devoured the front of the room, but rested on the far side; the back of the room was clear. He crawled low and slow through the doorway and along the back wall as the smoke squeezed a strangle hold on his throat. His tearing eyes were better closed than open. Every day for five years, he had ended his morning run in this room, on this floor. He knew every peg in each plank of pine. In a blind move, he inched his way along floorboards, but as he did, he placed his hand in a pool of lacquer from his college rocker blistered by the heat. "God damn it!" he cried, his response merely reactive; nobody else would hear, or care. In a house engulfed in flame, his first burn came from the liquid on the floor.

He shoved his scorched hand into his armpit for protection from the heat while he continued to crawl on his knees and with one remaining hand. Just past the corner of the room was the small built-in cabinet. From his knees, he rocked back onto his heels, opened the cabinet door, and pulled out his locked antique box. He squinted to dredge up tears to wash the smoke from his eyes, then stared at the box. In an instant, a fireball burst through the door, ricocheted off the walls, and sucked all the air from the room. He pancaked on the floor with his prized box under him, shielded. When the ceiling fan crashed onto the chair beside his head, he realized he did not have much time. The best thing for him to do was to slither backward along the same route by which he had entered. Small, but steady, streams of water hissed on surfaces around him as they worked their way down from the ceiling through the hole left by the fan. With his head resting on the box, he used his burnt hand to slide it along.

The flames had not yet reached the hall by the time he slid back through the office doorway. He lifted his head one last time to look around the family room. When he did, an explosion rocked everything around him. The timbers, twisted and charred, shrieked. When strips of cove molding and hall sconces landed on him, he kicked and flipped like a fish out of water to push them aside before they could burn through his clothes. Through the smoke and flame, he squinted to watch the banister peel from its baluster supports, and like a giant helix, the twisted mass crumbled to the ground. The crash of the staircase jarred the outside door behind him, his only exit route. If a couple of six-cent wood screws on one top hinge lost their grip, Kip had nowhere to go. The white noise of the red-hot fire crackled in his blistered ears. Panic rallied his senses. He mustered strength, then courage. Beneath a layer of toxic smoke, he pushed himself back onto his knees and hand, then crawled like a bear caught in a trap before another explosion flattened him to the floor. Scared and desperate, he grabbed his box, jumped back on his feet, and ran toward the door. If the solid outer door fell now, it would knock him out, and he would go up in flames along with his house.

The blast Kip heard, had occurred outside, toward the back of the carport, near the storage shed. Beleaguered firefighters responded to the arm signals from Lieutenant Gilliard. Immediately, two hoses, connected to a hydrant at the distant curb and hardened to their full two-and-a-half-inch capacity, shifted water toward the carport. While the nozzle man held his aim on the trees and the slack man wrestled with the hose, Kip bolted to safety.

Outside the house, past the heavy outer door, he gasped for air, unnoticed by any of the bystanders. He staggered, wheezing and coughing, stumbled into the pine woods, and collapsed facedown on the ground. Within minutes, the fresh smell of pine straw and the dampness of the sand revived him, but he lay there motionless; each heavy breath hurt less and less as he regained his wind. For him, it was a narrow escape; he wondered if Sandi and Chris had been so lucky. A few feet away, he saw his rescued box upside down beside a pine tree.

On the lawn, Toby Gilliard barked out instructions over his handheld radio to shift three hoses in the direction of the blast.

"What the hell was that?" the rookie fireman asked.

"Beats the shit out of me," Ronnie Heatherton hollered back over his shoulder. "Coming from the shed, it could've been almost any goddamn thing. Paint. Fertilizer. A can of gasoline. Could've been all that shit ignited at the same time. Doesn't make any fucking difference. This shit's getting bad. I ain't never seen anything like this. If we get any more wind, all this shit's going to light up the entire river line from here to Bay Street."

Their aim was on target, but the firefighters could not knock out the flames that bobbed and weaved in the dark like a prizefighter in the ring. Every time the jet of water landed a blow, the flames would slip to the side and punch in a different direction. When the wave of fire rolled over the broad peak of the rooftop on the house, the teams abandoned their aim on the carport and targeted the house. As the house burned, random explosions from the shed distracted them and sent cans airborne like Roman candles.

The smoke layered the water-soaked ground like jelly on toast. Kip squinted to wash away the burn; he tried to relax the pain. He wiped the plug of gray-black soot from his nose and rolled onto his left side, rested on his elbow, and shaded his eyes from the inferno's brightness. He stared, still dazed. He tottered to one knee, then staggered to his feet. The shadow of despair began to cover him when another explosion erupted. The earth quaked, once more from the vicinity of the carport; everyone in the yard dove for cover. The twisted remains of a large propane tank came hurtling through the charcoaled rooftop of the shed and crashed into the side of the Rescue Unit Truck like buckshot on pine. Fire hoses converged to eliminate the immediate danger. Lieutenant Gilliard redirected one of the hoses back to the carport, now defined only by four remaining posts around a sizeable crater. Nothing else remained of the carport or the shed. The burned walls, flattened by the burst, were gone. Within minutes, the posts fell into the crater left by the explosion, now a five-foot pool of water.

Kip emerged from the concealment of the trees. He mingled with the onlookers clustered across the lawn, his eyes glued to the liquid, silvery heat that quivered above the orange-and-yellow flames as they continued their belly dance over, around, and through his prized house.

Then, for the third time in this night filled with the horror of fire, another tremor shook the north end of the house, which then collapsed into a water-soaked smoldering heap. Another blast from the carport sent a shower of burnt wood, twisted chunks of ripped metal, and shards of glass flying like shrapnel across the landscaped lawn. Even the bravest firefighters hit the dirt. What had been a five-foot crater where the carport once stood was now a bowl fifteen feet deep with a rim of dirt around the edge. With hoses trained in the general vicinity, the crater quickly filled with water and dampened any threat of yet another blast. An exhausted Toby Gilliard assessed the damage and returned the focus on the pockets of flames that remained inside the house.

For three hours after the last of the bystanders departed, the crews secured the scene. The lawn, the picture-perfect carpet of green zoysia, was now a quagmire of sod and sand, churned to rutted mud by heavy trucks. Firefighters stripped off their heavy coats and hard helmets, dog-tired from their nonstop efforts for over six hours. Rolling the hoses, crews paused frequently to sit and rest, while they swapped tales of the bravery and courage they had displayed through the night. The teams had successfully quarantined the blaze, sparing all the houses between Spanish Point and Beaufort. In the end, the only damaged house was the Drummond house, or more appropriately known as the Moncrief House at Adventure Landing. It was a total loss. The wood, the tabby foundation, the tin roof. All that remained was the white Georgia marble on the circular front portico and the white Charleston rockers spaced neatly between the fluted Ionic colonnades of the front porch. At the far end of the building, one door frame and door stood ominously alone. It was the door Kip had used for his escape hours earlier.

Lieutenant Gilliard, along with Captain Sidney Watson, surveyed the scene, while the young photographer from the Beaufort Gazette took pictures and jotted notes in a small pocket steno pad as he talked to the firefighters. At one point, Toby Gilliard approached Kip. They exchanged a few words, hugged, patted each other on the back, and moved about the wreckage on their own.

Kip wandered about like a zombie. He kicked at embers, a futile attempt to rescue precious memories from the blaze. With his burnt hand that looked like a meatloaf, swollen and raw, he used a rake he left in the yard the weekend before to push aside bits of the house that still smoldered. There was nothing more for him to do there and no place to go. Toby had offered Kip a ride to the hospital to have his hand checked, but he declined. Gathering the box which nearly cost him his life and a metal water bowl from the yard engraved with "Sparta" on the side, Kip walked down his drive, past two fire trucks and crews, who flashed the V symbol with their fingers in a final requiem of the night.

Without the adrenaline that kept him wired through the night, Kip pulled himself into the cab of his truck, where he wrapped his arms over the top of the steering wheel, then laid his head on top of it. In the privacy of the cab, he collapsed.

Soon, with tears on his cheeks, he started the truck and drove off. He looked once in his rearview mirror and saw nothing but blackness under a pall of smoke and steam.

CHAPTER 23

Sunrise coaxed the song from the birds and the dew from the lawn, and swept the dark of night from the scene of the tragic fire. Beaufort lay nestled in a blanket of daylight, much as it had the previous day. Shades of pinks and orange colored the sky. On Port Royal, trickles of water snaked their way through the carbon skeleton of Kip Drummond's house. All that remained was the smoke-stained portico, the seared veranda, and the single, water-soaked doorway on the south end.

The sun tiptoed a quarter of its arc in the eastern sky before Kip awoke on his office floor at half past nine Saturday morning. He had slept covered by his old shrimp net, his head on the cushion off his chair. His clothes reeked of smoke. His body ached. His eyebrows were singed. His eyelids were stuck together with gunk from his eyes. With his desk as a crutch, he hoisted himself up off the floor and plopped into his chair. He bowed his head, chin in chest, his hands cupped loosely over the edge of the desk. He struggled to piece together the sequence of events of the past fifteen hours. His first, his very first, recollection was the voicemail from his wife, but he was not sure if the call was real or part of his nightmare. He leaned back in his chair and scooted closer to the desk. He placed his left elbow on the desk to elevate his burnt left hand, wrapped in a damp T-shirt; it throbbed as if someone had smashed it with a sledge hammer. With his good hand, he picked up the receiver off the phone and pushed the voicemail button. After a few seconds, which seemed like an eternity, Sandi's voice started. It was clear, not choked. She spoke with emotion. Her words, he could not believe, and he felt he could never forget them.

"Kip, Christopher and I are leaving you." He hung up. That was all he needed to hear. It was not just a bad dream. He remembered the message enough that he did not need to hear it again, not now. There were no other messages. He studied the photo on the corner of his desk. Memories washed away like a sand castle with the rising tide. He breathed slow, deep, deliberate breaths. A soft knuckle-tap on his closed office door broke his concentration. The knob turned, and Gunny peered in.

"You all right, Mr. Drummond?" Gunny asked.

Kip looked up. "Seems kinda hopeless doesn't it?" Seeing Gunny was a strange, but good, medicine.

"You know, Gunny, we never finished our discussion last evening. We were here talking about my decision last night when Mr. Stansel came running in."

"Don't go bringin' dat up now. We can continue dat discussion 'nother time, after you get some good rest and takes care of t'ings."

"What's there to take care of except you and the people of this factory?" Kip pressed the sides of his head with his palms and squeezed like a vise, until the pain from his burns got the better of him. He tightened the T-shirt around his wound.

"Before Stansel came in, I had not finished telling you and the others about the sale. First off, I'm going to repay you with interest. Then, I am taking the rest of the money and establishing a trust for all the employees. The trust will provide payments to all of them in amounts equal to double their current wages for the next two years. That will give everyone two years to find a job or go to school or get more training. Most of them can give up their second jobs, too." Kip was fully awake now. His eyes looked off in a wistful stare as he tapped his desk with the pencil in his good hand.

"So if you do dat, Mr. Drummond, what you goin' do about a business or a house?"

Kip looked back at Gunny. "Come on. You've been poor before. Hell, your people have been poor all their lives. Have they given up? No, they never have, and they never will. They work harder, play harder, and pray harder. My guess is that's what I'm going to do."

Kip winced with pain. He pulled his wrapped hand to his chest as he stood and walked out from behind his desk. He walked with a pained hunch in his back, his reward for his night on the floor and the events preceding it. He stepped around the shrimp net and cushion and moved toward Gunny.

"The Reader said there would be a major event, a major change in my life. Some of the forces behind that change I could not do anything about, but the key remained inside me. I think I know what I am going to do."

"I know the first thing I am going to do and I am going to do it right now. I am going to ask your forgiveness, Gunny Brewer. Forgive me for all the hurt I have caused you, your family, your people, this town, everybody. I wish there was more I could say or do. The past six years have haunted me."

Kip thrust his hand forward, looked straight into Gunny's deep-set brown eyes and, with a lump in his throat, said, "Will you forgive me? Please."

Gunny hesitated. His eyes locked on Kip's in a stare of scrambled emotions. Hate. Rage. Disgust. Distrust. Surprise. Sorrow. Pity. As much as Kip's world had turned upside down overnight, so had Gunny's.

Kip did not pull back his offer or his hand. For him, Gunny's handshake was the most important thing in the world right now. He waited, and he feared rejection.

Gunny slowly extended his hand. "I'll never forget what you did . . . in de end. I appreciate what you done to help me and my people."

Kip exhaled his relief. "Gunny, make sure the word gets out to all our employees. Effective Monday, the factory is closed for business, but the people can make arrangements to visit Tripp Stansel, my lawyer on Port

Republic Street. He will ensure everybody gets paid starting Monday and every week after that for the next two years. I better get going." Kip walked back behind his desk and pulled open his bottom drawer.

"Take care yourself, Mr. Drummond. I'll see you 'round town, I'm sure."

"Sure, Gunny. I'll be seeing you."

As Gunny walked down the metal staircase, Kip told him to hold up. He took one last look around his office, then grabbed two things from his desk and headed down the stairs. He heard the sounds of the gospel songs, the ladies singing, but there was nobody there. He looked long and hard at the factory floor. Everything appeared normal, like any other Sunday. Today the smell of seafood seemed stronger and fresher to him than it ever had before.

Kip looked at the frame in his hand, the family photo from his desk. "Maybe there is something still out there with meaning. Maybe I best go find it." He started down the steps. Still weak and stiff, he used the iron-pipe handrail to make it safely to the bottom, where Gunny waited. With his good hand, Kip reached into the antique box he rescued from the fire. He pulled out an old leather wallet and handed it to Gunny. "This is yours. I should have returned it years ago."

Gunny looked at Kip, then reached for the wallet. He stared at it, then opened it. Inside he found three one-dollar bills, his old driver's license, a membership card of the Marine Corps Association, and a picture of him and Joetta at the Marine Corps Birthday Ball. He rolled his tongue across the inside of his cheek, slapped the wallet against his thigh, and walked off.

Sad, ashamed, Kip followed a path of sunlight to the opening in the double bay doors by the dock. Outside, his eyes adjusted to the bright, new day. He then noticed the weekender boat tied up at the far end of the dock. It was the Carpe Diem, the boat where he had found Sparta. He took one step toward it, then realized now was not the time to reopen that wound. He turned back toward the live oaks in the area where he parked his truck. He eased himself inside and leaned back in his seat. As he left the lot, Kip clicked on the radio: 103.1 FM, WGZO, "The Drive" — the usual oldies station.

At the bridge, as the music echoed through his head, Kip wondered where Sandi had gone and if she was going to stay. The words from her voicemail emerged and played louder in his head: "Don't try to find me. Don't think you can change my mind." Her voice, the memory of her voice, was louder than the Bill Withers song on the radio. Where had she gone? Was she going to stay? Kip thought. He didn't know. He crossed the bridge and turned left.

During the weeks that followed, Tripp Stansel was able to complete the transfer of funds as promised, but he could do nothing to contain the rumors that sprang up like mushrooms around Beaufort. Milan "Gunny" Brewer began the cleanup and excavation of the Moncrief House at Adventure Landing, the property Kip Drummond bequeathed to him. As workers began to refill the crater left from the explosions in the carport, one of them noticed the edges of a wooden chest inside the charred remnants of a box covered in tar. With Gunny's permission, the workers recovered the charred box and, inside it, the wooden chest, strapped with thin metal bands. When they opened the chest, they found it filled with Mexican silver coins—exactly like the one Chris had found and Jamie Gentry had analyzed as the Mexico Felipe II 8 Reales. There were eighteen hundred and two coins in all, with an estimated value of $1.2 million.

Gunny did not hesitate to donate the box, the chest, and their entire contents to the Penn Center. He made the donation on behalf of Mr. Thomas "Kip" Drummond. The charitable gift, though formalized in stacks of legal documents, came with a simple, single-sentence message: "May the history of slavery in the Lowcountry be preserved along with the traditions of the Gullah people who made Beaufort the 'Bin yah.'" At Gunny's request, the Penn Center used the funds to establish a jobs training program.

Professor Barney Thayer, assisted by other local historians, researched the find. Their analysis cast a spotlight on the history of the area. Collectively, they determined that the carport sat above a piece of ground which had once been a part of Fort Lyttleton. Patriots buried powder and munitions in the area before destroying the fort to keep it from falling into the hands of the British during the Siege of Port Royal. The explosions during the night of the fire apparently were more than propane. The analysis suggested that the surface explosions ignited the buried kegs of powder. The secondary explosion of the powder exposed the chest of coins encased in the wooden box sealed with tar, buried deeper in the soil over a century earlier. It was the chest of contraband that Sir John Hawkins ordered his slaves to bury and guard in 1565. Hawkins never made it back to Beaufort, and the chest, in fact, became the Gullah Treasure.

ACKNOWLEDGMENTS

Once upon a time...

In the beginning...

From the very start...

there was a cast of people who offered encouragement in the *Haint Blue* project. Ah, yes, my parents who sparked life. My sister and brother who helped build the life. Many teachers, coaches and mentors who helped form the life. Then the countless numbers of people — friends and foes — who have challenged me to apply those lessons learned along the way. Names, in general, far too many to recall, but there were a few who went above and beyond in their efforts to keep me on task.

Many, many thanks to the following:

To Phil Bardsley and Alex Dunlap, who took time to read and provide feedback on several long drafts and shorter revisions. And a special thanks to Ralph Davis who helped add a pinch more of Lowcountry as he read through the manuscript.

To Lois Gilbert, for her guidance on the manuscript development.

To my copy editor, Lee Titus Elliott, for his detailed eye and words of wisdom.

To Barb Campbell, office manager and friend, who provided the initial spark that evolved into the story that became this project.

To Wendy Wilson and Janelle Proctor who provided feedback on several chapters despite the fact that I kept them in the dark on how the pieces would fit together.

To friends and authors, Jim Jordan and Jim Auten, for luring me into the tunnel and holding the light at the other end.

To Wayne Magwood and the Magwood family for sharing the family photo of an old oyster factory which appears on the book cover.

And, to the two inspirations behind Philip-Forrest Publishing—Eleanor Thacker (Sr. Mary Philip) and Forrest "Treeze" Sharrock—I tips me hat! Their spirit lives on in so many ways, in the many people they motivated in years past.

46776003R00174

Made in the USA
Charleston, SC
24 September 2015